SPARKY OF
BUNKER HILL
AND THE
COLD KID CASE

ROSALIND BARDEN

MYSTERY AND HORROR, LLC
CLEARWATER, FLORIDA

TABLE OF CONTENTS

DEDICATION

My sister Caroline

THANK-YOUS

Thank you to Gwen Mayo and Sarah E. Glenn of Mystery and Horror, LLC, who took in my short stories in need of a home and worked with me tirelessly to bring this book into being. Thank you to Ralan Conley who led me to Mystery and Horror, LLC by way of his amazing website, Ralan.com. Thank you to Sisters in Crime Los Angeles whose invaluable resources and encouragement went a long way to making this book happen. And thank you to all the people who keep Old Bunker Hill alive by sharing their memories, researching the fascinating history, and preserving the photos, films, and stories of this wonderful lost world.

Chapter 1

There's something to this 13th business. That's my birthday.

You see, on my birthday my mother died. That's how I ended up with the "cousins" or whatever they were, who didn't want me. Then 'round about my tenth birthday a year ago way back in 1931, I came home from running around Bunker Hill like always, to find the cousins' apartment empty. The landlady said they moved. And no, she could care less where they went and started putting the squeeze on me for past due rent. What could I do but scram?

I'd been managing fine ever since, scrounging here and there for eats, slipping through cellar windows to sleep, running with other neighborhood kids who were good for a candy handout.

Until today, you guessed it, my birthday again.

Just because I was a street kid didn't mean I didn't keep track of days. I did, and I knew my birthday was coming up. I saved a mighty fine candy stash for that purpose. Bright and early, I got my metal box full of candy from its hiding spot in my favorite sleeping cellar. I headed toward Court Hill Park, which was really part of Bunker Hill, to have my own personal candy bender while I watched the sun rise. I can't imagine a sweeter way to celebrate a birthday, can you?

It was so early, the park was empty of the old folks and other types who usually hung out there. Bliss, peace, with the only stain being City Hall looming up from the Los Angeles flatlands below, City Hall being full the of the types who liked to round up the likes of me and throw us in "homes," and I use that word in a non-funny joke way.

Never mind City Hall today. I was about to settle down to my favorite bench with my candy box stash, when lo and behold, there's another kid on my bench! A girl, really little, barely past the baby classification. She was in a thin white nightgown with some nice blue stitching, bare feet, blonde curls. Didn't look like a street kid. Too clean. But, who knew? Maybe she lived with cousins who tossed her out. She was slumped over. Sleeping probably.

My biggest fault, though some may say hot baloney, was being a big softie. She was having a rough morning, so I decided I'd share my candy stash. We'd have a good all-around bender together. Then I'd help her sort out what she should do next, where she could go.

"Hey, kid!" I called out in my friendly voice (yeah, I have different voices, and believe me, you don't want to hear my not-friendly one). "How 'bout some candy! Looks like you could use a shot or two."

I jangled my box and you could hear the candy inside rattling around nice and pretty-like. Not a peep from Goldilocks. Funny. No kid I knew could resist the sound of jangling candy. Well, she did look asleep. So, I nudged her. She tipped over on the bench and one arm flopped over the side.

About now, I was thinking something's strange here. When I touched her, she was cold. Like ice. You could say, okay, makes sense, she'd been sleeping out all night. Maybe. But the way she fell over? I got closer, lifted her head, and got a pair of open, milky eyes that used to be blue staring at me. And yeah, her head was ice cold.

I was so shocked, I made the big mistake of yelling, dropping my candy stash, and taking off running. I should have just done the running part and left it at that.

You see, it was a huge mistake because I'd written, "Property of Sparky. Touch this and you will DIE!!," on my candy box, and then inside the lid, "You are dead NOW!!" and so on. That gave the motive.

All the local cops knew who the street kids were, and me most of all. Of course, my yelling woke up the oldsters who had to come wandering out of their rooming houses to see what the ruckus was about.

That's how I became a hunted fugitive, wanted for killing another kid in a fight to the death over candy.

Did you know that as soon as you're on the lam, 99% of your friends desert you? It's true. Cops were swarming, asking other kids if they'd seen me: "Sparky, you know that screaming little girl who's always getting into fights? The freckle-face with ratty hair? Looks like it's murder this time, so we need your cooperation. We need you to contact us as soon as you spot her, tell us anything you know."

Those rats! They pointed out my favorite sleeping cellars, the back of the cafeteria where I liked to get handouts, and even the nice old couple who sometimes gave me sandwiches. They were killing me! Cutting off my lifelines! I wanted to lunge out and attack those rat fink kids!

I was slipping and slinking from hidey-hole to safe spot, under parked cars, inside trash bins, being invisible in bushes. Would I have to ditch Bunker Hill? For good? But I'd been on the Hill all my life and didn't know the city, Los Angeles, except for a few places down below, like movie palaces on Broadway. The cops'd be sure to hunt for me there. I was feeling real fear for the first time.

My fear made me stop too long, get distracted, and the next thing I knew, some little twerp was yelling, "Police! Police! I see Sparky!"

It's not only him, but a bunch of kids, kids I knew and played with a hundred times. They were all jumping up and down yelling for the cops. I planted my fist in the little twerp's kisser. That shut him up.

After he peeled himself off the pavement, he ran screaming, along with the rest of the rat finks. For good measure, I shouted after them, "And I'll kill all of you next!" That'd keep them away. Maybe.

Good ol' Bobby was still there. He was smiling in his hopeful way. I kind of hated Bobby, but I hung around with him more than any other kid. He'd give me his last stick of candy. To me, nobody else. That's the way Bobby was. Regularly, like once a week, he proposed to me. Once he even tried kissing me. That's when I socked him good and down he went. That's why his nose was crooked, making his angel face not so perfect anymore. Didn't faze him. He kept on proposing, and he kept telling the other kids I was his "girl," which made me think he warranted another whamo.

"Sparky, don't worry, I'll protect you," he said.

Maybe, maybe not. But who else could I trust?

Then those yelling rat fink kids were coming back, running fast up the street with a wave of cops.

"Get behind me," Bobby said.

I squeezed under a fence where he pointed and burrowed into some tomato plants. Bobby sat casual-like on the sidewalk in front on the fence, screening me with his own body. Good ol' Bobby. I suddenly got some soft thoughts, like maybe I could consider his proposals sometime. Maybe.

The cops and kids screeched to a halt in front of Bobby, and before they could even ask, he was shouting, "She went that way! I see her! There she goes!"

He pointed down, down, down Second street, down to the below world at the bottom of Bunker Hill. The cops, the kids, tore off down the steep hill.

"Are you okay?" he asked, all full of care and concern. He helped me out of the tomato plants and wiped the squashed tomatoes off my face. Then he ruined everything by saying, "You know you're my girl."

He shoulda gotten another first-class power punch for that. But he did do me a favor. A big one. So, I took off running instead, up and away from the cops.

Bobby called after me, "Anything you want, I'll help you!"

I ran to the top of the Hill, to Bunker Hill Avenue. I don't usually hang around there. It's full of the really fine houses that were built a long time ago, fifty or so years back. Before my time. Some rich old people still lived in those mansions, fixed them up, and hired an army of people to paint all the crazy towers and curlicues and columns on those things so they almost looked new. Other people were turning them into rooming houses. Made sense. You could fit a hundred grownups and kids inside those monster-sized mansions with space to spare.

There were big ol' houses like that all over the Hill, but you could tell this street, especially back in the day, was extra high-class. I steered clear of the area, like I said. Too open, too unfriendly to street-types like me.

But my other hiding spots were ratted out by my ex-friends, so I had to find somewhere new.

Where would the cops think was the last place a kid would want to hide?

Bingo. The Creepy House.

It was different from the other houses, actually not as old, maybe about ten or so years, not from the last century like the others. It was a weird house: all dark tile and made of strange square shapes.

Kids said a vampire lady lived there with a pet leopard and fed it any kids who wandered close. She was supposed to take baths in kid blood to keep herself looking young too. There was also a half-man, half-goblin who lived there as her slave. Rumor said she used to be a famous actress and built Creepy House before the movies started talking. For sure, she was "different." And that last part came from no kid. That was from nosey ol' Mrs. Tomes, so of course it made sense to take all the other stories seriously.

Dangerous as it was, guaranteed, no cop would ever suspect I'd hide there.

Taking my life in my hands, I slid under the iron fence railing and crept through the yard, which was full of looming plants with thick green leaves. Here and there I saw a strange fat red flower instead of the gladiolas everyone else had on the Hill. The yard was overgrown and dark, like a haunted jungle.

I found a door, unlocked. I slipped in. It was a kitchen. I was shocked that it was bright and modern. White tile, sparkling chrome. No boiling pots of kids. No dripping bloody kid hands and feet dangling from the ceiling. Maybe the neighborhood kids and Mrs. Tomes were wrong.

But maybe not. I wasn't letting my guard down.

Seeing as I'd dropped my candy stash, I was hungry. I set about opening the bottom cabinets. I saw a lot of dishes with strange, bright patterns on them, but no food. So, I clambered up onto the counter to snoop in the top cabinets. Jackpot. The first one had a tray of some kind of little cookies. I put my kisser to the edge of the tray and started shoving cookies in. The cookies were not sweet at all. Tasted kind of like baked hay, but my stomach was too empty to care.

"Well, would you look at that!" and a laugh.

I almost choked on the cookies. My feet slipped, the tray went flying, and I was holding onto the cabinet shelf with my fingertips. I twisted my head around to look, and there, blocking my exit to the outside world was the strangest woman I'd ever laid eyes on.

She wore a wrap made of different furs, and over her short dark hair, she had a cap with colored glass beads that swung as she laughed. In her hand was a foot-long cigarette holder like in the old, old movies, but there wasn't a cigarette in it. She was thin as a wisp, face painted as pale as a plucked chicken, with a ton more black paint around her wide brown eyes.

Next to her, sure as kids said, was a half-man, half-goblin: short, bald, with a scar over one eye. He was laughing too.

Chapter 2

So much for keeping my guard up.

"Are you this person?" from the lady. She held up a paper printed with my name "Sparky" and "Wanted" and "Murder" and a bad drawing of me that made me look like a rabid lunatic.

"I didn't do it! I swear!"

In my panic, I lost my grip and fell to the floor. The woman and the goblin swarmed over me. I kicked at them, but the goblin was strong and held my legs tight.

"I'm not going to no cops!"

"Relax. Quit wiggling around. I don't care if you killed ten people. It's none of my business. Well, it does make you more interesting, right?" the woman said, smiling.

I was still yelling about cops, so she added, "Do I look like a friend to cops to you? Does Gilbert?" and she cocked her heard toward the goblin.

She had a point, so I stopped wiggling.

Maybe it was time for me to relax, case the joint, weigh the odds.

"Okay, all right. No cops." I gave them my nice little girl smile to let them know I wasn't going to bite. At least not yet.

That seemed to make them happy, so the goblin let go of me.

"Come see the house," the lady said, laughing.

What? She wanted to show me her house?

Me, a wanted murderer? Didn't make sense.

I wanted to scoop up the cookies I dropped all over the floor, but hungry as I was, I decided I'd better keep alert. If things got weird, or more weird than they already were, and I spotted another door, I could bolt. Meantime, I'd play along.

The house was big, bigger than I thought it would be. You

couldn't see much of it from the street because of all the strange plants growing around it. But it was a certifiable mansion.

Maybe you wouldn't think it, but I was a mansion expert. I'd been inside plenty of old Victorians around that Hill, like Mrs. Tomes' house and other houses with old people who were good for cookies and a sandwich. Don't forget the mansions turned into rooming houses. Their basements made the best sleeping spots for Sparky.

Okay, so I hadn't been inside the fancy, fixed up Victorians (well, except for the quick, second-story in and out after dark, so I'd hardly be taking a nice long look around, if you get me). But, compared to all the others I'd been in, during the day, Creepy House took the prize. And you heard that from the mansion expert.

It seemed like there was one parlor after another. Each parlor had huge windows made of colored glass, except for smaller, clear glass transoms above the big windows. Some windows had pictures painted on the glass, and cut-glass patterns. I couldn't see outside, except for slivers of light and a bit of outdoor green through the transoms. Electric lamps were burning in every room, otherwise it would have been dark as a cellar inside.

If I'd left electric lamps switched on like that in my cousins' apartment, they would have kicked my fanny from here to Pasadena for wasting money. I guess this lady didn't worry much about money.

And another thing, normal people kept windows wide open in the summer. Because it gets hot! It was strange she kept them all shut except for the transoms, but those little windows were only open a crack. It made the air too stuffy. How could she stand to wear all that hot fur?

Nothing made sense in this place. No air, no light, couldn't see outside. Made me nervous, but I had to admit the colored glass was pretty.

I relaxed a little when we got to what the lady said was the "solarium, or sunroom for short—kinda fancy, Sparky, with all those French doors." One long wall was made of nothing but those French doors she was talking about, which were clear glass. Their transoms were cut clear glass that made rainbow light patterns around the room.

I could see out the clear glass French doors, but only to her green jungle. The glass doors at either end had so many plants, trees, and leaves pressed against them, I think you'd need an axe to chop them open. The middle set of doors looked like I'd be able to open them. Good. Another escape route.

Still, it was as if the outside world had disappeared. Kind of scary, like I said, but kind of good since the outside world was full of cops out to get me.

The huge sunroom and all the other parlors we'd walked through had layers of patterned rugs on the floors with not a moth hole in sight, plus crowds of cushions, seats, and vases with peacock feathers that everyone said were bad luck. The bookie I ran for palmed a peacock feather so he could touch it to his suckers' tickets. Then, they'd more than likely lose so he wouldn't have to give them payouts. Bookie seemed to be doing pretty well, so there must be some truth to the peacock feather curse.

I didn't tell the lady that. Her and the goblin hadn't eaten me yet, so no need to press my luck.

"You can call me Tootsie," the lady said. "And that's Gilbert." The goblin nodded at me, smiling. "And those are me."

She must have seen me staring at the paintings and photos and window glass pictures, all of the same gal who did look like Tootsie. Some were photos of her head only, some were huge paintings of her head to toe wearing all kinds of different getups. The biggest was in the sunroom where we were standing. It was a painting of her and a leopard. I wondered if that was the one who ate kids.

"There she is," and the lady pointed to a leopard sitting in a corner of the sunroom.

Oh, no. They tricked me. They were going to feed me to that spotted cat. I hollered and turned to run, but tripped over one of her million floor cushions.

As I scrambled to get up, I heard her and the goblin laughing. Fiends.

"She's stuffed now! Gilbert, show the girl."

Before I knew it, the goblin called Gilbert trotted to the corner of the huge sunroom where the dangerous leopard was sitting, picked it up pretty as you please, then trotted back to me and stuck its nose at my face.

"Harmless," he chuckled. "And heavy!" With a huff, he put it on top of the cushion I tripped over.

Sure enough, that thing was stuffed. Up close, I could see its eyes were glass. Plus, it didn't move. Didn't try to eat me. How about that?

"Her name is Clara Bell," the lady said. "She was like my sister. Always there for me. Always listening to me."

I felt like saying, hey, that's because a leopard can't talk back. But I kept that to myself. These people were strange, that's for sure, and I was a wanted murderer, so I had to feel my way around, see where I stood.

Instead, I pointed to another leopard I noticed, half under a table. It was flattened into a rug and stretched out on top of the sunroom carpets. Only its head wasn't flattened. Its snarling mouth was wide open, showing lots of sharp teeth. "How about that one? A good listener too?"

"Oh, no." Her voice got suddenly hard and angry and her eyebrows crinkled. "That one didn't work out at all."

"Too touchy. Ill tempered," Gilbert added.

"I have no idea what Clara Bell saw in him."

Since I could be called touchy and ill tempered, let's just say my worries weren't put to rest. Best not cross this broad. I decided to steer things back to the other cat.

"So, Clara Bell, she was nice, huh?"

"Oh, yes," and Tootsie's voice went back to soft. "I couldn't bear to part with her. So, I had her stuffed. But she's not the same. I don't like to pet her anymore." She looked so sadly at the leopard, then turned away and moved to another room. Gilbert looked sadly, not at the cat, but at her. Then he hefted the stuffed kitty up and hauled it back to its corner of the sunroom.

I decided the leopard wasn't so bad. I'd investigate it more later, see if I could find the stitching. The flat leopard warranted a closer look too. There were lots of peculiar things to check out in this mansion, if I could stick around for a bit. If I wanted to stick around.

The goblin trotted out of sight after Tootsie. "Mademoiselle! Mademoiselle! The little girl could use a scrub, some hot water. Very much so! Hum?"

I heard his voice repeating this a few times from other rooms, until Tootsie said in a far way kind of voice, "Oh, I suppose."

I could tell where this was going, and I wasn't too thrilled.

Let me tell you my opinion about baths. Waste of time. As soon as you clean off, dirty you are again. Especially if you lived my life, crawling under houses, digging in barrels for the slop that's meant to be hauled away to pig farms. Sometimes the nice old people demanded I use a wash basin to clean up. For a sandwich, okay, I'd put up with some scrubbing behind my ears.

Once my Bookie told me I "stink so bad," I couldn't run for him anymore until I "cleaned up my act." The crumb. He knew running was my only source of the green stuff, so he had me in a tight spot. I cleaned up in a rooming house's bird bath. Best I could do in a pinch. He said, "Hey, you're worse than you were before!" But he let me keep running for him.

Back Gilbert the goblin trotted, all eager smiles. I had to head this off.

"Really, I'm fine. Okay just the way I am." I was up off the floor now, backing away, hands up. I think in jail, they make you take a bath too.

Like a magic act, Tootsie reappeared, her sad face gone, eyes twinkling again. "You're right Gilbert, I think a bubble bath is precisely the thing."

Bubble bath? What?

"No, ma'am, really. Fine. I'm fine."

"You don't want a bubble bath? Everybody likes a bubble bath. I used to love a nice long bubble bath with Clara Bell. She loved trying to catch the bubbles with her teeth. Yeah, Gilbert, let's get this Sparky girl some bubbles."

I made to run, but that goblin scooped me up like he'd scooped up the leopard. He carried me under one arm like I was a sack of fake money. Let me tell you, I squirmed and fought, punching his arm.

"Enough! No wiggling, little girl! It's a bath for you!"

Did I tell you he had some kind of strange accent? Like something in a monster movie I'd seen in a Broadway movie palace. Then him barking at me like that? And that scar across his eye? It did make me pause. Maybe I escaped the leopard, but what next? Was it really a bubble bath, or a bubbling stew pot?

Tootsie? She laughed. "Hey, Gilbert, watch yourself. She's dangerous. A wanted murderer."

Making fun of me on top of everything. Being wanted cuts your options. Big time. I stopped wiggling. Like I said, no more options.

With Tootsie chattering about Clara Bell and bubbles (she caught them with her claws too, don't you know), Gilbert followed her with me under his arm to a white-tiled room all clean and shiny with a big white tub in the middle. Even the bathroom window glass was milk white.

"Maybe we should get her to a nicer bathroom," Tootsie asked the goblin, which confused me to no end. This was nicer than any bathroom I'd seen, including the time I got lost sneaking around City Hall and stumbled into the Mayor's suite, but that's another story.

"No, no, Mademoiselle. She's so dirty. Utilitarian is the bathroom we need."

"Ohh-kee-doh-kee. Gilbert knows best."

She turned on the water and it didn't take long for it to come out steaming. I'd never seen water come out of any pipe so hot so fast. I supposed I gaped. Tootsie laughed. She was enjoying this whole show. At my expense.

"Gilbert, I'll go look around for some bubbles." She swished out the bathroom door.

The goblin put me down to fiddle with the tub taps. Not so smart. I turned to flee, but he called after me in a loud whisper, "Please, little girl! Please!"

Like I said, I was a big softie. His voice sounded so desperate, I turned around, and his face looked worried. "Please, let's make Mademoiselle happy. It's such a small thing, a bath. Please."

I hesitated, looking from this Gilbert the goblin, to the door, and back.

"Where else do you go? Huh, little Sparky?" He had a point. "A bath won't kill you, uh?" That I didn't know for sure, but he did have a certain logic. "For now, stay. What else you going to do? For now. Come on, little girl."

Fine. I shrugged and sat on the floor. No options. Might as well stay. And let me tell you, a street kid could do worse. Like I said, this mansion took the prize. It was weird, sure, but it was fancier than anything I'd ever been invited to stay in. By a long shot.

Gilbert relaxed and went back to fiddling with the taps. "Good pipes in this house. Strong plumbing. You will like. Hot, hot water." He went on like this as the tub filled.

Whatever bubble finding Tootsie was doing was taking forever. I could hear sounds from other places in the house, thunks and footsteps. The goblin leaned against the wall and hummed to himself. After a while, he tested the water, then turned on the tap again to add more hot stuff. That made the tub too full, so he rolled up one sleeve, reached his arm down into the hot water, pulled up the rubber stopper until enough water drained. He did this a few times, sighing and looking toward the door.

I think I dozed. Then I was awake in a flash with her voice singing out, "I found it!" She waltzed in holding up a bottle filled with something purple, and some kind of shiny, flimsy gown.

Gilbert sprang to life, his face all light and cheery in an

instant.

"I got this bottle of bubbles in Paris, but haven't used it since . . . well, never you mind. You'll love it. It is absolutely intense." She dumped about half the purple stuff into the tub. It stank.

She held up the gown. It had a dragon all down the back. The dragon was breathing fire. "You can wear this after your bath. Gilbert, I think we'll have to burn those clothes." She nodded her chin toward me.

"Yes!" He liked that idea. "She dresses like a boy."

"Well, we all have our costumes, don't we?" she chirped.

Then out the door they went, with Gilbert giving me one last worried, pleading look before closing the door.

Fortunately, the door had a lock lever. The first thing I did was turn it, and I didn't relax until I heard that nice solid snap. Safe. The white glass window was cracked open, like bathroom windows usually were. Good. Another escape hatch if I needed it.

I'd meant only to scrub off a little in the sink. But, I had to admit, even for me, I was a particular mess. All the hiding in trash bins since I became a fugitive must have done it. Besides, the sink was too high for me to do anything but a little hand washing, and there was no stepping stool in sight.

The bath water stank, like I said, but in I went, minus the clothes. I'd only had those threads for two days anyway. They were stolen. By me.

The purple bubble water made me feel like gagging at first. But then the whole business started growing on me. If I churned the water, I could make a foam of purple bubbles. And it was fun to bat the bubbles around. I could see Clara Bell's point, batting the bubbles with her paws, chasing them with her teeth. Maybe I got a bit enthusiastic with the splashing, since half the water ended up on the floor. I never said I was neat and tidy.

There was a wire basket on the side of the tub that held a sponge and a couple of scrub brushes, including one with a long handle. I used that to get to all those itchy spots on my back. I used the smaller one to try getting the leaves and sticks out of my hair. Didn't have much luck.

Not perfect, but good enough. I must have gotten something off, because the water was almost black when it cooled. Time for me to call this cleaning quits.

There was a chrome rail attached to one wall with too many towels for me to count. I pulled a few off. They were lots bigger and thicker than pretty-boy Mayor's. I guess he wasn't the hot stuff he thought he was, with his second-rate towels. Made me chuckle for the first time since this birthday of mine took such a bad turn.

On with the dragon gear. It was strange, but not the strangest thing I've had to wear in a pinch.

I thought the lady and goblin might be waiting on the other side of the door, but they were nowhere. I found my way back to the kitchen, thinking to polish off the not-sweet-at-all cookies that'd fallen to the floor along with me when Tootsie and goblin found me, but the cookies were gone. The floor, the counter were clean of crumbs. I tried the icebox, hoping I'd find a cake. No luck. Itty bitty onions. A dish of tiny pickles that tasted funny. Strange things I didn't know what they were. Lots of hard boiled eggs. At least there weren't any bloody little kid parts.

"That's only a dressing gown. Let's get you some real clothes."

Her sneaking up like that scared me so bad, I dropped the dish of weird pickles I was eating to keep from starving to death. I once ate dirt to keep from starving, but I don't like people to know that. So, don't tell anybody, okay?

The pickles rolled around the floor, but she didn't seem to notice. "Come along, see my closets."

She flitted out the door. I followed.

At this point, I could have taken off. I could have run for it out the kitchen door. But, like the goblin said, where would I go? No options. I decided to keep playing along. Nothing bad had happened yet. The food situation wasn't good, but maybe it would get better. I had nothing to lose.

I followed her through the leopard sunroom, through parlor after parlor. She wasn't wearing the furs anymore. Good thing, because that fur made me hot just looking at it. She'd changed into something completely different, a purple flower print summer dress thin as tissue paper with a matching cape type thing that scooped down the dress's scooped back all the way to the floor and then some. She wore matching gloves so long, they went up past her elbows. Why would she make a cool dress hot with those gloves? And people thought I'd lost my marbles.

Finally, we reached a wide staircase with strange banisters that were made like two rows of squares that didn't match. More squares dangled overhead from the ceiling.

"A famous artist made that," she said when she turned and noticed I'd stopped to stare at it. "He gave it to me. People used to do that. Give me things. Come on! Gilbert! We're going to the closets!"

The goblin appeared with a dustpan in hand, so Tootsie must have cut short his cleaning. But he wasn't mad. He was all cheery, like it was a party. "Why, yes, Mademoiselle! We must go to the closets!"

Me and goblin followed her into a hallway. Off this hallway was a maze of rooms and more halls stuffed with clothes, hats, spangles, do-dads, feathers. The rooms had closed, colored glass windows, like downstairs, with only the smaller, clear glass transoms left open. Up here, it was even hotter and stuffier. And darker. Each room had a dim light burning so you wouldn't trip over all the velvet and lace and shoes with bows.

She opened her arms wide, smile wider. "These are all my costumes from all my shows! Do you love 'em!"

"Sure," I said, "There's lots and lots." It was amazing. Some of her outfits looked like what she was wearing in those pictures on the walls.

"Of course, she loves them," Gilbert said. "Everyone does."

"Here's pirate girl, milk maid, vamp, vamp, vamp, lots of vamps. I need to find you a nice dress."

"I don't wear dresses."

She whipped around. "No? Why?"

"I tell you, she dresses like a boy," Gilbert frowned.

"I have to run around a lot, be on the move. I can't let any skirts get in my way."

"Well, she is a fugitive, so maybe that's a point," Tootsie said. "Let's see. I've had to disguise myself as a boy in lots of pictures. Pirate boy? No. Little prince? No."

I kind of liked the prince outfit. Blue satin with sparkles sewn on it. But I kept my mouth shut. When someone's giving you a freebee, you have to take how the dice rolls. Start making demands, and the bet might be off altogether. Yeah, I'd learned a thing or two.

"Ah, sailor boy. That's cute. And it does have pants."

I didn't like that as much, but what did I tell you about freebees?

"Underthings. You'll need those too."

"She'll want little girl things," goblin said, worry in his voice.

"Oh, don't fret! I'll find something. Let's look through my older things, when I was younger and thinner. I was pretty small."

"You're still small. For a grown-up," I said in an off-handed way. Bookie told me all women liked to be told how small and tiny they were.

Sure enough, her happy face became Christmas happy. "Did you hear that, Gilbert? Still small! And that cow had the nerve to tell me I'd gotten thick. The nerve."

"You see, I tell you all the time you are the smallest girl in Hollywood. That cow is thick like a ditch digger."

This made the two of them laugh.

She opened several pink and white striped boxes and let a waterfall of lacey things fall to the floor. They were pink, red, black, purple, green.

"Here's a white one. That's a little girl color, isn't it, Gilbert?"

He shrugged his eyebrows in a I-suppose kind of way.

"These knickers are really small, so don't worry, they won't slide down to your knees. Here's the camisole that goes with it." And she tossed me a T-shirt made of lace.

These didn't seem like any kind of normal underthings to me. But, free clothes were free clothes.

"On to the dressing room, kids!"

With my free clothes in my arms, I followed her and Gilbert to a room with a pink ceiling, pink rug, tons more lights, and walls of mirrors.

I snuck in a fun house on Broadway once that had a room like this. The mirrors made a million reflections of me, over and over again. It was strange, scary. I didn't like this dressing room any better, but her and goblin seemed used to it.

In the middle of the room was a pink dressing table with drawers. Pink bows were tied to its legs. Another mirror sat on top of it. "Have a seat, Sparky," and she pushed me down on a pink puffy chair in front of the dressing table. "Your hair is a mess. Full of twigs or something. What's this?" She pulled out a nail. I had no idea how that got there. "Your hair's too long anyway. Short is the fashion."

"She's right," Gilbert said to me, like he was an authority.

"I'll cut it for you. I used to cut my hair all the time. I'm good at it." From a drawer in the dressing table, she pulled out a huge pair of shears, which made me flinch. Maybe I wasn't so safe after all.

"Mademoiselle, please, why don't I help with that?"

"I'm fine!" She snapped at him. "Look, steady hands. Not a bit of shaking." She held her hand up with the shears.

"Well . . ."

"I'm fine!" She started snipping. I closed my eyes. I

couldn't watch. Let me tell you, those were some tense moments, not knowing if I'd feel the cold blade slicing more than my hair. Maybe her hands weren't shaking, but if anybody'd looked, they'd'a seen my hands shaking plenty.

"All done!"

I dared open my eyes.

Not bad.

I looked strange. But not bad.

"You look exactly like the hair I had when I played the imprisoned princess in 'Canterbury Tears.' You remember that one?"

I didn't. I had no ghost of an idea, but my wheels spun, trying to think of something to say, quick.

She noticed my pause, and her happy face dropped. "You don't know who I am, do you?" I saw Gilbert's face drop too, and his eyes darted to her, looking worried. I was getting the idea he spent a lot of time worrying.

I didn't know who she was, not really. But I decided to say what I did know.

"Of course, I do! You're the star. Everyone knows."

"They do?" her voice soft, uncertain.

"Sure! Everyone says, 'That's the house where the star lives!'"

She let out a breath and touched her hand to her face. "Did you hear that, Gilbert?"

Gilbert's face was happy again. "What do I tell you! Everyone knows you! That cow lies!"

"Is that why you came here? To see me?"

Not exactly, but I shrugged in a you-caught-me way and hoped for the best.

She shook her head. "Naughty thing. Now I have a fan creeping around the house. A wanted fugitive fan. Oh, Gilbert. It's too much sometimes, isn't it? The fame."

She tucked her hand under his elbow, and the two of them wandered out of the dressing room. He was still carrying his dustpan. She murmured, "They remember me. They still do," and Gilbert repeated, "Of course they do! I tell you all the time that cow lies!"

I left out the part about the crazy old actress in the Creepy House bathing in kid blood, but she didn't need to hear that.

With them gone, I donned my new threads behind a folding screen painted with long-necked, pink flying birds. The pants were long, but I fixed that by rolling up the hems into cuffs.

I didn't have a pair of shoes, but I didn't mind. I never wore them anyway.

It took me awhile to find my way out of the clothes maze. Again, the two of them had vanished.

By now, I was super-duper starving. And tired. It had been a long day.

I wandered down the stairs and found my way back to the leopard parlor. I curled up at Clara Bell's furry feet. Light still sparkled through the green jungle leaves, through the French doors' clear glass and the cut-glass transoms.

Being summer, with days going on forever, it was hard to tell how late it really was. The room was still hot and stuffy. It made me drowsy. I was staring at the rainbow patterns that the sunlight made through the cut-glass transoms, and then before I knew what happened, I woke to someone wailing.

Chapter 3

I jumped up so fast, I knocked over Clara Bell and landed face to face with the grinning cat's pointed teeth. Then I was the one yelling, until I remembered where I was.

The light coming through the cut glass was softer. Had I slept all the rest of the day, through the night, until the next morning? Must have.

Someone was still wailing. Then it stopped. Whatever was going on, it put my nerves on edge.

I shoved Clara Bell upright again. No kidding, she was heavy. A pinch of sawdust fell out of her and landed on my hair.

I was swishing sawdust out of my hair, my stomach was growling gallops, and there the wailing started up again. Boy, oh, boy I needed something, anything to eat. (Was sawdust from a dead stuffed cat edible? Nah, better not risk it.) But first things first. I had to find out what was up with this wailing. Were the goblin and the weird lady slicing up kids after all? Or leopards they didn't like?

I carefully stepped around the flat leopard on the carpet. Wasn't sure if it would squeak if I stepped on it. You never knew. My Bookie hid a squeaker under a rug outside his office, so he could hear if anyone tried sneaking up to plug him full of holes.

Using my street kid savvy, I slithered along walls, ducked behind huge ceramic birds with long legs and beaks, and crawled under rows of chairs and sofas. I spotted the source of the wailing. I darted into the room and crouched under a Victrola cabinet to get a better look.

The room had tall windows, but like the other windows, you couldn't see a thing out of them because the panes were made of squares of colored glass. The room was crammed with anything musical: piano, harp, and violins and guitars hanging from the walls and some from the ceiling. There were plenty of paintings and photos of her too, in poses like she was singing.

That's what the wailing was. This Tootsie was singing, I supposed.

She was wearing a long shiny green gown with purple trim and a matching green turban. Her arms were spread wide, making the gown's long, pointed sleeves hang down to the floor. In one hand, she held a lacy purple hankie. Her head was thrown back, her mouth wide open, wailing, wailing.

"No, no, Mademoiselle. I hear a flatness. Tiny, yes, but please, let us make sound more from our diaphragms, shall we?" A small man with almost no hair and round spectacles said this. One of his hands held a little stick and the other fiddled with papers on a metal stand in front of him. "Your voice is so beautiful, but a little more diaphragm and it shall be divinely beautiful, no?"

Beautiful? This guy was full of hot baloney and applesauce.

She nodded like she was out of breath. With all that hollering, she must have been. She dabbed her face with the purple hankie. I noticed her makeup was twice as heavy as it had been yesterday. Looked like she had an inch of black painted along her eyelids that swooped up in an Egyptian curve heading toward her ears.

"Deep breath, Mademoiselle!"

She breathed in deep, deep, threw her head back, and belted out another one. She was loud, I'd give her that. She'd be a great barker calling in the tourists for one of the side shows down the hill on Broadway.

But I won't tell her that.

The little man was staring at me. No, can't be. No one sees me when I'm in hiding mode.

He tapped his stick on his stand and held up his other hand to stop Tootsie. He kept staring at me. Those spectacles must give him super vision.

With a croak, Tootsie cut her wail short.

"Mademoiselle, what is that thing?" He pointed his stick at me.

Did he recognize me, the wanted fugitive? Should I run? I felt frozen in place.

She twisted around, her arms still flung wide. She squinted, leaned over toward where he was pointing his stick, squinted some more. Her black lined eyes finally saw me and popped wide open. I could almost see her face thinking. Good gal.

She remembered I was wanted for murder. I breathed out in relief. I hoped she came up with a good story.

She straightened up and looked at the little man with a smile. She still had her arms flung out. She could hold a pose like a champ. "Why Beele, that is my new house boy."

"It looks like a girl."

"Well, we can't always be choosy, can we?"

"Does it have a name?"

She twisted back to look at me, her face in thinking mode again. Then she looked back at this Beele. "No, I haven't decided on one yet. I want the name to be something amusing."

He nodded and made an "um" sound like he bought the story. Good. Then his eyes peered at me again. "Why is it creeping beneath the Victrola?"

Her Egyptian eyes batted at me, batted at Beele. She came up with a story faster this time. She was getting into the swing of things. "I instructed it to search for my missing earring. The one with the garnets that would have more perfectly matched this costume rather than the poor substitutes I am wearing now, which is probably why my voice isn't its usual perfection—divine perfection—this morning. I instructed it specifically to be thorough. Excruciatingly thorough."

Poor substitutes? Those ear bobs she was wearing looked like emeralds to me, and the real kind, not paste. My Bookie sometimes bought "merchandise" 'round the midnight hour, so I'd seen plenty 'a paste rocks and the real deals. I'd acquired a few paste fakes, and not-so-fakes, for him too. Sometimes Bookie got like he was a teacher and explained the difference. Yeah, those were some real emeralds all right.

Beele nodded like this excruciatingly thorough business made him happy. The creep. But he wasn't completely happy. "Ah, but Mademoiselle, its staring is interfering with our practice. I believe, and correct me if I am wrong, I believe it is throwing off your beautiful voice."

"Yeah, I think so." She twisted to look at me again. "You heard the man. Scram!"

Don't have to tell me twice. That was a close call. I was up and running, following my stomach towards smells of baking that'd caught my attention. My stomach led me back to the kitchen.

The goblin was bustling and humming, apron on, hands wrapped in dish towels that were wrapped around a pan of the most delicious smelling just-baked I don't know what they were, but my stomach laid down a reservation on five of them right off the bat.

He lifted the pan away from my grabbing hands.

"Tsk tsk, my little Sparky. Go have a seat and I will serve you properly. There will be plenty for you. Mademoiselle cannot eat these. Her figure, you understand."

Fine with me. But, I hoped the wait wouldn't be too long. I was so hungry.

I squirmed in the chair at the kitchen table. Everything was shiny chrome, neat and clean. Nice, but food's more important. The wailing started up again. It drove me twice as crazy now that I was twice as hungry and so close to a fine plateful of eats.

"What's the noise about?" and I nodded in the direction of the wailing.

"No noise, practice! All the pictures are talking now, did you know that?"

Of course, but I played dumb with a blank look. Better to keep him talking. The more info I knew about these people the better.

"Oh, yes. Mademoiselle must keep her voice in shape. Of course, she has made many jazz recordings in the past. They have been very popular with her fans, despite evil people dismissing them as 'vanity' recordings. Horrible, horrible, jealous people with sad lives that must attack those with talent!"

I didn't mean to get him talking this much. Didn't want my breakfast delayed. I nodded encouragement. Get this show on the road, pops.

"Yes, yes. The talkies, as the people call them, have much singing. She is absolutely perfect for so many of the singing parts. The star parts, of course."

"Of course. I want to see those pictures, with her in them."

He smiled broadly, his cheeks red from the hot oven. "Yes, our dear little fan. I saw you sleeping by Clara Bell. You seemed so peaceful, I didn't want to disturb you. I hope you don't mind. It makes our Mademoiselle so happy to see your affection toward Clara Bell. She does worry about the poor thing being neglected, but Mademoiselle can't bear to touch her Clara Bell anymore. And then you came. Like an answer to a prayer."

"Yeah, sure." My stomach was on those fancy buns or whatever. To hell with Clara Bell. I wanted eats!

With a flourish he laid a plate with a strange gold and red pattern on it before me, but I barely noticed the pattern for the five fat buns shining with sugar. And in the next instant, he had a steaming cup of, was that? Cocoa? Hot cocoa?

Let me tell you, hot cocoa was some fine drink. I'd had it exactly once, at Mrs. Tomes' house, before her housekeeper Mrs. Mabaline decided I was no good and refused to make it for me again. "We have to humor our Mrs. Mabaline," was all Mrs. Tomes had to say about it. A real letdown, but at least I could still get a few cookies from a visit, seeing as the Mabaline lady always made them anyway. Not that she was happy about me eating them.

Should I stick my snout in the cocoa cup, or shove in some buns? Tough choices. I decided I could do both, and had one hand on the cup at the left side of my mouth and one hand on a bun at the right side of my mouth and was about to enter paradise, when a thought occurred to me.

What if that cold kid had been here?

She was clean, was wearing a nice nightie without any holes I could see. She was thin, though. Maybe they did pluck her off the streets.

What if they'd washed her up, dressed her, then fed her buns and cocoa cooked with poison? I saw a picture show about that very situation. The bad guy in the castle fed the little prince the best-looking sugar bun you ever saw, but it was full of poison. At exactly the last second when the kid was about to stuff the bun in his snout, the good guy swooped in on a chandelier and snatched away that poison bun. There was no swooping good guy who saved that cold kid on the Court Hill bench. No good guy to rescue me either.

I put down the cup of cocoa and pushed it away from me, with a shaking hand. It was all I could do to say, "I don't want cocoa. It gives me hives or something." I spotted a dish of the same buns on the counter. "I want those, not these." I put the one I was about to eat back on the plate.

The goblin raised his eyebrows. "Those are for Mr. Beele, but we'll give him these. They are the same anyhow." He switched plates and took away the cocoa. Oh, boy, that broke my heart. But there's serious crime happening in the neighborhood and I had to take all precautions, no matter how terrible.

Deciding maybe they wouldn't be poisoning Mr. Beele, I shoved an entire bun into my mouth.

"Funny, your friend asked for Mr. Beele's buns too."

I froze mid-chew. Friend? My mind zipped to the big cop who particularly wanted to put me in a "home," the cop I called

Mug.

"Fre-? Wha?" I mumbled through the bun in my mouth. I started choking and coughed.

The goblin pounded me on the back a few times until I coughed up that delicious bun all over the floor and my sailor boy outfit.

He wasn't mad but chuckled as he swiped a rag over my shirt and the floor. "Ah, the little boy said he didn't want you to know he was here. I think maybe you are jealous he got an autograph from Mademoiselle before you did. All these little fans coming around. I hope Mademoiselle does not get too overwhelmed. Fame is such a burden." But he smiled as he said this. "So many fans reminded Mademoiselle she must keep up her voice. She hasn't had Mr. Beele here for so long. It is good to have him back, and see her preparing for parts again. Like old days."

"Did this little boy say his name is Bobby?"

"Ha, ha. Yes. That's the one. He said he followed you here. He is very fond of you. Quite the young gentleman."

"Yeah, that's Bobby all right. Where is he?" Did they stuff him like the leopard and shove him in the basement? Or was he a rug? I must have been off my game if Bobby followed me and I didn't notice. Being wanted for murder was making me fall apart, lose my edge. But, yeah, where was he?

"Ah, he left. He did not want to alarm you. He knows you are wanted for many crimes."

Wait a minute. "Many? It's just the one murder."

I was about to shove another bun in my mouth, and it's a good thing I didn't because the goblin slapped a morning paper on the table and the headlines would have made me choke all over again.

"One Girl Crime Spree!!" was the headline and with two exclamation points. There was a photo of me from the last time I was in school. I was sticking out my tongue. How'd they get hold of that? There was a drawing of the dead girl too, looking sweet like sugar and not so dead. Next to her, I looked extra rotten.

The rag played up the murder-over-candy angle, and then a bunch more bad things I'd done: break-ins, milk stolen from stoops, holdups, a missing piano, and a bank robbery down the hill on Spring Street. There was a photo of a tommy gun in a basement. The rag said the cops found it in my "lair," and I'd used it the holdups and bank robbery. The rooming house basement in the photo was one of my hideouts, but I had nothing to do with that gun. Meantime, the Mayor managed to get his movie star grinning photo on the front page too, saying something about the good citizens could feel safe with him being all on the case and baloney like that. Yeah, and his pretty-boy photo was bigger than mine too. What a ham.

Okay, so maybe the milk was me, and yeah, I wiggled through windows now and again to get something to eat, something to wear. Maybe once, or maybe twice, or maybe, oh, forget about it—Bookie had me sneak into a place to look for jewels he'd heard about. Once after I found only paste, he called me "a waste of time." I didn't like that and won't do a second-story job for him ever again.

"But I didn't do any bank robbing or stickups. Where would I hide a piano?" I pleaded with goblin.

He chuckled. "I think you would not be able to pick up that big gun. I think it is almost as tall as you."

This was serious. This was more than being in the wrong place at the wrong time with the dead kid. I was being framed. But why? What was going on?

I'd been wasting too much time messing around this weird house with the dead leopards. I had to take action. First order of business: I'd better find Bobby, make sure he was still alive and not chopped up in a suitcase under the goblin's bed. But I didn't want goblin to know what I was up to.

I made a pocket out of my shirt front, and shoved the rest of the buns in. "I got stuff do to, I mean, I wanna go play with that leopard. Maybe some hide and seek type stuff around the house. That okay?" I asked the goblin as I made my way out the kitchen.

"I am making a special treat for lunch. Be sure to come back to the kitchen while it is still warm!"

"Yeah, sure." Warm food. Sounded real nice. Could I come back for lunch? Was it a good idea, or a really bad idea? I'd worry about it later. I had to get out on the Hill, find out what was going on.

My path was blocked by Tootsie and Beele. His bespectacled eyes were hungry for those buns. Their smell was like hard liquor to a boozer. Then his eyes saw me and the buns I was holding in my shirt front, and the stain down my sailor suit from when I coughed up the other bun. He frowned. "Here is this thing. Again."

Tootsie followed his stare. "Ah, yes, I have decided on a name for our new addition. Mysteeree, like Mystery."

That was the dumbest name I'd ever heard. "What?"

Now I had Beele's disapproval, not that I had enough of it

already. "You disagree with the name Mademoiselle has spent much thought choosing for you? Ungrateful. And you were to work. To find the missing earring. I hope you have not pocketed the valuable."

Oh, now, come on. "I, ah, I found it and put it back where it belongs. Like I was told. Doing what the boss lady says."

"Excellent, Mysteeree! Go run along and double-check that you've done everything exactly how I've asked."

I hope she wasn't going to keep calling me that dumb name. "Yes, Mademoiselle! Immediately!" I had to squeeze past Beele, who didn't look like he approved of me escaping his gaze. As I took off, I could hear him say, "Obedient servants are the only acceptable kind. Beating is often for the best."

I was only too glad to get away from that character. I didn't like his suspicious eyes getting a look at me. What if he started putting two and two together? I hoped he kept buying Tootsie's Mysteeree house boy hooey.

After quickly shoving the buns down my throat from my hiding spot behind Clara Bell, I was fortified and ready to go. The kitchen door was out of the picture with likes-to-beat-'em Beele busy eating his buns there. I could try the French doors since I was right here in the sunroom. Or maybe that was too likely, something goblin and Beele would figure out. I had a better idea.

I steered around the flat leopard again and headed to the bathroom. I was amazed to see the black mess I left in the tub was gone and it and the floor and everything else was sparkling white like it was brand new. Must have been the goblin's magic.

I clambered on the toilet to reach the white glass window I remembered from yesterday. It was still cracked open. It didn't take much for me to open it all the way. Since the bathroom was on the first story, it was a nice and easy drop into bushes with orange pointy flowers and long green leaves reaching as tall as the windowsill. Like I said, she had some strange plants.

Being careful of the pointy flowers, I climbed out of those plants and wandered around the dark green jungle until I found the fence. After making sure I'd be going into an empty yard, rather than one full of people yelling for cops, I squeezed under the iron fence railing. There were advantages to being a kid. Tight spaces were no problem.

Bobby lived on Bunker Hill Avenue too, only at the other end. I took my time wiggling from one yard to the next, avoiding dogs and curious toddlers. If not a yard, I crawled around whatever sideway or byway I knew didn't get a lot of people walking through.

Let me tell you something about Bunker Hill. It's a maze. A maze on top of a steep hill that stuck up like a sore thumb smack dab in the middle of downtown Los Angeles, right in front of the fancy new City Hall building. It's like Bunker Hill was rubbing City Hall's nose in its old houses and old dirt. That's how I thought of Bunker Hill.

City Hall didn't think too much of Bunker Hill. Too old. Too in the way. Sure, plenty of the Hill was rundown. Sure, characters like my Bookie operated here. But mostly, it was regular people, and a lot of old people living in the old mansions that got turned into rooming houses. Some had lived here all their lives and remembered when Bunker Hill was a fancy place, when rich high rollers were building all these great big houses.

Mrs. Tomes was like that. She was born in her old house! She lived like she always did, though maybe she had more than just Mrs. Mabaline waiting on her back in the day. She never took boarders into her house, and she still kept it looking like it always had. Well, sort of. She got it painted last year. It's pink now, with violet and mint green trim. Mug laughed at it. Called it a "pink tart." I don't know. I thought it was all right. It was different. Wasn't that good?

The Victorian houses on Bunker Hill Avenue—like I said, those were the nicest. My Bookie agreed the people there really kept them up. He should know. He's had a few of them robbed.

Bobby's parents went overboard with their house, if you asked me. They tried to make the place exactly like it was when it was built, minus the gas lights and plus an electric Frigidaire, if you know what I mean. They're not that crazy about being old-timey.

But they did have some guys scrape away years and years of old paint on the house. Why? Because they decided they'd repaint it in its "original Victorian colors," inside and out and had to properly "prepare" the old wood, or something like that. Bobby told me they practically fainted when they found out the house used to be this weird pea green and yucky blue color. The inside colors were even worse. Now they don't know what to do since they told all the other Bunker Hill Avenue snobs they for sure were going back to the "original colors."

Meantime, the house looked like a goof, with half the paint scraped away. Ha ha. His parents were funny, in a strange way. Considering the parents he had to put up with, sometimes I thought I was lucky.

Sometimes.

Bobby read all the time. And sure enough, when I squeezed into the bushes on the other side of his backyard fence, he was lying on the grass and reading a book.

By a twitch in his eye, I could tell he saw me through the gaps in the iron fence rails.

"Hey, there," he whispered without moving his face from the book. He knew how to play it cool.

"I heard you were at Creepy House," I said, keeping my voice low.

"Yeah. I followed you there. Wanted to make sure you were okay." He kept his eyes glued to the book. If his parents happened to look out a window, all they'd see was him sounding out words from the book. His parents were big on books, school, stuff like that. He had their number down pat. Good ol' Bobby.

"Thanks. I wanted to make sure you were still alive too. Make sure that goblin and the crazy lady hadn't cut you up and eaten you."

Bobby's head came up for a second, before he caught himself and looked down at the book again. "Gee. Thanks," he said with a catch in his voice. I think he was touched I was looking out for him.

"Yeah, well, you did me a big favor yesterday, hiding me from all those fake friends of mine and the cops. I owe you a few."

Bobby smiled but then wiped it off his face before any spying eyes noticed. "You don't owe me anything. I'll always be there for you. You know you're my girl, Sparky."

Not that again! "Hey, Bobby, I'm in serious trouble. Now the papers are saying I stole a piano and robbed a bank with a tommy gun."

"Sparky, it's gotten worse. Special editions came out saying you murdered a whole bunch of people. A hobo found dead on the beach last January, that's one of your victims. The coroner changed his mind about the lady who died walking up Bunker Hill during the last heat wave and said it wasn't heat stroke after all, but you. Remember the elevator that broke on Spring Street and three people were killed? You were behind that too. Sabotaged the elevator cable. Papers say you're a 'one girl killing machine.'"

This was bad. "Someone's out to get me, Bobby."

"Sure looks like it. The Hill is swarming with cops. Not so much on this street, but everywhere else. I think you need to go back to Creepy House and keep hiding. Those people don't seem so bad. Strange, but not bad."

"Nah, Bobby. I gotta get answers. I gotta clear my name. I haven't killed one single person, dog or cat or goldfish, ever!"

"Let me go with you. It's dangerous out there. I'll protect you."

I was afraid he'd say that. "I'm not dragging you into this, Bobby. You'll end up in the slammer or swinging from the end of a rope if they decide you're my crime partner. I'm going it alone."

Bobby was so upset he forgot himself, put his book down and looked at me. Just as fast, he remembered himself, and had his nose back in the pages. "Sparky, I insist!"

But I was already in the other yard and on my way to the bad man who hangs around Court Hill. He's out and about early in the mornings. Maybe he saw something. Bobby wouldn't want me near that guy. Like I said, bad. All the kids knew to steer clear of him.

And maybe it was him that'd iced that girl.

Chapter 4

It took me forever to get to the park on Court Hill. Bobby wasn't kidding about cops swarming everywhere.

They were posted by all my favorite hiding places. I nearly stumbled over one lying flat in my most reliable crawl space under one of the old mansions turned into a rooming house. I had to do some extra quiet scrambling to get away from him. I even spotted a cop with a tommy gun watching the top of the Angel's Flight tram tracks. Would he really gun me down if I made a break for that little train running up and down Bunker Hill?

Along the way, I hid in a box of trash meant for a backyard incinerator. In all the trash, I found a beat-up straw hat. I needed a disguise, so I slipped it on. I still kept low, but at least no one would see my face.

"That you, Sparky, the killer kid?"

It was him. The bad man.

He spotted me peeking out from bushes at the top of Court Hill near where my favorite bench overlooked the city. The bench where I found the dead kid. He was sitting in it now. Like a skinny spider, his long thin arms draped over the back of the bench, and his long thin legs stretched out on the grass. Why was he hanging out on my bench and not his usual spot on his rooming house steps? He had the best view of the park, and anything going on in it, from those steps.

"That hat doesn't exactly hide you. No other kids I know wiggle through the bushes like you do." He was laughing. "You coming to see your old friend? I can hide you. Keep you safe from the coppers. Any favors you need, all you gotta do is say the word." His smile was huge.

I didn't move from the bushes. Had to keep myself hidden from cop eyes for as long as I could.

"Well, yeah, I do have a couple 'a things to ask now that you mention it," I said from my hiding space.

His face got brighter. "I love questions. Proceed, my miss."

He calls me that. I hate it. Worse than Bobby calling me his girl.

"I think you killed that girl."

His eyebrows shot up like he was shocked and offended. "My miss! I am shocked and offended. I can't imagine why I'd do that and have half the Los Angeles police force after my tail. But they did question me up and down a good part of the day yesterday. They looked at my finger prints, spoke to my alibi."

"You're lying. You got no alibi."

"Oh, but I do. My landlady's new cleaning girl. Fresh from foreign parts by way of New York City. I'm looking out for her, helping her. Do you know how hard it is to clean a floor with a bottle brush? One meant for little, tiny decorative bottles? That's exactly the type of work that builds character. And she needs a lot of character building. Oh, yes, she was cleaning, all that night in question as a matter of fact. She needed my supervision the whole time. Every minute. Sadly, she didn't do a good job, so I couldn't pay her with the new shoes I promised, though I truly wanted to help her. I'm kindhearted, so I think I'll give her another chance." He smiled.

I couldn't stand this guy.

"Well, I guess that makes you a hot lotta no use to me if you didn't see nothing."

"Oh, now hold on, my miss." He held up one of his long thin fingers that I hate so much. "Did I say I saw nothing? My window looks out over this very park and very bench. You know I like getting up early. I saw the whole scene play out. You, darling you, and your sweet box of sweets, tossing them up in the air and running screaming."

He did see. But how much? "Go on."

"There was more. Before then. Before she landed on the bench."

"Keep going."

He got his disappointed look that I hate too. "Oh, now, now, my miss is a greedy one, isn't she? Isn't it polite to give, if you get? Well, isn't it?"

Here it comes.

"Need I remind you that you are a wanted fugitive? Wanted now for multiple murders. What did the latest edition say? 'Bloody Crime Spree of the Century.'"

My heart kept sinking. My head told me he was lying, but my gut said, no, I think the bad man saw something. And right now, I needed something.

"Whaddya want?" I don't think I'd ever heard my voice sound so dead to my ears.

"Oh, poor thing. You seem sad, my miss. But don't worry. I truly want to help. So how about you come to the bench and we'll talk some more. No tricks. I promise." He spread his long, thin hands in an innocent kind of way and smiled big.

I didn't believe this no-tricks business. But I needed to know what he saw. "Okay."

After carefully wiggling out of the bushes, and looking this way and that to make sure the coast was clear of cops, I went to the side of the bench farthest from him. I thought I was keeping alert. I shoulda known better.

The second I got there, his long thin hands shot out across the bench and shoved me so hard, I flew down to the grass, landing flat on my fanny. For an older guy, he's spry.

He jumped up and down giggling. "Got you! Stupid, Sparky! Got you!"

"Hey, you said no tricks!"

"But I didn't mean it." He slid down to the ground and put his face up close to mine. "Wonder what happened to your candy box? Huh? Wonder? I'll tell you what. I have it. It's in my room. I ate the candy in it. I savored it, long and slow, all this morning. Ummm. That cleaning girl. Know what? I had her scratch your name off the candy box. Gone! Then I wrote my name—mine! I laughed so hard. And you know what? I still have some of your candy. But it's not yours. It's mine now. I'm going to eat it and laugh thinking about you." He laughed hard, in case I didn't get the message.

"Liar! You don't have my candy stash. The cops do!" I pulled away and got ready to sock his snout.

"But do you know that for sure?" He smiled in his mean way I've seen more times than I'd rather tell you. "You know what, Sparky? I don't think you wanna know what I saw. I think you wanna stop playing. Maybe I should yell, 'Police!' Huh?"

Being a wanted fugitive is a bunch of rats. A big bunch of rats.

Fine. I'd play.

"No pouting, my miss. I double-promise what I know is worth your while." He giggled again and rubbed his hands. "Since you're on the ground already, I think, um, let's see. Yes! Eat that grass. Go on. Like a cow. Oh, yes, a cow. You have to 'moo' too." He laughed and clapped and hopped up and down. That's his idea of fun.

I did it. Okay? Not that I was happy about it.

Did I tell you there was a time when I had nothing to eat? Zero. Maybe a few times. He had sandwiches, candy. He always had something for kids that were stupid, or hungry. But half the time, he didn't give what he promised. I got a lot smarter finding food after that. I never thought I'd have to sink to playing his games again.

I jumped up from the grass. He'd had more than enough. "Okay, you talk."

He chuckled. Not a good sign. "Tsk, tsk. Didn't anyone tell you that being demanding is unattractive in a girl? I'm afraid I'm wanting much more, for such valuable information."

Everyone knew Sparky got mad. Sparky punched. Sparky didn't get upset and sobby like a girl. But I did now. Couldn't help it. "But you promised! You double-promised!"

"And what are you going to do? Huh? You know when they give you to the hangman, I will make a point of being in the audience. Oh, yes, my miss, they let people watch the execution. I will watch as you drop, twist and choke. And I will laugh. And while I'm laughing, I will eat your candy." He stuck his face close to mind and laughed, loud, like I supposed he planned to do when I was thrashing around at the end of a rope.

Playtime was over. Before he knew what was happening, I lunged and socked him hard on his big snout. He screamed and shoved me away. "Police! Police! Sparky's attacking me!"

Who's acting like a little girl now?

I threw myself over the edge of Court Hill, which is really more like a cliff. I landed in brambles and all the wild growing things that the city can't seem to tame. I scrambled along them, and kept scrambling. All the while, I spat and spat out the grass he'd made me eat. At least with all the cops running to Court Hill, the way was clear for me to slip in the opposite direction, to Bunker Hill proper.

I made it back to Creepy House. I wasn't sure I could get up to the bathroom window without something to stand on, so took a chance and tried the sunroom French doors. Unlocked. I ran inside, hid behind Clara Bell and clutched her tail to my face.

I hate to admit it, but I cried and cried, quietly as I could, but I did cry. As fast as I wiped my tears away with the furry black end of Clara Bell's tail, new tears popped out.

Did bad man really have my candy? When the hood was pulled over my head, and the hangman's noose tightened around my neck, would I hear the crinkle of my candy wrappers? I knew the sounds of my favorite kinds. Would those be the ones he'd pick to eat while I dropped and thrashed? Would those candy wrappers be the last sounds I'd ever hear?

The cops must've had my candy. Not him. But the world was being so crazy lately, maybe somehow he had gotten my stash from them. Maybe Mug gave my candy to him. No. Mug would never give him my candy. Mug'd eat it himself, if anything. Bad man had to be lying. But what if he wasn't? The more I thought about it, the more I cried.

"Is that you, Sparky?"

Tootsie.

At least she wasn't calling me that stupid Mysteeree name. She'd changed clothes. She wore all black in a shiny fabric that was probably something fancy, like silk. No skirt, but wide flowing pants like women in the movies wore, but not women in real life. At least none that I ever saw. She wore a black turban thick with sparkles, and a huge sparkling, panther-shaped brooch that was pinned to her blouse through a lace hankie. Her belt had sparkles on it too. Her ear bobs sparkled most of all. Diamonds. Panther pin too. Can't mistake that sparkle. Not the belt or the turban, though. Those sparkles: paste.

She knelt down next to me. "I'm so happy you've taken to my dear Clara Bell. But, hey, are you crying?" She touched my face, being careful not to touch the leopard's tail.

"Don't tell Bobby," I sobbed.

"You mean your little boyfriend?" She paused and gave me a long hard look. "Hey, what happened?" Her voice wasn't soft anymore. "You can tell Tootsie. Come on, what happened?"

She was a sharp one, I'll give her that. I didn't mean to say anything, but it all poured out before I could stop myself: my candy I hoped he was lying about, the cow-grass routine, everything. I kept crying like a girl, embarrassing myself completely. But I couldn't help it.

"Well, doesn't that beat all. What a bucket 'a slime. I know exactly what to do. We'll get that information for you. You just watch and learn. Come on. We're going to my closets."

She took me by the hand and pulled me away from Clara Bell. I wanted to take the leopard's tail with me, but that would've meant ripping it off. I don't think Tootsie would've liked that much.

"Here take this." Tootsie unfastened the black lace hankie from behind the diamond panther pin and handed it to me.

It was a nice hankie, but I had to blow my nose all over it. "Sorry."

"Forget about it. I got a million of those things. A linen maker gave me a lifetime supply if I'd use them in public. Don't go out in public much, but I still got those hankies!"

We made our way up the grand staircase with the squares hanging overhead. I could hear Gilbert banging around the kitchen and could smell wonders I could only guess at.

"Let's not tell Gilbert, okay? This'll be our little secret." She put a finger from her lips to mine. "Sealed."

She pulled me through her closet maze while I kept sniffling into the hankie.

"Gotta get you out of that sailor suit. Too many people probably saw it. We need something no one will suspect." She pulled out a long pink dress. "Yes! You'll be my baby sister."

The dress looked like something a baby would wear. I knew I was too old for it, but she seemed to have a plan, so I let it go. I was still too upset to put in my two cents.

"I'll be your big brother. She pulled out a cap, shirt, shoes, stockings and short pants that looked about ten years out of fashion, but I supposed they'd do.

Then on to her mirrored dressing room. She had a jar of something she called "cold cream." She rubbed it over her face to take off her face paint. I was amazed how fast it took off her big black Egyptian eyes. Then with her finger tips, she rubbed on color that was about five times darker than her pale skin. Next, she brushed on pink powder here and white powder there. She clipped back her short hair with pins and popped the cap on her head.

She turned to smile at me. "Don't I look like a sun-kissed young boy? Like your Bobby? I copied him."

The change was amazing. "Yeah, you do look like him, kind of."

She laughed and disappeared behind the folding screen painted with long-necked, pink flying birds to change into her costume. When she was done, she jumped out from behind the screen and shouted, "Voila!"

I clapped. She really looked like a boy now. She bowed. She seemed to like the clapping. I could see her looking at the reflections of herself bowing in the room's mirrors.

"Your turn now!" She turned my face this way and that in

her hands and pulled at my hair that was dirty all over again. "I have no idea what you do with yourself to get in such a state. I need to dump you in the tub again, but, never mind, we don't have time. I'll fix you up."

She rubbed cold cream over my face and my dirty hands until they came out clean. Then she rubbed color that was lighter than I usually am over my face and hands. "You're a baby, remember. You've not been out in the sun much, so you can't have all those freckles." She put what seemed like a ton of the pink powder on my face. It made me sneeze so hard, she had to re-do part of my face. "Don't look at yourself yet!"

She hurried out the room and came back with a sun bonnet like a little kid would wear and a wig made of blonde curls.

"That looks too much like the dead kid." I pointed to the blonde curls.

"Okay, fine." She went out again and came back with a wig that was exactly the same, except with pale brown curls. "This make you happy?"

"Okay."

She pinned back my hair exactly like she'd done to her own, and fitted the wig over my head. "Don't look yet." She had me put my hands over my eyes so I wouldn't see myself in all the mirrors. "But don't touch your face! Just cover your eyes, but no touching the makeup. It's a lot of work to cover up all your freckles. There you go."

She guided me behind the pink bird screen so I could change into my baby clothes. "Don't forget your slippers." She handed me thin satin shoes with pink ribbons on them.

Behind the screen, I switched from the sailor suit, which was a ripped wreck by now, and pulled on the toddler dress while Tootsie called, "Be careful not to muss the makeup!"

When I came out, she squealed with delight. She ran the powder brush over my face and hands again. "I told you not to muss the makeup." Finally, she stepped away so I could see myself reflected over and over a million times in the walls of mirrors.

This was the most embarrassing I'd ever looked, the most embarrassing thing I'd ever worn. Maybe I wore something like this when I was a baby. But if I don't remember, it didn't count.

"Well?"

"Yeah, I look like a big baby. I suppose it'll work." Maybe.

"You suppose! Of course it will! Come on! Gilbert's in the kitchen, so we'll go through the front doors."

"No. Can't let anybody see me coming outta this house,

even dressed up like a baby. Especially dressed up like a baby. They'll wonder what's going on and maybe put two and two together."

She paused, thinking. "Like the secret escape plans in 'Castle of Love.' I know exactly what to do." She led me by the hand back down the stairs, shushing me and tiptoeing. Then she took me through a door that went down dark stairs. The cellar. I could hardly see. Then we were up another set of stairs, wooden and creaky. She pushed open a pair of storm doors and we were in the sun again. Or as much sun as could come through the thick jungle in her backyard.

"We can get under there." I pointed to the gap under the fence that I wiggled through earlier in the day. "I think you'll fit."

"I'm not crawling through bushes like you do! There's a back gate that leads to the alley where Gilbert drives my car to the garage. We'll go through there."

Fine. Hopefully, our disguises worked.

I tried steering her through the back ways, but all of a sudden, she cut to the sidewalks, right out in the open sunshine. I chased after her, but it was hard moving in a baby doll dress, especially when you're trying to duck behind cars and trees.

When I caught up, what do you know, but she was chatting with of all people, gossipy Mrs. Tomes!

Chapter 5

Mrs. Tomes was on her front porch, which really was the wrapping-all-around-her-house porch, since that's what it did. She was having her afternoon tea. I'd have thought sharp ol' Mrs. Mabaline, her housekeeper, would've caught on quick, but there she was offering cookies to Tootsie. She was even smiling, something Mrs. Mabaline never did for me.

Me? I was cowering in Mrs. Tomes' rose bushes. Disguise or no, Mrs. Mabaline would spot me in a hot second. I was on the top of her no-good-kid list. I'm sure she believed I was guilty of all those murders.

About when Mrs. Tomes started launching into her hours-long story of how her dead husband was related to lots of presidents, Tootsie smartened up and made an exit. With both mitts full of cookies, Tootsie skipped down the porch steps saying, "Gee, thanks, ma'am's! These sure are swell! You know how to treat a hungry boy!"

Both of those ol' gossips waved at Tootsie. Waved and smiled. Unbelievable.

I followed Tootsie, keeping low by crawling. I had to be careful not to show above the rose bushes so Mrs. Tomes and Mrs. Mabaline wouldn't spot me. When I reached the end of their yard and the rose bushes, I slipped onto the sidewalk again, but I kept low, kept crawling. Can't be too careful.

Tootsie was even whistling. What was that all about?

"Hey, you gotta stay away from those two. They're dangerous."

"Seemed harmless to me. Besides, I have to work my character, test to see if my audience believes in me."

"This isn't a movie. This is my neck in a noose here!"

"You worry too much. Life is a movie. We have our costumes, our parts, and now we have to deliver the show."

Like I said, unbelievable. But at least she handed me the cookies. They were the ginger ones with candied sugar ginger bits falling off the tops. I stuffed them in my mouth and licked my fingers one hand at time, never missing a beat with my crawling.

"No cookies for me. Have to watch my figure. I like that crawling you're doing. It makes your baby character convincing. Fingers in your mouth are a nice touch."

I woulda said something smart, but I was busy chewing.

"Listen, Sparky, there's one thing I've learned and I want you to keep this in mind: it's better to be difficult and different than be a safe little person who bothers no one and no one cares about and everyone forgets. Remember that, okay?"

"Yeah, sure," I said between chews.

All of a sudden, she stopped. I rammed into her leg and nearly choked out my cookies.

She bent down toward me, but not too obvious, and whispered out the side of her mouth, "Copper up ahead. Stay cool. We need to hide."

There, across the street and a couple of houses down, was Spooky. A cop.

That wasn't his real name. Don't know what was. He was leaning his head against a lamppost, like he usually did. Looked like his forehead was pressed against a paper tied to the lamppost. It was a wanted poster. For me.

He'd never given me trouble before. Rumor said he was a young cop who went to the war, and then never left 1918. When he came back, the police chief felt bad for him, so he posted him to Bunker Hill, where it was nice and quiet and nothing much went on, compared to other places.

Except for lately.

"Hold on the hiding. Let's keep going, but casual and easy. Spooky's a little different for a cop. He'll keep to the lamppost. I think."

Tootsie nodded, and we made our way like nothing was out of the ordinary. Tootsie cut her whistling.

I thought I caught Spooky's eye watching us. Would he blow his whistle? He sure had seen the poster. His face was plastered against it. And casual as we were walking, or me crawling, we had to be a strange sight.

He said nothing. Moved his eyes back to the poster. Good ol' Spooky! When this all blew over, if it did, I'd remember to slip him some candy as a thanks. Who said Sparky didn't look after her friends?

The sidewalks made me nervous, but we didn't have any more scares on our way to Court Hill, except for a lady giving a sour face to Tootsie and saying, "You should have that toddler in a carriage. Shame on you making her crawl on the dirty sidewalk!" After the lady left shaking her head and tsking, Tootsie bent down toward me and whispered, "A baby carriage would have been a perfect prop! But I don't have one. I'll have to ask Gilbert to get one when we're back."

"I'm not planning on dressing up like a baby again anytime soon."

But Tootsie was back to whistling and swaggering like a boy, so she paid me no mind.

When we got to Court Hill, I waved to Tootsie to hide with me behind trees at the edge of the park where we had a good view.

Sure enough, the bad man was standing next to my bench. But Mug was there now and a bunch of other cops. They didn't look very happy. Bad man was waving his arms around, face angry. I caught a "That Sparky!"

Ratting on me. Whaddya know? No surprise there.

Didn't look like Mug was buying it. He started poking the guy with his club, hard. Bad man balled his hands into fists, but then smartened up and backed off. Mug jabbed him one more time in the guts, making him sit down hard on the bench.

Mug was a big cop. Big stomach, big head, big all the way around. The local knuckleheads knew not to mess with my Mug. Even my Bookie played nice, all bowing and scraping to Mug.

After Mug made sure the guy was nice and quiet on the bench, he waved his club to signal the other cops to move out. And away they went, laughing in a mean kind of way at bad man.

I can't say the cops have ever been real fond of him.

We waited awhile until the coast was good and clear. Then Tootsie tugged my hand and the show was on.

Tootsie was doing her boy swagger, cap at a slant almost touching her right eye. She didn't look like Bobby anymore, but like one of the tough older boys on the Hill.

I stayed away from those boys. One at a time, I could handle them. I might've been little, but I had fists like pistons, and anybody dumb enough to wanna find that out, would. But, in a group, those boys would get nasty, pushing me over, swarming me and kicking. They beat the holy stuffings out of Bobby once when he came to my rescue.

After that, Bobby's parents got touchy about him running around the Hill. Okay, maybe me breaking his nose with my power punch had something to do with that too. But he didn't rat me out to his parents. Not Bobby. He told them he tripped and fell on a tree. They didn't believe him, and figured the tough boys messed up his nose too.

Just so you know, I did tell Bobby I was sorry about his nose. And Bobby said he was sorry about trying to kiss me. So, we're square. Kind of. He keeps calling me his girl and trying the kissing routine. Bobby's not perfect.

Nowadays, Bobby's parents wanted him to be either: 1) in the library, 2) in school, or, 3) at home reading. So, he had to be careful slipping out. Bobby said he wasn't afraid of the older boys, and would still "fight them to the death" to protect me, or something like that. But I don't think he should. If he got in another scrape with them, they'd mess up his nose lots more than I ever could, even with my best power punch. Those boys, they fought dirty.

Tootsie wouldn't know any of that. So, I didn't say anything about her looking like the mean boys.

The bad man didn't notice us at first. He was busy frowning and rubbing his stomach where Mug jabbed him in the guts. When we were almost on top of him, Tootsie started in on her whistling.

He jumped. Must have thought it was the Mug come back.

He settled down when he saw it was only us. "Sparky. A baby now? You're not good with disguises, my miss. I think you should give them up. And what's this? Well, well, well, a boy, eh? How sweet." He smiled big.

That so? I guess bad man didn't have the same problem with the older boys that I had. Not a drop of fear on his face, which made me think the older boys were the ones afraid of him. Interesting. Didn't know that.

Tootsie was standing right next to where he sat on the bench, even though I'd warned her not to get close to him.

He smiled and waved his long, thin fingers at her.

"Watch out," I whispered. But she stood there still as a statute and even smiled back at him.

"Sparky says you know something that might help her," she said.

He pouted. "Always wanting. Boys and girls."

Before I knew what was happening, his long arm shot out, grabbed her and flung her to the ground. She skidded when she landed. Oh, no.

He jumped up and down, laughing. "Big, tough boy, are

you? Whatcha gonna do down there on the ground, huh?" He could barely talk, he was laughing so hard. "Tell you what. Tell you what. I won't jump up and down on you and squash you flat if you quack like duck." He paused. Tootsie didn't quack. He didn't like that much. "You, quack!" His jumping got closer to her, like he was about to jump on her head. "Quack!"

I waved my arms at him. "Hey, it's okay! I'll quack. See. Quack, quack!" I made the best duck sounds I could muster.

This made him even more mad. "Shut up! You made this boy come, so the boy must quack!"

While he was turned to shout at me, Tootsie got busy fast. She pulled out something she had hidden under her belt, in the small of her back. It was black and floppy. I couldn't make it out clearly. She got up into a crouch and swung the thing. It whacked him across his hind end.

"Wha?" He turned back toward Tootsie as she straightened up all the way. His face was in the wide open now, so she swung the floppy thing hard. Home run! I heard a squishy sound when it hit.

His long fingers went to his cheek and he leaned over, moaning. Not so smart. Now his back was wide open. Tootsie didn't miss her opportunity and swung the black floppy thing hard down on his back.

"Stop!" and he fell forward on the ground. She stomped her foot on his arm. He started to grab her leg, but she swung the black thing at his hands. He jerked his fingers back. He wasn't quite as stupid as he looked.

"Ready to talk, smart guy?"

"You're a horrible boy! Horrible!" he whined.

She swung the floppy thing at his face so it almost touched the raw part on his cheek she'd already squashed. Then she swung it away, teasing. I could see the thing better now. It looked like a silk stocking, the nice kind my Bookie never gave his girlfriends. She had things inside that made lots of shapes I could see through the black silk. Was that a panther? Her panther pin? Was that fancy stocking full of her jewels?

She swung it again, and this time it brushed his squashed cheek. I could see it was bleeding. He whimpered.

"Ready? Or you feel like some more?"

"I didn't see anything!"

The stocking came back, brushing harder. "Wrong answer."

"I just saw a car. That's it."

Tootsie swung the stuffed stocking around and around like she was winding up to hit it out of the park.

"Okay, okay. It was a big sedan. City Hall sedan, like the high-ups in the city drive, that are always coming in and out of the City Hall."

"Yeah?" That was me asking. This was interesting. City Hall. Huh.

"I figured it was something I wasn't supposed to see. At 5 am, a city sedan prowling around Court Hill? Nah, I didn't want them to see me seeing them. I went and hid."

"Come on. I know you saw more. Don't hold back." I wasn't letting this germ off easy.

"I don't know. I told you, I hid. I'm not that stupid."

"Maybe I should give him another close shave? What do you think, Sparky?"

He wasn't having any more of this. He stared screaming, "Police! Police! Sparky is murdering me! Police!"

"Let's scram," I said. She looked like she wanted to get in a few more swings, so I grabbed her arm and started running, hoping she'd forget about the guy and run with me. Luckily, she did. And just in time too.

We ducked behind the trees as Mug and his crew came running, blowing their whistles.

I couldn't make out everything bad man was saying, but I caught, "Baby . . . Sparky . . . horrible boy . . . murder . . . look at my face!"

I heard Mug plenty clear. His voice was as big as he was. "Baby? You trying to steal a baby? I had enough of you."

Down went Mug's club, bull's-eye on the bloody spot Tootsie made with her jewels. Bad man was so surprised, he squeaked and started scrambling away on all fours like a dog. Mug gave him a kick in the rear to help him along.

"Next time I hear from you, you don't wanna know what I do to you. I'm just waiting. Just waiting." Then Mug started to laugh. I thought I heard him yell back, sobbing, "I'm gonna tell on you!" But that only caused more cop laughter all around.

Tootsie had to hold her hands over her mouth to keep from laughing too. I added my hands to her mouth because she looked like she was ready to burst, especially when the cops passed right next to us on their way back to Bunker Hill. Last thing I needed was her giving us away.

When the cops were out of sight, and the guy had crawled to his rooming house steps, I whispered, "Let's scram. It's too hot here. We gotta move." I pulled her arm.

As we slipped out of the trees, I looked back and saw a girl helping bad man up the porch steps. Was she the cleaning girl? She looked older than me, but not by much. He draped his arm over her and leaned his weight on her, making her almost drag him up the steps like he was an invalid. Once they got up to the porch, he pushed her and it looked like he was yelling at her. He lost the invalid act and stomped in the house, slamming the screen door. He left her out on the porch sobbing.

I knew the feeling, girl. But too bad for you. Nothing I could do. Had to scram.

I dropped the baby crawling bit. Too slow. Tootsie forgot about swaggering and whistling and seemed distracted, so I led her through the side ways and back ways, out of sight of prying eyes. "If the cops see us, they might connect the dots with me dressed like this and you dressed like that, and the guy's baby and bad boy story. Gotta keep off the public sidewalks."

Tootsie was different, besides not acting like a boy anymore. It was like she was a balloon with all the air pushed out. She wasn't saying anything, seemed like she wasn't paying attention. She followed wherever I tugged her arm, which was good. Like I said, Bunker Hill was a maze. You had to know your way around. And that I did.

I wondered if Tootsie was acting funny because she hadn't had lunch or any of Mrs. Mabaline's cookies. I hadn't any lunch either, but Mrs. Mabaline's fine cookies were a feast that could keep me going for days, and had. Maybe it was time for a rest, to figure out what was going on.

There was an old Victorian house near Mrs. Tomes, but it wasn't nice and painted pink like hers. It was run down and no one lived there except a strange old lady and her housekeeper. There was lots of gossip about that lady, so being how kids were, they liked to snoop in her yard and spy. Sure enough, the rotting wood fence along her back yard had a kid-sized hole in it that was big enough for Tootsie to slip through too. Mean Old Bob and his nephew did the yard work for the strange old lady. No matter how many times they nailed a patch in that fence, a kid came along and made another hole. You should hear Old Bob yelling when he found holes.

Once we were through the fence, I picked out a spot near the old backyard incinerator where mean Old Bob and his nephew never cleared, so there were lots of big weeds to hide in.

"Let's rest for a bit, okay, Tootsie?"

She nodded and sat down, but still didn't say anything.

The heat of the day was covering everything: the weeds, the sky, the trees, the old incinerator. I was glad we were off our feet. Though I was getting a little thirsty.

"You okay?" I asked.

She looked off toward the fence, but seemed like she wasn't really looking at it. "Why doesn't anyone do something about that man?" she said in a faraway voice.

"The bad man? For one thing, there's lots of types like him, and lots of other crazy types too. Not enough jails for all of 'em. I'm sure Mug would do more than tap him with his stick, but that guy's got connections. Least, that's what the other old people in his rooming house say. The landlady gets a check in the mail like clockwork every month for double the rent as long as she puts up with him. She can't afford to say no, so there you go. Maybe he's got rich folks in Pasadena. Who knows."

"Then why would he be afraid of seeing a City Hall car if he's so untouchable?"

I thought about that. She had a point. "He could've been lying about being afraid. But either way, I think he only spilled half the story. But that might be all we can get from him. It's a good start, though, right?"

She nodded and then said, "We won't tell Gilbert about this. You understand, Sparky?"

"Sure. And we won't tell Bobby too, right?"

But Tootsie was distracted again. She moved her hand lightly along her arm. Her arm and front of her shirt were dirty from where she skidded on the ground. "I have a cut," she said softly.

I saw the mark she was touching. "Aw, Tootsie, that's a big nothing. You're barely even bleeding. One time that bad man tricked me into climbing a dead tree for a nickel. Didn't tell me it was rotted. The branches just crumbled and I fell. Broke my arm. That hurt, let me tell you. Never got my nickel neither."

"That's terrible, Sparky."

Tell me about it. "That's why I'd rather run for my Bookie for spare change."

Oh, oh. I got her attention now. "Bookie? You run for a bookie?" Her face went from a sad kind of blank to mad. I sure didn't need her slamming Bookie with that jewel filled stocking of hers. Though, even while she was breaking his face, he'd be impressed by her weapon.

I decided I'd better change the subject from my Bookie

quick.

"Hey, some slugger you got there," and I pointed to the stocking. She was holding it in her hands, turning it over and over.

Her face changed again, from mad to happy. She sat up and reached her hand down into the stocking. "Oh, yeah, Sparky. The real jewels give it extra cutting power. See how fine and thin the stocking is? That way the jewels will cut right through the silk, without actually cutting the silk and falling out, so the guy doesn't even see what got him." She pushed her fingertips against the silk so I could just about see through it. Her finger nails almost came through the silk, but not quite. She raised her eyebrows at me and smiled.

"That's a first-class weapon, Tootsie." And it sure was.

She pulled out one of the jewels and handed it to me. It was a pin made out of a huge colored stone. I wanted to say emerald, but the green was too pale. Or maybe it was a special type of emerald. Bookie would know for sure. This green rock was set in gold and a dozen gold arms stuck out around it, like how you see the sun drawn in pictures. At the end of each arm was a red stone I'd say was a ruby or I'd eat my hat, or my baby bonnet.

"All of these were gifts," she said holding up her stocking. "I used to have lots of admirers."

"These are some real rocks, Tootsie. Not paste."

She squinted at me. "How's a kid like you know real from paste rocks? You're not really a criminal, are you?" But she smiled when she said this, like it didn't really matter to her. "Never mind. You keep that," and she waved toward the big green stone pin I was still staring at.

I was shocked. That pin was worth serious dough. Didn't she realize I was a street kid? Had she forgotten about the wanted murderer bit? "I can't keep this! Someone will just steal it from me. Shoot me first and then steal it." Bookie would be first in line to do it too.

"Fine," and she snatched it back. "I'll keep it in my safe for you. How's that?"

I shrugged. I thought about telling her to keep her safe good and hidden because there's plenty of second-story characters breaking in houses looking for things like safes. But she seemed to be in a funny kind of mood. So, I decided I'd better not say anything that might scare her. Or make her want to beat up Bookie.

But, hey, it was Bookie who got my arm fixed. So he's not all bad. Okay, maybe it was some girl he was with who saw me on the sidewalk with my arm all bent and felt sorry for me. If I'm honest, I'd admit he got mad at her and snapped, "Quit bugging me. Let that flea-bitten kid crawl off and die somewhere." But she kept stroking his arm and purring, "Aw, come on, baby, call that doctor who helped me. You know. That doctor guy." So, there you have it. She's been outta the picture for a while now. Bookie's girlfriends never stuck around. Me? He put me to work, my arm still plastered up and everything. I didn't mind. Bookie paid me. With actual money.

"Let's go. I'm thirsty already," I said as I got up and tugged her arm. She was sinking back into being quiet again, so she followed me without a peep.

By the time we came through her back gate into her jungle yard, I was beat and felt like my mouth was a desert, like in a movie I once saw. The star was super thirsty. Then the movie showed what he was thinking: a desert of sand with a camel that laughed at him. Well, maybe you'd have to have seen for yourself. I thought it was pretty funny and laughed really loud which made grownups in the seats next to me do the shhhh thing.

Tootsie looked like she was asleep and awake at the same time. She hadn't said a word since we left our hiding spot in the weeds. I didn't know what to make of this Tootsie. She could be really fun one minute. But then in the next minute, it was like the light's on but nobody's home.

Gilbert must have heard the back gate click when we got to Creepy House because he popped out of the glass sunroom doors, the ones that weren't blocked by her jungle plants.

That scar over his eye was bright red and his face was blotchy, like he'd been crying. Goblin ran to Tootsie and grabbed her, because it looked like she was starting to fall.

Chapter 6

"Oh, Mademoiselle! You were gone! I could not find you! I feared, I feared! You must never do that! I was so frightened!"

He led her into the sunroom. There, standing inside, I saw Bobby. He looked mad. His arms were folded. He was glaring directly at me. Oh, boy.

Did I tell you Bobby was bossy? Just when I'd think I might consider his marriage proposals someday, he'd start getting bossy again, and then I'd decide, no way. I don't like anybody telling me what to do. Well, I put up with Bookie bossing me. But that was work, and he was the boss and was paying me. So that's different. Bobby was just a pill.

I took my time coming into the house, moving my feet super slowly. I could hear Gilbert's voice as he took Tootsie upstairs, "I will call our vitamin doctor. He will know what to do. You must rest. Oh, I was so frightened."

I was hoping Bobby would get bored standing there in the sunroom glaring at me. But he didn't. As soon as I put my foot inside, he said in his you've-been-bad-voice, "You look like a baby."

"It's a disguise. You're not supposed to recognize me."

"What were you doing?"

"Investigating."

"You should have told me, so I could help. Gilbert practically had an attack. It's a good thing I came here, otherwise, he might have fainted."

"Oh, so you're on first-names with the goblin and everything."

"Sparky! You're not listening to me!"

True. My mind was on the kitchen, so I ignored him the best I could. I brushed past him, even though it looked like he was trying to block my way.

He followed me into the kitchen, all the while going on and on about how he could have helped and how I shouldn't be wandering out by myself.

I was so thirsty (like the desert in the movie I was telling you about, complete with laughing camel), I climbed up on the counter, turned on the kitchen tap, the cold water one with a "C" on it, and put my mouth right under the gushing spout. Ahhhh.

"Sparky! You don't have to do that! I can get you a glass. Look, you made a mess all over the counter and Gilbert tries so hard to keep this place clean."

Now that my thirst was taken care of with the best cold water out of a tap I'd ever had in Bunker Hill, my nose noticed something. I slid off the counter, and there it was, a pan on the kitchen table covered with a cloth. What did it hide? The smell coming from it made my mouth water and made me tingle all the way down to my feet.

I whipped the cloth off before Bobby could stop me. What was that? Big fat noodles laid flat like thick stripes and covered with red sauce that smelled so good, like hot spices.

"Sparky, we don't know if that's for us. We have to wait until we're invited to eat."

No-ho. That's not how things were in the real world, which Bobby didn't seem to understand. If somebody left something out all by its lonesome, not watching it, not paying any attention to it, then, open season.

I dipped my hand into the corner of the pan. The sauce was still hot. No matter. I scooped up a fist-full of noodles and sauce and pushed it into my mouth. Oh, my. Oh, my, my, my.

"Sparky! Gilbert will notice that. You can't eat with your hands. Just stop, just sit down. I'll get you a plate and a fork if you're going to be that way."

He actually slapped my hand. He'd done that before.

Okay. I sat down on the chair, didn't touch the pan like a good girl. The second he turned his back, I was scooping again while he was saying, "I hear Gilbert coming. We've got to hurry! Where's the plates!"

Moving fast, he found the plates, forks, napkins and a big spoon. He slid them onto the table and himself into a chair as Gilbert ran into the kitchen and straight to the phone. Hands shaking, he dialed.

I hadn't noticed the phone before. It was white like the rest of the kitchen, so blended right in.

"Doctor! It's an emergency. Mademoiselle has collapsed! You must hurry!"

The doctor must have been saying something on the other end of the line, because Gilbert started nodding and saying, "Yes, yes. Yes! The drink? Lemons! Yes! Hold on."

He put the phone down, said, "Lemons. Lemons!" and looked right and left like he was lost in his own kitchen.

Bobby popped up. "Let me help!" He opened the Frigidaire and stared at the little bowl of onions and lots of empty space.

"No, there's nothing in there," Gilbert said. "I hide the food so Mademoiselle doesn't come down late when I sleep and eat things. The lemons, yes, I put them in the cold cabinet."

He opened one of the lower cabinets and a cool, musty smell came out. It must have an opening to a crawl space or the cellar to let cool air come up so potatoes, onions or whatever's in the cabinet would last longer. Sometimes I'd gotten into kitchens by climbing up from under a house through those types of cabinets.

I didn't see any potatoes in that cabinet. Only some onions and lots of lemons and limes. There was also a jar with a murky white liquid in it. Gilbert grabbed that, tried to grab a bunch of lemons but dropped them and they started rolling all over the floor.

"I got 'em!" That was Bobby, now on all fours scrambling after the lemons.

Me? I was still eating the noodles. To make Bobby happy, I was actually eating out of the pan with the fork. Not that he noticed, since he was chasing lemons.

Gilbert was still very excited. "Oh, my! Oh, my! Wait! Here's a bowl. Let's put the lemons in the bowl. That's right. But we must not forget limes! Doctor says limes! The vitamins!"

He finally noticed the noodle pan with my fork in it. But he wasn't mad, or maybe he was too busy thinking about limes. All he said was, "Oh, good, you found the lunch," but in a way like he was only half paying attention.

Bobby was piling a wide blue bowl to the brim with lemons and limes, while Gilbert ran back to the phone and yelled into the receiver, "I got the lemons and the limes and the drink! Hurry over here!" Then he slammed it down so hard the receiver bounced off the hook, so he had to slam it back. He started saying things in a different language.

Then he grabbed the bowl, "Thank you, Bobby! Such a good boy!" He grabbed the jar of awful looking liquid, and ran out the kitchen. A couple of limes fell off the bowl and bounced back into the kitchen. Bobby picked them up and carefully put them back in the cold cabinet on the shelf with the other limes (not the lemon shelf), and closed the cabinet doors. Bobby was very neat.

Bobby sat back down like he was in a daze. Suddenly, he noticed me eating out of the pan. "Sparky!"

"I'm using a fork. Like you said."

"But you're not supposed to eat directly from the serving dish. See this?" He held up the spoon, which was particularly big. "This is the serving spoon. Everyone shares it to get the food out of the serving dish. But you don't eat off the serving spoon or serving dish."

He used the big spoon like a knife to cut out a big chunk of noodles around where I was eating. He plopped it down on a dish and scooted it toward me.

"It is rude to eat off dishes and utensils that other people use because then they end up eating your spit and stuff. It's inconsiderate to other people's feelings."

"Oh, so you don't want to eat any of my spit."

"I wasn't talking about me. I was talking about other people."

"I don't see any other people here. Just you. You don't wanna touch my spit."

"That's not true! You know how I feel about you. I don't mind your spit"

"Liar."

He grabbed the dish of noodles he'd just given me, pulled it over to himself, and started sticking his fork into it.

"Hey! That's mine. Give it back!"

"Settle down. I'm proving to you that I don't mind your spit."

Too late, I had my hands on the dish ("Gimme!"), he was pulling back ("No!"), but I was louder ("Gimme!!"), so he gave up and let go.

"I can't believe you. Fine. Have it back."

"You belong in the nut house."

"No, you belong in the nut house."

"You need to go to the nut house first," I retorted.

"No, you need to go to the nut house first."

"No, you!"

The phone rang. That shut both of us up. It kept ringing.

"I should answer that," Bobby said, but in an uncertain kind of way.

"No! What if it's cops?"

"What if it's important? We need to find out."

He ran to the phone, I ran after, but he picked it up before I could stop him. I stayed close to listen in.

"Hello?"

"Who is this?" a man's voice said from the other end of the line.

Bobby could get huffy really fast. So, he said in his no-messing-around voice, "Who is *this*?"

Silence. Then, "Where's Gilbert?"

"Ah, he's busy."

"Who are you?"

"None of your business! Who are you?"

There was a pause so long, we both thought the call was cut off and Bobby almost hung up the receiver. "I'm the doctor. Get me Gilbert."

Bobby put the receiver back to his ear. He was looking at me and shrugging, and mouthing, "I don't know!" I didn't know what to do either, so all I could do was shrug back. As long as it wasn't cops, then I didn't really care.

Bobby pulled himself together, got his no-messing-around voice back, and said, loudly, "Gilbert is busy. I told you that. Get here right away or there will be a problem!" He slammed down the phone. "That'll teach him," Bobby said.

But Bobby was frowning. He sat down and didn't say anything. I could tell he worried he'd done something wrong. It's like Gilbert said. Bobby's a good boy. He didn't usually talk back to grown-ups. I wonder if he partly did that to impress me. Maybe.

"Hey, Bobby, have some of these noodles. They're really good." I picked up the serving spoon and waved it in front of his face, so he could see I was doing the serving spoon-serving dish thing. I scooped up a huge chunk of noodles and slopped them down on an empty plate. "For you. Eat up!" I pushed the plate toward him.

After a couple of bites, he perked up. "This is good."

"It was better when it was hotter, but still okay."

"It's called lasagna," he said.

"Las what?"

"Lasagna. It comes from New Jersey. Before that, it came from Italy. And before that, it originally came from China. It's Chinese. Marco Polo brought it, not to New Jersey, but to Italy. Then Italians brought it to New Jersey. But, really, Lasagna is

Chinese."

"Wow. Really? Like chopsticks?"

"Kind of."

Bobby read a lot of books, so he knew a lot of strange things. He liked school too, which wasn't normal. Sometimes, his parents even hired a private tutor to come to his house to add more school on top of the school he already had. To me, that wasn't fair. He was already doing his time in school, and then this tutor showed up and it's like the judge threw him in the slammer all over again. Bobby said he liked the tutor. He liked extra school. He wanted to grow up to be a professor. That's what his parents were. Professors of old stuff. You could actually get a job and make good money doing that. Being a professor of old stuff. It's a crazy world.

"But how come I don't see any lasagna in Chinatown?"

My Bookie took me there once. He bought me lunch in a real Chinese restaurant because I kept complaining I was hungry. He told me the best way to plug my mouth was stuff food in it.

Bobby had to think about the lasagna in Chinatown question for a minute. "Maybe lasagna is like ancient Chinese. Chop suey is like modern Chinese."

"Oh."

"But, then again. Some historians say the Marco Polo story is baloney. They say the Greeks invented noodles, and the Italians borrowed it from them. Or maybe noodles are really from early Rome. It's possible parts of all these stories are true, or maybe not. When looking into ancient history, it can be hard to figure out what really happened. Because it's so long ago. Maybe someday, there will be an exciting archeological dig in an ancient temple that will give the answer. I'd like to be on a dig like that."

Didn't really make any sense. But I guess since Bobby read a lot of books, he knew. Like a professor of old stuff.

Bobby stopped chewing all of a sudden and frowned at me. Oh, oh. What did I do now? "You've been to Chinatown?"

I shrugged.

"You shouldn't go there. It's dangerous for girls. There's dens of iniquity. Things like that." He stopped and stared hard at me. "You're not still hanging around with that bookie? I told you before, I don't approve."

I was spared more of his chastising when a man carrying a small black suitcase walked in through the outside kitchen door.

Quick as a wink, I pulled a napkin over my face, covering everything but one eye. Can't have him match my face to the wanted posters and run to the cops.

He stared at us and we stared at him.

I'd say he was the coolest customer I'd ever seen, and I'd seen a few. He was thin. I mean thin-thin. He was so pale, he was almost as white as the kitchen tile. He had black hair that was slicked down flat on his head. His suit was made of some kind of dark green material that was really thin too. But it wasn't a cheap suit. The opposite. He smiled at us in a way I could tell he didn't like us one bit.

I didn't like him. The way Bobby glared at him, I knew he felt the same.

Bobby stood up, forkful of lasagna still in his hand. I could tell he was trying to block the man's view of me with his own body. Good 'ol Bobby.

Bobby said, "Identify yourself."

The man laughed. "Oh, the voice on the phone. How charming. I'm the doctor. If you don't mind?"

He walked through the kitchen like he knew where he was going. When he went by Bobby, he walked a little too close, and it looked to me like the doctor bumped into him on purpose, which made Bobby stumble and have to catch himself on the chair. He almost dropped his forkful of lasagna. For someone like Bobby, if all that sauce had fallen on the floor, it would have been a major disaster.

The doctor laughed low and quiet, but I could still hear. Then he disappeared into other parts of the mansion.

Bobby sat back down. "I don't like him."

"Me either." I waited a bit before I took the napkin off my face. Can't be too careful.

Bobby wasn't eating his lasagna anymore, but he was still holding his fork. The sauce started dripping down to his hand. With an, "Oh!" he realized and finally put his fork back on his plate. He stared at it.

I didn't feel like eating any more either. Truth was, I'd stuffed so much of those noodles into my mouth, whether they were Chinese or not, I felt like I was going to explode.

"Hey, Bobby? You wanna play? There's lots of weird stuff here."

This got his attention. "Okay."

I was about to lead him into the leopard parlor, but he said, "Wait, I have to put the rest of the lasagna into the Frigidaire. I should wash our dishes too." Okay, fine.

After he got done cleaning up, it still took a while to get to the parlor because he wanted to look at the pictures, the stools, the big vases along the way. "Some of these vases are antiques, I'm sure of that."

"Forget those. Take a look in here. There's a leopard on the floor. There's another one, but not flat. They used to be her pets or something."

"Those aren't leopards."

"What do you mean? Look at the spots?"

"They're cheetahs."

"What?"

"Cheetahs. They have spots like leopards, but otherwise are totally different. Cheetahs have been kept as pets for centuries, starting with the ancient Egyptians. I don't think leopards have the temperament to be pets. They'd probably eat their owners. Cheetahs, on the other hand, can be tamed. There are paintings of cheetahs in the pharaohs' tombs."

We sat down by the flat leopard, or cheetah, or whatever, and stroked its fur. "I'd like to go to ancient Egypt," I said.

"You can't go there. That's the past. You can go to modern Egypt, though. It's still very interesting and all the old stuff is still there. I plan to visit Egypt someday. Maybe we can go together."

"Sure, if you're paying."

Bobby stuffed his hand into the flat leopard's mouth like he was trying to see how far his hand would go in. But a tooth got him, "Ow!" So he started pulling on the ears, trying to see inside them. He seemed to be thinking of something else, and I had an idea what.

"Sparky, be honest with me."

Here it comes.

"What were you and the lady doing today?"

"Her name is Tootsie."

"Okay. What were you and Tootsie up to? Where did you go?"

I twisted the leopard's arm. Since it was flat, I could get a good twist going full circle. "We were following leads. Investigating."

He stared hard at me.

"I found out that a City Hall car was driving around where the dead kid was, on that very morning too."

Bobby dropped the leopard's head. 'City Hall! That's serious." But then his wheels started turning. "The dead kid was on Court Hill. Were you talking with that weird old guy?"

I didn't say anything.

"Sparky, I've told you to stay away from him. What happened? What did he do?"

I was really twisting that leopard arm now. "He didn't do anything! Tootsie had a sock with stuff in it and she slammed his face with it."

I left off the part about the sock really being a silk stocking and the stuffing being real jewels. He wouldn't have believed that and would have started wondering what else I was lying about. Then he'd start suspecting the worst, like what if bad man had made me jump up and down on one leg while oinking. Yeah, okay, I did that once.

"She beat the stuffings outta him and made him talk. You shoulda seen her go at him. No mercy or anything."

"Wow. But, was he telling the truth?"

"I'm sure of it. She beat him to a pulp." Maybe the bad man was lying. Maybe he offed the little girl. Maybe the car was just a story. But, somehow, I didn't think so. "Yeah. Maybe he wasn't telling the whole story, but he was being straight about the car."

Bobby stared at me, considering. Then I could tell from his face that he decided to buy it. "Okay, Sparky. But next time you go to Court Hill, I'm coming with you. I'll protect you from that bad man."

I knew Bobby liked to think he was the big man, but that bad man was bigger. If Bobby'd been there, he'd'a had his hind end kicked and good. But I didn't tell him that. "Sure, Bobby, I'll do that," I lied.

"City Hall. This concerns me. I think I'll ask my tutor what to do. He knows a lot about government going all the back to the Magna Carta."

"What! You can't tell your tutor. What if he's a spy or something?"

"I'm sure he's not a spy. He's a university student."

"What if he goes running to the cops?"

Bobby thought about this. "Maybe you're right. Okay, then I'll go to City Hall tomorrow and demand answers."

This was getting worse and worse. I wished I'd made up a different story. "Bobby, you can't have anyone know you're talking to me. Mug'll beat you with chains until you tell them where I am, and then it's me, Tootsie, the goblin, and you too, all swinging from the gallows."

"I won't talk. Mug can never get me to talk! Fine. I won't go to City Hall, but you promise me that you won't either. You stay here and don't do anything."

He stopped talking and looked at the sunroom's glass doors. "This house is crazy. I can never tell how late in the day it is with that overgrown yard blocking the light, and all the rest of the windows having that colored glass I can't see through. I told my parents I'd be at the library. I'd better go home before they call the police and say I'm missing."

He stood up and looked down at me. "Promise? No running around to Court Hill or City Hall or anywhere?"

"I promise," I lied. He seemed to buy it and off he went.

"Make sure no one sees you coming outta here!" I called after him.

"I know, I know!"

Bobby did know. He's the one person I could trust most now. But I couldn't be honest with him.

Tomorrow, I was going to City Hall.

The house sounded dead empty. No sign of Tootsie, or Gilbert, and thankfully not that doctor.

I was getting tired, but no matter. I crawled under the flat leopard, being careful of its teeth and claws. The room didn't feel as hot and stuffy as it had. Strange, but I wasn't complaining. Down low to the floor, it felt even a bit drafty. But it was comfy under the leopard. Lots more comfy than most places I'd slept. And off to dreamland I went.

Then someone was shaking me. Something was on top of me. I panicked, thrashing.

Chapter 7

"Little Sparky, it's me! Wake up!"

Gilbert.

"Okay, hold your pants on."

The something on top of me was the flat leopard. I crawled out from under it.

"Sparky, let's not sleep with this leopard, yes? Clara Bell is better. Mademoiselle is not so fond of this one. Maybe she will not be happy to see you so happy with him. Clara Bell makes Mademoiselle happy."

"Yeah, fine." I did kind of like sleeping under the flat leopard. But, not my house. And I was staying here for free. With free food. I wasn't going to argue. "Clara Bell it is."

Before I could yell about being hungry, Gilbert said, "Come, quick, into the kitchen. Breakfast is waiting."

I didn't smell anything. And sure enough, there wasn't anything. Only toast and lots of jam. Okay, and maybe some OJ too. "Where's those buns you made yesterday?"

"None today. Doctor says the smell of cooking cannot reach Mademoiselle. She is in too fragile a state now."

"I think that doctor is a quack and he's starving her." And me too.

"You mustn't say such things! Yes, she needs to keep her figure for auditions, but Doctor is most concerned about her nerves. We must all be most careful of her nerves."

"Fine. Whatever." I still thought the doc was a third-class quack.

I should have still been on the alert for poison. That would have been smart. But I hadn't died from the buns or from the Chinese noodles yesterday. Bobby ate the noodles too and he hadn't turned green and fallen over.

Besides I was hungry. Okay, I'd chance it.

The toast was first class, I'd give Gilbert that. The bread was sliced thick, thick, and Gilbert didn't seem to care how much jam I piled on top. There was orange jam, purple jam, yellow jam, and pinkie-purple jam. I think the pinkie-purple jam was my favorite.

"That is strawberry and blackberry jam, my little Sparky. I made it myself. When the markets have the best fruit, I take advantage and make lots of jam. I am so happy to have someone to appreciate it."

"Yeah, thanks," I mumbled through a mouthful of toast.

A corner of newspaper sticking out of the trash bin near the door caught my eye. I waited until Gilbert's back was turned, fussing over making more orange juice by squashing orange halves onto a pointed strainer. Then I slipped to the bin and pulled out the paper.

"Fake Girl is Prussian Spy who ignited the Great War!!!"

What?

The story went on to say I wasn't really an eleven-year-old girl, but a short spy. I started the war (I wasn't clear on how I did that), and now I was plotting to start another. This was why it was so important that the citizens of Los Angeles alert the police the second they spotted me. The city was offering a $20,000 reward for my capture—alive or dead. There was the grinning Mayor's photo again. Would it kill him to be outta the papers for one day? He was holding up a check that I guess was for my twenty-grand reward.

That was so much dough, I could hardly even picture it. Made me tempted to turn myself in. Except the hangman would put a damper on my enjoying the loot.

Gilbert noticed what I was reading. "Sparky! I did not mean for you to see that." He snatched it out of my hands. "Papers print nonsense. I should not have shown you the papers yesterday. Do not believe these lies."

Of course, I didn't believe it. "I wasn't even alive in the war."

"I was, and I know you did not start the war. This is mad propaganda. You must stay inside and not leave until things are safe. It may be a long time. But, Mademoiselle is happy to have you here, so please, you must stay. When Mademoiselle's nerves are better, I promise I will bake more buns just for you, big cakes, pastries like from my home." He smiled big, but in a worried way.

Can I say that I'd never had an invite like that, ever?

Wanting me to stay. Wanting to bake buns and cakes for me? Either I was really lucky, or I don't know what.

They could still cook me. But so far, they hadn't shown a sign of wanting to hack me up or boil me. Couldn't figure out why they wanted me around. No one wanted me around. Maybe they both had a foot in the loony bin. Best explanation I could come up with.

Still, there was no way I was staying cooped up in this house. I was City Hall bound.

"Sure. Can I play in her closets all day?" If he thought I was busy playing, lost up in her closet maze, he wouldn't look for me and realize I'd given him the slip.

His face lit up. "Oh, yes! Mademoiselle will love to have you play in her closets. But first, you must have a bath." He looked me up and down, frowning. "I do not know what you do to make yourself so full of dusty dirt."

Another bath? Didn't I just have one? "I'm fine. Don't need any bath. Maybe later."

"Please. To make Mademoiselle happy? Her nerves?"

Was it his nerves or hers when it came to baths?

Can I lay it on the table? I really didn't want to take a bath. Really didn't. But here's the pickle I was in: wanted murderer, nice house, free food, crazy people but they seemed to like me being around. It really put the squeeze on a girl, if you know what I mean.

"Yeah, fine, whatever."

"Wonderful! And I won't make you soak in those purple bubbles. I don't think you liked them."

Actually, the bubbles grew on me, but I didn't need him wasting time looking for that purple bubble bottle. The quicker we got this over with, the better. So, I shrugged like it was fine.

Gilbert, humming away, bustled with the bathtub taps, the towels. He disappeared upstairs and came back with a sickening dolly dress with big bows and lace. I was about to make a stink, until I got an idea. So I played cool and went along with the program.

I got the washing business over with as quick as I could without making it look like a rush job. Had to have the dirt off my face and hands at the very least. On with the dress, then back to the kitchen for a quick, "Hey, Gilbert, I'm going up to the closets."

Lo and behold he hands a bag to me. Cookies. "They're not baked by me, because I cannot have the baking smells for fear of her nerves, but they are still very good. A fine shop delivers them."

Did I land in paradise or what?

I went up to the closets long enough to complete my disguise. I had to be sharp about it because if the bad man could recognize me, who else might?

I found a cutie-pie straw hat with fake flowers. A blonde curly wig was attached to it. Too much like the dead girl, but I had to put my worries away. It's like my Bookie said: "Business is business so suck up the candy and forget about it."

I took a deep breath and shoved the wig with hat on my head. It didn't make me happy, but, like Bookie said, I was sucking up the candy.

I found a pair of Little Bo-Peep shoes that seemed to fit the outfit. I grabbed a big fake sucker that was sticking out of a box. Why not? Like I said, I was sucking up the candy.

On to the pink room with all the mirrors to make sure I looked the part. Not bad. I found the pink powder Tootsie used on me yesterday when I was being a baby. I decided it'd fit the job today too. I was playing a nice girl who stayed in the house all day doing sewing and reading books, stuff like that. I'd be plenty pink, not sun baked like Sparky.

I wasn't as good with powder dusting as Tootsie, I'd admit that. But, close enough, for being in a hurry.

Cookie bag and sucker in hand, I slipped out the sunroom doors this time. I could hear Gilbert busy humming and cleaning up in the bathroom, so the coast was clear. I'd have crawled under the fence, but that would've messed up the costume, so I took the gate by the garage that Tootsie showed me yesterday.

As much as I could, I stuck to the back ways. But not being able to crawl in the dirt limited my choices. So, I had to take a risk and go on the sidewalks.

I ran straight into Mug's big belly.

He had his slab-of-meat hand on my arm. I nearly dropped my sucker, my bag of cookies, as surely I'd take the drop at the end of the hangman's rope.

He was laughing. "Hey little girl, you're in a hurry."

I looked up at him. He was smiling, but not in his mean Mug kind of way. Was it possible? Did he really not recognize me?

"Whaddya got there?" He snatched the bag of cookies from my hand. He looked at the bakery's name on the bag. "That's a swell bakery. Really swell. Mind if I have a sample? See if they're up to snuff for you?"

He didn't wait for an answer, and I was in too much shock to say anything anyway. Mug reached in and his hand came out with not one, but two cookies. He popped them in his mouth. "Mmmm! Some fine cookies."

Then he seemed to notice me all over again, and peered down at me. Oh, oh. But instead of cuffing me, he asked, "You okay, little girl? You look lost or something."

"Oh, Mr. Policeman, I think I lost my sucker." Don't ask me why I said that. It was the first thing that popped in my head. I tried to talk in a sweet girly voice.

Mug laughed. "You got your sucker in your hand!"

Of course I did. I acted surprised and licked it like I was so happy to find it. The lollipop was made of something like plaster that made me choke. I tried to giggle to cover up my gagging.

He laughed some more, patted me on the top of my straw hat, and then said, "You got too many cookies in the bag. I don't want you to get sick eating all of 'em. Here, let me help you out by lightening your load." With that big hand of his, he reached in and scooped out all the cookies he could hold. I couldn't believe it.

He handed me back the more-than-half-empty bag, patted me on the head again, and said, "Go run along now." He walked off, throwing the cookies down his gullet like he hadn't a care in the world.

I felt like turning around and whacking him with the lollipop, but I'd pushed my luck to the limit already. Had to keep moving.

The Court Flight train would have been the easiest way for me to get down to the bottom, near City Hall. But when I peeked around the corner of a building toward the top of the tracks, I saw there was not one cop with a tommy gun, like at the Angel's Flight train, but two cops with two tommy guns guarding it. Nuts to that.

I went a block over. I nearly bumped into Spooky leaning against a lamp post, but he didn't move, didn't look at me. He was busy keeping his head pasted to a poster again. I could see part of the poster. Something about the millions dead in the war being my fault. The biggest type shouted out the reward, which had grown to $25,000. How about that? I slipped one of the cookies under his belt, for helping me yesterday.

Since Court Flight was out, there was no choice but to go by sidewalk. So bold as a brass button, I skipped down the Hill like a girly girl with a lollipop might do. It didn't make sense if you thought about it, but when you skipped, you're less likely to fall and roll down the Hill than if you walked. It was really steep at the Court Hill end.

No one stopped me, so when I got to the bottom of the

Hill, casual and easy as I could, I strolled to City Hall. I passed the hobo who hung around there. He was dozing in the grass. I didn't bother with the fancy front steps, but went around the back, where the cars went in and out.

City Hall was new, compared to most other buildings downtown. It was shiny and white. Modern. It wasn't my usual territory, so I didn't know all its ins and outs. Bookie had me run envelopes to a man called Chum-Chum who worked with his pet goldfish in the back of a speakeasy near City Hall. I'd make the drop, turn around, and was back up the Hill for Bookie's next errand. Like I said, it wasn't my territory, so I didn't stick around. And, can I tell you something confidential-like? If you met Chum-Chum, you wouldn't wanna sick around him either.

The most time I spent there was when Bookie sent me on the second-story job, and I ended up in the Mayor's bathroom looking for jewels that turned out to be paste. I guess the Mayor was what his girlfriends called a cheap date.

I wish I knew a back way into the car park, but I didn't. So, I had to keep strolling casual like out in the wide open. Let me tell you, it wasn't easy doing the casual stroll dressed like a flower girl with a big plaster lollipop. I stuffed most of the cookies I had left into my mouth to fortify my nerves. They were good. I can understand why Mug snatched so many. They were like a dream of sugar paste melting in my mouth. Before I could help it, I said out loud, "Mmmmmm, um!"

"What are you doing here!" It was José. He was the boss of the car park under City Hall. He grabbed my arm and pulled me into the garage, then hustled me further back into the shadows.

"Sparky! Are you crazy?"

Let me tell you something about me and José. He owed me big time. Really big time. That's why I had the nerve to stroll into the City Hall garage.

Not too long back, José let his love of laying bets on the speedway races get a little out of hand and he owed my Bookie, let's say, more than a few of his city pay checks. In other words, money he didn't have and wasn't going to have. My Bookie, not really being a very understanding person, was planning on taking care of this problem shortly. Since I spent a lot of time around Bookie, I knew all of this.

José was Bookie's problem, not mine. To me, José wasn't a problem. He was an okay guy. He got me into City Hall when my Bookie was hoping for jewels that turned out to be paste. He helped me, so I wanted to help him out.

It was easy to switch the payment from another sap, who was dead or soon to be, so it didn't matter to that guy. I gave the credit to José instead. Bookie bought it. "How about that? The garage monkey paid. Wonder where he got the dough? Maybe he stole from the brass. Like the jewels." He gave me an extra suspicious stare. "You sure you didn't pocket the Mayor's real rocks and pass along some paste to me?"

"José probably stole some cars. That's where he got the money. He's a garage monkey, like you said."

That was more plausible, so Bookie was satisfied. For the time being anyway.

When I let José know he was off the hook, he was so happy he sobbed, like a man back from the dead and born again. Which he was.

Now I came to collect.

"José, you owe me. I need some information."

"I don't know anything. I just work in the garage. You gotta git. I'll end up in the slammer if anyone sees me talking to you. I don't know what kind of trouble you got yourself into, but it's serious. Way too serious for a little guy like me."

This wasn't going well. "Okay, fine. I'll tell Bookie the money belonged to the dead guy and you never paid his pocket a hot cent."

This got him quiet really fast. He got so nervous, he looked like he was going to start jumping. "Okay, okay. What you want?"

"There was a car, a big City Hall car, driving around Court Hill at 5 am the morning that dead girl showed up on the bench. Who was driving? Who was in the car?"

José rubbed his mouth and I saw his hand was twitching. "Listen, I'm a nine to five guy. I don't know what goes on here after hours."

I took a page from my Bookie's book. I stood there staring at him and didn't make a sound.

"I'll look at the log, but I'm telling you, it won't have after hours!" There was a bunch of papers held together with metal loops hanging from the wall. He almost dropped it when he pulled it down, he was shaking so much. I could hear him cussing low and quiet because he kept tearing the pages as he flipped through them.

"See here," and he held the papers down for me to see. The page was for the day I found the dead girl, and the day before.

"Nothing at 5 am. Zero. I told you, it's after hours."

He was right. The log stopped at 5 pm and didn't start up

again until 9 am the next morning.

"So, you're saying that anybody can come in here and steal cars and go joy riding all night and that's okay?"

"No. I didn't say that. Don't put words in my mouth!" He was shaking all over by now. He looked over his shoulder, out the entrance to the garage. Across the street was a tall thin man with a long neck like a vulture and teeth like a chomping horse. He was laughing with a group of guys in fancy looking suits and ties. As he laughed, his blond hair bobbed up and down. His great big Adam's apple bobbed too. José did a little jump when he saw this vulture man.

"You have to go. That guy there," and he nodded his chin toward the man, "You can't let him see you. He's dangerous."

"I don't remember seeing him before."

"That's because you don't spend time down here. If you did, you'd know to stay away from him and stay away from this whole place. Now you gotta go!"

"I don't remember you told me what I need to know. Maybe you want me to go to Bookie?"

"Little girl! What did I ever do to you!" He was staring to cry. Grown up men do that when they talk to Bookie, too. Fine. I'd play along.

"Talk."

He whimpered. "Okay, okay. But it wasn't me that told you anything, right?"

I nodded.

"Sometimes, the brass, the high-ups, they wanna take high rollers, big shots, girls, whatever, out on the town. All hours. They don't bother signing in and out of the log. The brass, they're too important to fill out forms. The drivers they use aren't the guys on the city payroll. They use private drivers."

"Like who?"

"I make a point not to know. Anyone who drives big shots and girls around at 5 am isn't an up-and-up kind of guy. Sometimes I come in and the cars are all dirty, bottles of hooch spilling on the seats. It's a lot of cleanup, let me tell you."

"What kind of cleanup did you do that day, the dead kid day?"

He stopped for a second and wiped his tears away, thinking. "There were some blonde hairs. Not much—inside one of the cars, on the front seat. That's nothing unusual. I get a lotta blonde hairs."

"There's a lotta cars here." I waved my arm to all the

parked black sedans. How you know that's the one?"

"When I came in that morning, there was only one car that was moved. It wasn't parked where it's supposed to be, and it wasn't parked straight. That's how I know which ones we gotta clean. All the city garage workers are trained on proper straight parking techniques. But these drivers the big shots dig up aren't trained like..."

I cut him off before he started reciting city training manuals. "I wanna see this car."

"It's all clean. There's nothing in it now. Besides, it's out there." He nodded his chin back outside. The long-necked guy was doing a few final handshakes before the swells climbed into a big black sedan. "That's the car."

Nuts. It was looking like I'd learned everything there was to learn.

"Can you go now, please?"

I nodded.

"There's a back door. You can't go out where you came because Whisper-Whisper's there."

"Who?"

"That guy! Move!" He was pushing me now, out a door, down a hallway, out another door, up some stairs, and finally out in the sun, at the side of City Hall. Then he disappeared, running back down the stairs.

The hobo was awake and taking a sip from something inside a paper bag when I passed him again. He was singing a little tune to himself, "Money in my palm, money in my shoes." He nodded at me and raised his paper bag in salute.

I was feeling tired and not sure what to do next. The sun was high now and the heat was settling in. So, I sat down on the curb next to him. He looked me over. My dolly dress was a mess by now with all the skipping down the hill and being pushed around by José. My plaster sucker was cracked down the middle.

"Had a rough day?" he asked me.

"You could say that."

"I'd offer you a sip of sauce," he said, holding up his bag of something smelling like sugared paint, if there were such a thing, "but I think you're a bit young to start down that road." He took a long gulp. Looked like he'd had a lifetime of rough days.

I dug into the cookie bag. My fingers found one left. I handed it to him and he took it, turning it around and around like he'd never seen a cookie before.

"People don't usually give me these kinds of treats. A kick

in the pants or spare change, if I'm lucky." He popped the cookie in his mouth. "Say, this is something new."

"Yeah, they're supposed to be from some fancy bakery. Don't think it's a Bunker Hill bakery. Never saw a fancy bakery up there. Me, I'm a candy girl, usually. I get my candy from the Bunker Hill pharmacy. They have all the latest styles. You can say I'm something of a gourmet, candy-wise."

"Bunker Hill, you say? That's where you're from, is it?"

I kept my mouth shut. Maybe my disguise was keeping him from recognizing me, but best not give him extra info. I'd blabbed too much already. I really musta been tired, to get so careless.

"Nice place. Fresh air. Clean. Not like the sleaze around City Hall. Guess I'm one of the sleaze now," he sighed.

Nothing I could say to that.

"Say," I asked, "do you know a guy with a long neck that hangs around City Hall? Teeth like a horse?"

"Ah. You must be talking about our Whisper-Whisper."

"Yeah, that's the one. Why's he called Whisper-Whisper? I've never seen his face in the papers before, like the rest of the City Hall types. What's his deal?"

He smiled. "So many questions for such a little thing. Yes, I suppose you wouldn't see him in the papers. He makes a point of staying out of them, and the papers obediently comply. He's not one for publicity, but he pulls all the strings. They call him 'Whisper-Whisper,' because that's how he operates, though whispers, behind closed doors, late at night, in places like those," and he moved his chin toward what used to be the bars that kept close company with City Hall. They're speakeasies nowadays.

"You see anything early in the morning a few days back, like the day the kid turned up dead on Court Hill?"

He paused a long time. "I'm a drunk. I don't remember much from one day to the next. Guess I'm not much use to a little girl in trouble."

I peeled some plaster off my sucker. It came apart without much work. Long shot asking the hobo. But at least I knew more about this vulture neck guy, Whisper-Whisper.

The hobo looked up toward the Hill. "I used to live there too, Bunker Hill. Me and the wife and my little girls."

"You leave 'em? That what happened?"

He got quiet, lowered his head, and said, real soft, "No, that flu while I was away at the war. The girls. Both of 'em. Then my wife left. Well, didn't give her much choice after..." and he held up the bag.

Such a sad look came over his face. He sat still, his eyes lost in a different time. I don't remember that flu. Too young for that. But, I'd heard plenty about it. People dropping like flies, City Hall shutting down schools, pool halls, even movie theaters, Pasadena closing its borders, anything to keep the germs from spreading.

I wondered if they took the girls away to one of the hotels rigged up as make-shift hospitals, leaving their mama wondering, worrying, until official word came back they were dead. If he was away at the war, did he even know? Did he find out long after, when the letter finally got to him from across the ocean? Tough break.

He eyes came back to me and he seemed to wake up to today.

"Listen, a little girl like you shouldn't be hanging around the sleaze here. Your folks must be worried. Why don't you run along?"

Well, Sparky's a street kid with no parents, a wanted murderer who started the Great War and everything else. But I guess he didn't know that. Good. Then he wouldn't rat me out. Not that he seemed the type. Not a pal of the cops, if you know what I mean. But you never knew, really, did you, who you could trust?

"I'll keep an eye on you as you go up the Hill. Okay? Not that I'm much use, but I'll keep an eye." He smiled in a sad kind of way.

I nodded and took off. Don't need to tell me twice. Ol' Gilbert might start wondering why I didn't come down for lunch anyway. Best to head back to Creepy House.

"Thanks for the cookie!" he called after me.

Not a bad guy for a bum.

It was a hot lot of huffing and puffing by the time I dragged myself back up the Hill. I got sloppy. And I must have looked sloppy. I'd lost that straw hat somewhere on my climb and forgot that the fat blonde curls were sewn into it.

This time Mug recognized me right off the bat.

His whistle blowing and blowing and blowing woke me up to reality. Tired and hot as I was, I hoofed it. This way, blocked by cops, that way, Mug's big self was barreling toward me. Doom.

I scrambled down another street and there was Spooky. He moved. He actually moved. Well, only his head turned away from the poster saying I started the war his mind was still fighting.

His face looked like a ghost. But I noticed one thing: sugar at the corner of his lip. Cookie sugar. Fancy cookie sugar. My eyes moved to where I tucked the cookie under his belt. Gone. Well, would you look at that?

Sometimes you have to take a chance. I decided I'd trust him.

I could hear Mug's whistle getting closer, could hear the cop feet running faster, gaining. I dove into the geraniums and gladiolas and bushes in the yard next to Spooky's lamppost.

My life was in his hands.

Chapter 8

The cops swarmed Spooky. I heard lots of "Did you see her? Where'd she go?" But Spooky didn't move.

Mug was slower catching up. Through the flowers and leaves, I saw him, face red, wet with sweat, panting. He pushed the other cops aside to get to Spooky. He stopped to bend down, holding his knees and catching his breath. Then he straightened up and was back in business.

"Hey, Spook, we gotta get this little girl. You know the girl I'm talking about. Just to question her, understand? Nothing rough. Just talk. Keep her tucked out of the public eye until all this business settles down. It's for the best. Safer."

Spooky kept staring at the lamppost.

"Come on, Spook." Mug was using his nice, patient voice. "Help us out. Come on."

Spooky moved his head away from the poster.

"Atta boy, Spooky."

I wish I could've seen Spooky's expression, but all I could see was the back of his head.

He moved his arm to point toward a walkway across the street that ran between two houses. "Sometimes, she goes there." His voice was a scratchy whisper, kind of like how you'd think a ghost would talk.

I could see Mug's face. He lit up like Fourth of July and Christmas all rolled into one. "Thanks, Spook. You're a pal." And off they ran.

After the cops were good and gone, except for Spooky, I climbed out of the flowers and bushes. Some had thorns that ripped my getup even more.

Spooky's forehead was back against the poster and he was staring at it with his faraway eyes. Since his head had moved a bit from where it'd been, I could see more of the poster. The picture wasn't me. It was an old photo of a battlefield from Spooky's war. Same war the hobo was still fighting in his head too. The picture was lined with lots and lots of dead people. Spooky kept staring at it.

Not much I could say, other than, "Thanks, Spooky. I owe you a few." Then I took off.

It took me longer than I wanted to make my way to Creepy House. I had to do careful crawling through yards and thorns and spend time hiding under a car. When I got back, I looked more like a mangy dog than Little Bo-Peep.

This time, I went inside the mansion through the storm doors. I wanted to be under the floors, to listen for Gilbert moving around. I heard footsteps by where pipes came through the floor. Must be the kitchen. Good. He was still messing around there.

I made a dash out the cellar, up the stairs with the squares, through the closets and into Tootsie's pink dressing room. I dug through the drawers of her pink-ribboned table until I found the cold cream. I rubbed it over my face, my arms, my legs. I never noticed before how dirty I could get. Must have ruined a dozen of her hankies wiping myself at least partly clean. I wadded them up, and the Little Bo-Peep getup. I shoved them in a back corner in her closet maze where nobody was likely to find them.

I wasn't sure what to wear, so I grabbed the first thing I saw. It was a dress made of glitter. It went down almost to my knees. Good enough. It wasn't too long and trip-able, that's the main thing. I liked to have clothes that left me free to run in a pinch.

I was heading back to the stairs, when I ran into Tootsie.

"Hey, you're a vamp today, huh?"

She'd lost the lost look and was back in her happy mood. She only had a little makeup on, and she wore a long, loose dress with tigers on it. Pouncing tigers. She still looked a pale.

"Yeah. Something different."

"I remember the movie I wore that in. 'Slow Party Boat to Paris.' That was a hoot. We had such fun."

I looked down at the dress and back up at her. She's taller than me. "Wasn't this kind of short on you?"

She bent back her head and practically howled she was laughing so hard. "That was the idea! Don't be so wet behind the ears. Hey! Gilbert! You gotta hear what Sparky said!"

I followed her as she moved out of the maze toward the stairs. I heard Gilbert running up the stairs at the same time.

When he reached the top, he was panting almost like Mug because he'd run so fast. He had his apron on. "Mademoiselle?"

"Relax! I was going to tell you something funny. Sparky worried this dress was too short on me."

He looked at her, looked at me, seemed to understand what was going on, and then laughed. Then she started laughing again.

"Yes, the little one said she wanted to play in your closets. She's been there for hours!"

"This is what happens when you let fans loose in the house, isn't it, Gilbert?"

"Oh, yes, Mademoiselle. How do you feel?"

She brushed him away. "Stop with all the fussing. It's time for a little girl's lunch, I think."

"Of course! Of course!"

But she didn't follow me and Gilbert down the stairs. She drifted back through the closets. I guessed she was going back to bed.

"I'm so happy you made Mademoiselle smile," Gilbert said when we were back in the kitchen. "So much laughing and smiling since you came."

Made me wonder what the situation was here before.

Lunch was a sandwich. Not what I was hoping for, but Gilbert mumbled about the not cooking business again. Look at me, getting all high-horse. Complaining about a sandwich. Usually that's a fancy meal for me.

I was in a bit of a pickle. I'd found out some first-class information, but if I told Gilbert, he'd know I hadn't done what he said and was running around the Hill dodging cops. The best solution was to do more creeping and running, as soon as I caught my wind and finished my sandwich, which was pretty tasty, let me tell you.

"Is it okay if I play in her closets all afternoon?"

Gilbert was even more happy than ever to hear this. "Of course! But, please try to play quietly. Her nerves are mending. We must be careful."

"Sure, I'll be extra quiet."

Since I won't be there.

I felt sleepy after my sandwich lunch. Still, I headed to the closets, with the goblin calling after me, "Don't get lost!" He chuckled too.

The heat outside crept into the house's second floor and made the closets more stuffy than ever. Like the rest of the house, the bigger colored glass windows stayed closed and only the smaller, clear glass transoms above them were cracked open. That wasn't enough to let in a decent breeze.

Maybe it was okay to relax. But only for a minute. I mounded up what looked like a coat, and before I knew it, I was down for the count.

When I woke, not a speck of light was coming through the clear glass transoms. If not for the dim electric lights that were always kept burning, Tootsie's closets would have been as dark as a sewer at midnight with the manhole cover slapped down tight.

Were those voices? I followed the sound, crawling on my hands and knees through the closet maze. I dragged the coat with me in case I had to hide under it in a hurry.

Then I saw a brighter patch of light where the voices seemed to be coming from. I crawled low now, remembering how Beele the singing teacher spotted me. I came to a set of double doors that were cracked open. I draped the coat over me to cover all except for my eyes so I could peep through the doors. If the people belonging to the voices happened to look toward the cracked open door, all they'd see was a coat fallen on the floor, hopefully.

It was Tootsie's bedroom. All lavender and pink, with a huge bed that had what looked like a fake bird head about six feet high at the foot of it, and a fan of fake bird feathers maybe ten feet high, at the head of her bed. They were painted in peacock colors. In the middle of this huge bed was Tootsie. Sitting on the bed next to her was that vitamin doctor.

It was hard to hear what either of them was saying because they were talking so low, they were almost whispering. I thought I heard her say, "I can't manage." Or maybe it was, "I can manage." Or, no, it might have been, "I can tango." I wasn't sure.

He was stroking her hand and I think he was saying, "Let's talk." Or, could have been, "Let's tango." Somehow, I don't think I was hearing the "tango" bit right.

Nothing interesting was happening, except Tootsie was wasting her time with that vitamin doctor. I crawled with the coat, steering by the dim closet lamps, back to where I'd been sleeping. Back to dreamland I went.

The sound of my name woke me up. The sun was making a hazy light through the transoms. I heard Gilbert's voice, low and quiet, saying my name.

I wasn't ready to be found quite yet.

The coat was itchy and had a strange smell, but I realized

it wasn't a coat, but a dog costume. It looked like it was made of real fur. Dog fur? Yikes! Gave me an idea, though.

I dodged the sound of his voice, weaving here and there in the maze, until I could slip down the stairs with the squares. With him still whisper-calling for me upstairs, I went down the cellar steps and stashed the dog coat in a barrel near the wooden stairs leading to the storm doors. Hanging on a peg nearby, I spotted a pair of overalls that didn't seem too big. That gave me idea number two. I stashed them in the barrel too.

Then I ran back upstairs and into the kitchen.

Gilbert had the table set like yesterday: juice, lots of jam, and those thick, thick slices of toast. I dug in.

After a while, I heard him coming down the stairs. He was red in the face and mumbling in that strange language he spoke sometimes, when he came into the kitchen. "Sparky! There you are! I was looking so much all over for you! You mustn't hide like that."

My mouth was full of toast, so I tried to shrug in an innocent way.

He frowned at the glitter dress I was still wearing. "That is not for sleeping in. I made up one of our guest rooms for you last night, but couldn't find you. You weren't out last night, running from police?" He stared hard at me.

"No!" I mumbled through the toast in my mouth. I stuck up my bare foot so he could see the bottom of it. I'd cleaned it off plenty yesterday with Tootsie's cold cream.

He didn't seem completely satisfied, but what could he say, except for, "I suppose. Ah, Sparky, you are a wild one. Another bath for you and something else to wear."

Now this was going too far. I swallowed the toast down with a swig of OJ. "I've had two baths since I got here. I draw the line. No bath. And I'm fine with this dress. I like the sparkles."

He sat down in the kitchen chair across from me and made a long sigh. He rubbed his knees, then rubbed his forehead. "Very well. But tomorrow you must have the bath. Tonight, you will sleep in a proper bed. It is not for little girls to make nests here and there to find sleep."

"Fine." A bed. I wasn't used to that. Not sure I wanted one. But I'd worry about that and the bath later. I was behind with clearing my name already because I fell asleep on the job yesterday. "Can I play in her closets again today?"

This seemed to cheer him up. "I am so glad you have found something to amuse yourself with. Yes, that is good. Be very extra quiet today, though. Mademoiselle's nerves?"

"Sure!"

I gobbled down the toast with as much jam as I could shove in my snout. "See you later!" I took off running up the steps.

I listened to make sure Gilbert was busy puttering around the kitchen. Then I tiptoed down the stairs and slipped into the cellar. I switched places with the glitter dress and the overalls and dog coat in the barrel. After rolling up the overall's cuffs and adjusting the straps, it fit me good enough. I wore overalls a lot. There were plenty of them in every house, and they were handy because they're both a shirt and pants in one. Overalls had lots of pockets too.

The dog coat seemed to have gotten stinkier overnight. But I still slipped it on. It wasn't an ideal getup, that I'll tell you. But I figured, maybe disguising myself as an animal would work better than being a person.

Not taking any chances, I still kept to the byways and not the highways. Though I had to do some quick scrabbling across streets. Halfway across one street, who came around the corner, but a lady in her Sunday best with a Bible in one hand and the hand of a little girl in the other. Both of them were all prim and pastel with their little hats and veils. The girl had on patent leather shoes, don't ya know.

I wasn't one for shoes, like I said, but the very thought of a pair of those patent leather babies got me all green eyed with longing. Under a different state of affairs, meaning if I wasn't wanted for murdering about a million people, I'd tail the two of them, wait till dark when all good people were deep asleep, then do a second-story job, and that little girlie would kiss her patent leather shoes goodbye.

I wouldn't wear them, you understand. I'd keep them in one of my hidey-holes and pull them out now and again to admire the shine while I took a nip from my candy stash. My candy stash I used to have.

But I was wanted. That's the rub. No patent leather shoes, no candy. So, I kept scrabbling in my most dog-like way.

The lady spotted me and started screaming, pointing.

Put yourself in my shoes, or paws. What would you do? I started barking. Had to play along. I was in too deep already.

This got both of them screaming even more, raising the roofs of the whole Hill, so I took off, as best I could on hands and knees. I hid in a crawl space nearby that I'm familiar with, where I've spent more than few nights huddled, especially when it's raining outside.

No rain on this bright, sunny Sunday, but mom's and little girlie's screams drew the Mug. He came huffing over, face red, expecting something juicy.

But all she had to say is: "Satan! I saw Satan in the flesh! It is what Brother Fredrick warned! The world is coming to an end! Horned devils on our streets."

Let me tell you about Mug. He dealt with real things. Things he could punch or kick or slap a pair of cuffs on. Devils prancing around wasn't something he wanted to hear about. But, she wasn't some cheap floozy he could tell to scram. Church ladies were the type to storm to City Hall with complaints, demands, petitions. And this Brother Frederick and the whole congregation would likely join in. Mug was in a bind.

"Yeah, well, I need you to be calm and tell me exact details. What was this guy wearing?"

She started pounding him on the chest with her Bible. "It's Satan! Satan is naked!" She'd be halfway to the pen right now if she were a floozy. But she wasn't.

"Okay, lady. A naked man?"

"No! A demon from hell!"

The little girl started tugging Mug's sleeve and saying, "You're going to hell. You're going to hell," over and over. She was smiling, enjoying herself.

A neighbor came out of one of the rooming houses to join the party. "Officer! Why aren't you helping this poor woman?"

This only egged on the church lady. She launched into a whole spiel about hellfires. A few more nosy neighbors appeared, nodding and complaining about why don't the cops do anything. I was tossed into their mix too: "That girl the papers says is mowing down people right and left—she clearly came straight up from hell and all you police do is sit on your hands twiddling your thumbs!"

Mug looked lost.

Perfect. Seeing as he'd be busy for a while, I was safe to slide out of the crawl space.

But I was surprised when I couldn't slide anywhere. I was caught on something. There's not much light down in the crawl spaces I frequent. So it took careful squinting into the shadows before I realized someone had laid loops of barbed wire and I was caught in one of the loops. The cops. They must have rigged all my likely hiding spots. If only the church lady knew how the cops were messing with me. If this was sitting on their twiddling thumbs, I'd hate to see what real action was.

Fortunately, it was the dog outfit that was caught, not my hide. Being extra careful, I was able to pull my legs out of the barbed wire by leaving behind plenty of the long dog hairs. The barbed wire loops almost caught me a couple more times, but finally I made it out and was on my way. To my Bookie.

Chapter 9

My Bookie's office was a room behind a five and dime store. High on the back outside wall of his office was a little bared window. He kept it open all the time because it stank in there: booze, stogies, fear. But meaning to say, he wasn't the one being fearful. It was people who owed him money or otherwise were causing him some kind of problem.

I jumped, grabbed hold of the window bars, then used my bare feet to scramble high enough so I could hook my elbows around the bars and look in.

"Hey, hey!" I whispered as loud as I could.

He whipped around so hard, he knocked his chair over and nearly fell over with it. I had to try hard not to laugh. He probably thought he was getting plugged.

The crazy look in his eyes melted away when he saw it was just me. Then he sneered, "Whatcha doing in that stupid outfit. You look like a goat. Aren't you a murderer or something now?" He laughed.

But I saw a glitter in his eyes. The same glitter when he knows big money's coming his way.

"I need information," I told him. "And I'm a dog. Can't you see a dog when it barks at you?" I made a "woof."

"Ugly dog." He tilted his head to one side, looking at me. "Say, you got your hair cut or something. Makes you look less like a wild animal. Well, except for that goat you're wearing." He laughed some more. "Want information, eh? Don't we all." He pulled a rag of a newspaper up from his desk and showed me the big black headline. It was the usual over-cooked applesauce: "Murderer Rampaging! Body Count Climbs! $35,000 Reward!" Of course there was a photo of the Mayor holding a new check in one hand and pointing at it with the other, grinning. I'd like to knock those pearly whites clean outta that pretty face.

Thirty-five grand. I had to whistle. My dollars went up.

"Some reward, huh?" he smiled, his eyes glittering.

"Haven't I done a lotta good work for you?"

'Which I paid for. Paid too much."

He had a point. Not that I agreed with the "too much" bit. But still, come on. I'd been a good little runner.

"Listen, I just need to know any guys, drivers that take the drunk high-ups for unofficial rides in city cars with girls or whatever. Like at 5 am in the morning with dead kids."

He didn't say a word. Just stared at me. He cocked his head and smiled.

"Come on. I need to prove I'm innocent, get this heat off my back. This is me here. You don't wanna see my little bitty feet swinging in the wind, do you?"

I was sounding like people who owed him money, owed him favors, owed him everything they had. I hated sounding like them. Because I knew it never worked. But I was desperate and couldn't stop myself.

"How about this..."

He grinned now. This was what they all said, trying to bargain, offering a trade for something he could care less about.

"I'll trade you. I'll work free for you for a whole month."

His mouth curled up like he was trying hard not to laugh. This was also something he did. Every single time. Not good. Not good at all. But, I kept going. Hoping like all the others that maybe this time it'd work.

I tried for two months free labor, then three, then four. All the while he said nothing, and his smile was getting meaner and meaner. The glitter never left his eyes.

He cut me off, finally, like he always did, when I got to six months. "Listen, girlie, you're in no position to negotiate. City Hall car, you say? That's a lotta hot business, right there. Risky for me. And say, that reward would keep me in some fine new threads for a lifetime."

He gave me a long look, the glitter practically dancing in his eyes. "Let's say, for the sake of argument, that I consider your offer. You understand, I also need to consider that I can get any of a hundred street kids to do what you do. And to be my runner, even for a few tossed pennies, they'd kick the hangman's trap wide open for you. What do I care if your little itty-bitty feet swing in the wind?"

I guess I thought maybe he liked me a little. I felt like crying, right then and there. A lot of great big guys have cried in his office at this very point in the conversation. A conversation I'd heard so many times, it's memorized. I had to pull myself together, swallow the tears, not be like all the other losers who ended up here.

"What's the matter, Spark? What'd you think? I was your daddy or something?" He snorted like this was the craziest notion in the world. "Aww. Where's tough little Sparky? You crying or something?"

No, I wasn't. He always made a dig at the losers about crying.

"Okay, twelve months. Totally free," I said, in the hardest voice I could scrounge up. Not crying at all. No way.

"Okay."

What? Did he say, "Okay?" He never said that. This wasn't what happened. Maybe he really did like me, just a little.

"See how soft I'm getting? But, listen, there's fees, surcharges, interest and so on that I'll have to tack on to the twelve months. You've worked for me long enough to understand that, right? I'm a man with expenses."

This sounded more like the Bookie I knew. Interest, surcharges. That meant I'd be working free forever.

"Sure." I had to work hard to keep the croak from my voice, or else he'd realize I really had almost started crying. I still felt like crying. How was I supposed to eat if he didn't give me even a tossed penny? But that was something I'd have to worry about later.

He cocked his head to the other side, his glittering eyes watching me. He leaned on the edge of his desk, since his chair was still spilled on the floor.

He didn't say anything for the longest time. Then, "Yeah, I know a guy. Not too bright, but pretty. Knows how to drive. Is available at all hours for whatever ails." He laughed again. I supposed he'd made a joke.

"You know the rooming house next to that old place with the old lady living all by herself with all the gladiolas in the yard?" I sure did. Nice lady with the gladiolas. Nice to me. Not many are.

"In that rooming house, he's got a basement bed. House has a telephone in the parlor. He leaves the basement door open, so he can hear it ring, all hours."

And that's it. He kept smiling at me, eyes glittering.

I let go of the window bars and took off.

I smelled a rat. Maybe Bookie had a soft spot for me, but I'd never seen Bookie so generous. The whole setup didn't seem right. But a lead's a lead. I was a quick kid. But, I'd have to be even quicker and grow eyes on my back.

My Bunker Hill wasn't a huge place, so I was at the house with the nice lady and the gladiolas in a flash. The lady sometimes let me sit in her yard with the flowers and the little bees buzzing about. She'd given me cookies a few times, and some clothes a long-gone kid used to wear. Not a dead kid. She had photos of the kid all grown up, looking good. Trying to be an actress nowadays or something. The grown-up kid didn't have much time to visit the old lady. Maybe that's why the lady was nice to me. I was someone to talk to or something.

It took a quick case of the joint with my eyeballs to tell me the rooming house next door would be a cinch to get in. Most of these places were left unlocked so the boarders could come in and out without pounding on the door and waking the world up. This was probably the same. Not that I was so bold to walk in the front door. Especially dressed like a dog—a dog—I was no goat. I spied a likely parlor window. Being hot, this window, and all the other windows in the house, were wide open.

I had to do a bit of careful climbing over rose bushes that could've used a trim. Then I grabbed the window sill and hefted myself up enough to see inside. Just an old guy dozing in a chair. He'd be no trouble. If he did wake up, I knew I'd be faster than him, judging from that cane propped up on the chair's armrest. Maybe he'd think another boarder got a dog. Or goat.

I crawled the rest of the way up on the sill, then hopped down onto the carpet, which was so thin it didn't exactly muffle my fall. The old guy snorted, shuffled a bit in his chair, then dropped back deep into dreamland.

I tiptoed through the parlor. There's the phone. It was next to the arched doorway leading to the hall. And in the hall was a door. Probably led to the basement. The door was closed. Bookie said the driver left the door open so he could hear the phone ring. So, if the door was closed, did that mean he was out? I listened carefully. I heard a radio, soft, somewhere upstairs in the house. I heard a sigh, a creak, a lot of nothing except ticking clocks.

I opened the door and made my way down the basement stairs.

Fortunately, there were lots of basement windows letting in plenty of light, so I could see fine.

Not that there was much to see.

One corner had a stack of suitcases. Since I'd done the slipping into boarding house basements for a spot of shelter, let's say, more than a few little times, I knew the routine with the suitcases. Someone left, or more likely, someone died, then the landlady packed up all their worldly belongings, which never filled more than the one suitcase they brought in with them, and stashed it in the basement. All these suitcases sat there, waiting for some relative to come and pick them up. Never happened.

I'd spent many a long empty day poking through the suitcases, looking at the photos, wondering about their stories, borrowing any clothes that more or less fit the bill for me. As long as I put the suitcases back all nice and neat, no one was the wiser. No one, no relatives, no nobody wanted the dead people's stuff anyway. That was plain to see.

Down in this basement, along with the suitcases, there was a work table against another wall. It had a few tools on top, door knobs, a broken plate. There was a window screen with a broken frame leaning on the wall next to the table. Someone probably'd been meaning to fix it for the last twenty years.

That was it, apart from a few more odds and ends: a wooden crate with nothing but another wooden crate, empty, stacked inside it, empty mason jars, that sort of thing. It was the type of stuff I'd always seen in basements. No surprises.

The only wall with no windows had a closed door. I listened again, ear to door. Waited, listened some more. Nothing. Not a snore, not a shuffle, not a sniffle.

I turned the knob nice and slow and peeked in.

Safe.

No driver, but plenty to show he slept here. The one window, high up on the wall across from the door, gave me enough light to see this probably used to be a storage closet. All four of the walls were lined with shelves. Maybe those mason jars were evicted from the shelves to make room for one more boarder.

There was a cot, a few clothes folded extra neatly on the shelves, ties rolled up and lined up on another shelf, a pair of socks hanging by color on the metal rail at the cot's foot. Maybe that's how he hung them to dry.

Funny thing, though. There were socks on half the cot's rail. There were ties on half the shelf. There were folded clothes on half the other shelf. Like there was half as much of everything, but it wasn't here.

Under the cot I saw the same basement-stashed suitcase all boarders had, except this boarder was still alive. Next to it was a space with a lot less dust. A suitcase-sized space. But there wasn't a second suitcase. Only one. Where did number two go? I turned to give a quick look around the room. Like I said, probably used to be a closet for the mason jars. There wasn't much to it. It was easy to see there was only one suitcase here. Wherever number two went, it must have taken half the socks, ties and clothes with it. And him too.

I slid it out the suitcase that was left. Not too heavy. Not locked, so I popped it open.

A few letters, a few photos. A young guy and some girl. I guessed the guy was the driver. Yeah. The tie he wore in the photo had the same pattern as one rolled up on the shelf. He looked like a dandy. Kept his clothes nice and neat like you'd expect from a dandy. He was pretty, like my good 'ol Bookie said. The girl? She had the type of hair bleached so hard it looked white. She had it processed into waves so tight, they sure didn't look like hair. More like a helmet. She wore a dress that clung to her every bump and dip like a sock. A threadbare sock. He sure seemed happy standing next to her, his arm around her waist. She was smiling too, but in a sneering kind of way I didn't like.

The two of them wore the same outfits in all the photos, like they were taken the same day. In the background, it looked like the beach. Not that I'd ever been to the beach, but I'd heard enough about it. I saw a roller coaster in the background. Someday I'd like to take a spin on that. I wouldn't be scared a bit, even when it took me all the way to the top of the rise. I'd ride it down at a hundred miles an hour with my arms up way over my head, like Bookie said you're not allowed to do. He'd been to the beach lots, so knew the drill.

Oh, but look here! Another photo. This time, someone else was standing off to the side. A little someone. I held the photo up close to my nose.

Yup. It had to be. That dead kid. But, here, she wasn't so dead.

She was a third wheel, that was plain enough. Like she got in the photo accidentally, or maybe whoever took it didn't realize the kid wasn't welcome. The driver and the girl weren't looking at the kid, like she didn't exist. But the kid was looking at them, all solemn in a blank kind of way that made me wonder if she was hungry. I'd been there. I'd felt that blankness when you're so hungry you could hardly stand. Looked like the kid was leaning against the fence. Eyes not on the roller coaster, not on the beach sand, not on all the things you'd think a little kid would stare at. Only them.

Now I could see the deal. Was the kid too inconvenient for pretty boy driver? Did he do away with the kid, then dump her on a Court Hill bench thinking no one would notice or care? Or did the bad man creeping around scare pretty boy off before he could dig a hole and pop her in?

Was she his kid? Her kid? Their kid?

And where's the bleach job now? Did she tell him to do it? Did she know?

Yeah, she knew. With those headlines splashed all over with a $35K reward, she knew. She knew but she wasn't saying a peep, even with that reward dangling like a ten-pound block of the finest sugar candy you ever saw. So, what did that tell you?

She couldn't claim the reward because she was as guilty as him. Maybe she let him do the hard killing bit, but she was in it every step of the way with him.

It just burned me. Them two having a laugh about getting away with murder, while I twitched with my neck in a noose. Didn't that beat all?

My ears picked up a sound. A little tiny sound, hardly noticeable, but such a change from the dead quiet in this house, it might as well've been a brass band.

Had the rats come to roost?

No time to find out. No time to neatly pack the suitcase away.

With the photo of the three of them in my teeth (couldn't leave that proof behind), I climbed up the shelves to the little window. I couldn't get it open. Maybe it was old and stuck; maybe it was painted shut from the outside. No matter. I butted the horns of the weird dog outfit against the glass and it broke, easy as you please.

Since the costume was made of some kind of skin (dog? goat?), the sleeve was thick enough for me to brush the bits of glass aside so I could climb out. I still got a cut across my hand, but I'd gotten worse. I zipped behind the overgrown roses and cased the scene.

Exactly as I thought. Mug and plenty of his fellow cops were prowling around, trying to be quiet, trying to sneak up on me, since no doubt they'd been tipped off. They had a dog too, sniffing around.

Oh, oh. It looked like their dog caught a whiff of the dog or goat or whatever skin I was wearing. Its eyes popped wide and then it let out a huge bark and growl and tried lunging away from the cop holding its leash, making the cop fall half into the rose bushes. He started swearing up a storm. Mug and the other cops laughed at him.

Time for me to slip out of the dog-goat. And it was barely in the nick of time. Almost as soon as I ditched the skin and slithered away to safer bushes, that dog had the costume in its mouth and was swinging it back and forth like it'd caught the rabies for sure.

"What the hell is that?" I heard from Mug. You can say that again.

I knew my Bunker Hill well. I knew there's a gap in the fence along the side yard that led to the nice lady's gladiola house, a gap barely big enough for someone small like me to slip through. Now wearing only my overalls, I made a quick dash for the fence while the cops were else wise occupied fighting with the dog to get what was left of the weird hairy thing out of its mouth. They'd be puzzling over that one for a long time.

Before Mug was the wiser, I was under the fence and out on the other side, in the backyard of the gladiola house. There were more than gladiolas in the backyard. Tomatoes, string beans and a crowd of other vegetables were growing happy as you please. The lady was there now with her watering hose. She was smiling as she gave all the happy growing things some water. Like I said, she's a nice one.

I felt safe here. But I didn't want her to see me, didn't want her to get in trouble with the Mug for helping me, and have her get the hangman's rope too. Nah, she'd been too good to me.

So, I did more slithering in the wet dirt, caught a shot of the hose water, got to the other side where the artichokes grew thick, slipped into another yard, and then another and another, and ran across an alley. Off the alley, I spotted a rusting metal bin hiding behind bushes at the side of a house. I lifted the lid. It looked empty, except for spider webs. Hoping there weren't any spiders hanging around the webs, I jumped in.

I didn't have a costume anymore, so I'd have to wait for dark before I made a move—not that my costumes helped me much.

The scene was red hot. After a while, I could hear police whistles blowing, cop voices, cop feet running here and there. I heard Mug's big voice going on about, "That's the crazy thing those church people were yelling about." Then I heard some other cop talking about, "Fur stuck on our trap," and Mug saying, "Yeah. It's a match. What's that girl up to?" So they were checking their barbed wire, seeing what it caught.

Maybe where I was hiding wasn't so safe if the cops were checking every little nook and cranny. I was about ready to bolt, when the lid popped open. Cops. I was done for. But then, a pile of the wettest, stinkiest slop landed right on top of me. The lid slammed shut.

I'd been in some situations before, but this might've been the topper. If I thought that dog-goat smelled bad, I had another thing coming with this slop. I wanted to run, but then again, the slop was good cover if the next person popping the lid was a cop.

So, I stayed.

It seemed like I spent hours listening to the cops. I thought I heard that church lady yelling about the world coming to an end again, and then a man's voice and a bunch of other ladies yelling the same thing. Must have been the whole congregation.

There was a little gap between the top of the metal bin and its lid that let in a crack of light. I used the light to try wiping the slop off the photo of the dead girl and her parents, or whoever pretty boy and the blonde were.

Made me think of what my Bookie said to me. Before I knew it, all the tears I kept bottled up tight back at his office came pouring out. He was right. Where was tough Sparky now? I had to be careful not to start bawling, else the cops would hear me for sure. The cops or the congregation, take your pick.

Yeah, I knew Bookie was Bookie. That's the way he was. But, still. He talked the same to me, running the same routine, like to all the other beat down slobs who wound up on his office floor. Sure he gave me some information, but he ratted me out big-time. It was only luck that got me out of that bind.

I thought maybe he liked me a little. Had a tiny soft spot for his reliable little runner. Something.

Guess not.

The tears kept running down my face. I gave up trying to hold them back. As long as I didn't cry too loudly, I might as well cry. Even with the stinky wet slop and the noise outside, I must've cried myself to sleep. Like a baby. That's right. Sparky acting like a baby. Embarrassing. But I couldn't help it.

When I opened my eyes, it was good and dark. But I could tell through the gap between the bin and its lid that the moon was still low. Now was my chance before Mr. Moon started rising higher and shining too much light around the Hill.

I lifted the lid nice and slow, and slid out the bin like a mouse with feather feet. I still heard commotion, but farther away, like they were searching lower down the Hill.

I ran along where the street lamps were burned out and no one'd bothered fixing them. I hugged walls whenever I thought someone was coming. I darted onto a dark porch, then crawled through back gardens until I was hidden in the bushes at the edge of Bobby's yard.

I didn't know where else to go. If I went back to Creepy House, Gilbert would know I'd been doing exactly what he told me not too: running around and getting chased by cops. I was sure Tootsie and he heard all the commotion and whistle blowing. Bobby would be upset with me too, but I could handle Bobby. He'd get mad at me, but he'd get un-mad just as quick. Those Creepy House people? I didn't know them well enough to chance it. Look at Bookie. I thought I knew him, at least sort of. And what did he do to me?

I'd show Bobby the photo, see if he had any ideas. Meantime, I'd hide in the bushes until the sun came up and normal people, like Bobby, got out and about.

Chapter 10

I tried slapping myself to keep awake, but how it happened I couldn't tell you, but I fell asleep again. When I popped my eyes open, it was daylight and there were green leaves all around my head. I'd woken up in a few strange situations before. Luckily, I kept my wits enough to stay frozen and quiet until I remembered where I was and what I was doing.

Carefully, I wiggled around in the leaves until I was sitting up. I could see Bobby's yard. Nice green lawn, nice neat rows of tidy flowers. No Bobby.

I waited and waited. My stomach growled. I tried telling it to shut up, but it didn't listen. As the sun moved higher, it got stuffy in the bushes and the heat made the slop smell soaking my overalls rise high into my nose. Flies started noticing.

My eyes were nodding off again in the heat, when I heard Bobby's screen door closing with a nice, soft tap. He never slammed it. Must be him, or his parents, because they didn't slam it either. Their ex-housekeeper used to be a slammer. That's why she's ex.

"Sparky? Sparky? Are you around?"

It was Bobby, whispering. I saw him now. He was holding a newspaper and walking along the edge of the bushes, like he was making a study of the leaves.

"I'm here," I said as low as I could.

He strolled casual-like to where he heard my voice. "Sparky. I was just at the Creepy House. They're going crazy there looking for you. I told them you might be in my yard. You need to get back there. There's even more police than ever searching for you."

He held up the newspaper like he was reading the back page, so the front page and the screaming headlines faced me:

"Murderer in Devil Cult!" The Mayor was grinning in a photo with some church-looking guy, who wasn't grinning. He was glowering. And holding up a Bible.

Bobby turned the paper around and quietly read the headline story to me:

Infamous girl murderer is part of an ancient sect that worships "Satan as their god," according to the Reverend Frederick Blass, who tends his flock at Bunker Hill's Church of the Most Righteous Second Rising of the True Apostles. Dozens of Bunker Hill residents sighted a strange horned creature yesterday afternoon cavorting with whom our anonymous source claims is an infamous Prussian spy responsible for a series of horrific murders.

According to our source, who claims to be highly placed in "US Government circles," this she-spy fled Europe as a stowaway on a luxury liner after her plots at world conquest were foiled when our Yankee Doughboys bravely gave their lives to win victory in the Great War and keep civilization safe. Los Angeles has been in peril since the moment she arrived, first posing as a wealthy debutante from the East Coast, then a chop suey chef, and finally a street girl with the phony name of "Sparky." Her loss of the Great War only fueled her blood lust.

In an exclusive talk with this reporter, the Reverend Frederick, as he prefers to be called, explained she is part of an ancient cult, dating back to the time of Marie Antoinette, and may have been behind the plots against her. "They follow the commands of Satan without question. We believe she is receiving secret orders from Europe to cause chaos in our sacred United States, starting with Los Angeles, which is the new Eden for the Chosen Ones."

Mrs. Martine, a member of his flock, was the first to sight the horned beast on the streets of Bunker Hill. She told this reporter, exclusively, "The beast clawed at me and tried to snatch away my little girl. That Sparky person was there too, ordering the beast to attack us. I have often seen her running around the streets. She is always dirty, and I always knew there was devilry about her."

The entire congregation plans to come to City Hall this morning to confront the Mayor and City Council over what they say is "police indifference" to this crisis. In response, an anonymous source within the Office of the Chief of Police exclusively confided to this reporter, that, "We are operating on a

Oh, boy. I supposed the "underground figures" meant my Bookie.

"Sparky. This gets more and more serious by the minute. Mug and the other officers are rounding up kids and questioning them. No one is safe. I'll help you get back to Creepy House. Now. You need to stay there."

"Then you're not safe either."

"You know I'd go to jail for you."

Not this again. "Bobby, I have a lead." I reached through the leaves and slipped the photo into his fingers that were wrapped around the newspaper. He turned the newspaper over, like he suddenly decided to read the back page, and looked down. I could tell he was studying the photo.

"Is that the dead girl?"

"Yeah. Bookie," and my voice started to catch, remembering what he did to me, "he tipped me off to a boarding house where the guy in the picture stays. He drives City Hall types, off-hours. We gotta find out more, find out who the blonde is."

Bobby let out a long slow silent whistle. "I don't know, Sparky. Things are so dangerous." His eyes crinkled as he realized what I said. "I told you to stay away from that bookie. He's not good for you."

But he didn't have his usual steam and fire about me disobeying his orders. I could tell he was curious and thinking.

"Bobby, I'm fresh outta ideas."

I watched him move his hand that was holding the paper and the photo, like he was considering it, trying to pull answers from it.

After being quiet like this for a while, he whispered, "Marigold."

Marigold! Why didn't I think of that? But you know that saying: two knuckleheads were better than one.

Marigold was Old Bob's grandnephew and lived in his little house with a bunch of other relatives. Old Bob was in the habit of hiring local guys, like pretty boy in the photo, to do odd jobs, including driving his truck when he and his nephew, Marigold's dad, had more jobs than they could handle.

If anyone knew about a character like pretty boy, it was Old Bob. Of course, we couldn't ask Old Bob directly. He'd holler for the police, after first knocking our heads together and stringing us up by the ankles. I'd heard him yelling that particular promise to neighborhood kids often enough, including me. Rumor said he used to be some kind of cowboy working for the movies, doing things with horses. He was probably an expert at stringing up bad guys. No, we weren't messing with him.

But, Marigold, he was another story. He was a bit younger than me, not baby material, but kind of cry-babyish sometimes. He was an easy-going mama's boy with a hankering for candy who wasn't allowed to talk with me, but did anyway.

"Let's do it," Bobby whispered.

Don't need to tell me twice.

It wasn't an easy shot to Marigold's place. Bobby's parents decided, in light of murders and horned beasts running the Hill, he might not even be allowed to go to the library. So, he was stuck in his backyard. He'd snuck through the neighbors' backyards to get to Creepy House this morning.

Good 'ol Bobby. He's so straight and narrow most of the time, but he could be like a street kid when situations warranted. Bobby didn't look at it like that, though. He said he was being "an explorer." That's what he wanted to be when he grew up. A general all-around explorer, and a professor of old things too, like his parents. "Because being a professor will give me more credibility for my explorations."

Whatever.

The point was this: he'd dirtied his clothes creeping around in the am. When he came back to his house, he had to sneaky-like change clothes so the parents wouldn't smell something's up. If he did it again, he'd be running low on fresh threads and for sure the parents would give him the fish eye. He needed another approach to explain his disappearing.

"I'll tell my parents that it is vital I go to the library to research any past sightings of horned devils in Los Angeles and the deeper meaning that such sightings symbolize in California society. I'll say it is a matter of national security, and historical accuracy."

"Sounds like something your parents would buy. Very professor-like."

"Thanks."

The thing was, we couldn't just waltz up to Marigold's house, since it wasn't his house, but Old Bob's, and I've told you the problem with Old Bob.

Old Bob also had an attack horse named Dodger that bit me once. Rumor said the horse was in pictures and was something of a movie star. Didn't know about that. All I'd seen was the nag dragging kids around for birthday parties. That's another racket Old Bob runs. Pony rides, hauling, yard work, you name it. Rumor said he kept a six-shooter and other cowboy stuff in that little house. He threatened to plug me himself. Old Bob's dangerous all around.

Now, of course, I was wanted for murdering everybody, plus siccing horned beasts on the church folk of Bunker Hill. Showing my face at Old Bob's door would get me a blast from his six-shooter for sure.

"I'm drawing a diagram in my head," Bobby whispered to the bushes where I was hiding. "I can't crawl around and get my clothes dirty, again. So, I'll walk along Bunker Hill Avenue like I've not a care in the world because I'm going to the library. Hiding in plain sight."

"Cops might frisk you. They know you hang out with me."

Bobby put his chin in the air. "Let them have at me. All they'll find is a library card." Nice and easy, he turned his newspaper around so the photo with the dead kid faced me again. I poked my hand out of the leaves, snatched the photo back, and slipped it into the front pocket of my overalls.

"I'll stick to crawling through yards and under houses, like my usual lately."

"The alley behind Old Bob's place—I'll meet you there."

"Whatcha' gonna tell the cops if they catch you in the alley?"

He had to think about that for a minute. "I'll tell them I

was following an interesting flying insect that I plan to research in the library.”

Hard to tell if cops would buy that one, but Bobby was known for being an incurable book worm, so they might fall for him chasing bugs in an alley. He’d done stranger.

“Okay. But that attack horse lives in the shed along the alley. Old Bob always keeps the top half of the shed door open, so its head’ll be hanging out. It’ll bite us for sure, or raise a ruckus.”

More thinking time for Bobby. “You have a point. But, if Marigold is in his yard, like I’m thinking he will be with all the commotion going on lately, then maybe he can talk with Dodger, calm him down. We’ll have to chance it.”

Not the best plan, since it hinged on his parents letting Bobby out of his house to start with. But since everything went south with the dead girl showing up on the Hill, no plan’s been fool proof. “Yeah, we’ll chance it,” I agreed.

That settled, Bobby headed back into his house, and I disappeared into more leaves and backyards and whatever else would hide me.

It took me a lot longer to get to the alley behind Marigold’s place than Bobby because he was right about there being even more cops than ever. I even had to hide in a rain barrel to dodge one.

“You’re all wet,” Bobby said when I finally crawled over a fence and hopped into the alley, after first checking to make sure the coast was clear.

“Yeah, well, I had a cop situation. I guess your parents let you escape, huh? Hey, what’s with the jar?”

Bobby held it up. There was some kind of unhappy bug crawling and flapping around inside.

“Before I left, I thought to bring an empty jar with me. I poked holes in the lid with a nail to allow air flow inside for a captive insect to breathe. It’s a perfect container for the purpose. It didn’t take me long to find this insect. It sure came in handy when I ran into a bunch of police. I told them about my insect research plans and they let me go. This will also help back up my research story to my parents—it was touch and go with them, and they almost didn’t let me leave. With this jar, I’ll have proof of what I was up to. I’ll say insects might be involved with the horned beast sightings.”

Like I said, Bobby’s a brain. A strange brain. “Bookie could use someone like you that’s got all the angles covered. If you ever need some spare change...” My heart sank when I said this, remembering how Bookie said there'd be a hundred kids waiting in line to replace me.

"I hardly think I'll be working for that man! I've told you, I want you to stop working for him too. You'll be my wife someday, after we clear your name and all that, so I have a say in what you do with your time."

It's when Bobby got like this, I couldn't stand him. But I didn't try to sock him. I decided to let it go—for now—because, you guessed it, I needed his help more than I needed to sock him.

It was about this time when the horse decided to poke its head through the shed door's top half that Old Bob always kept open. The horse was so quiet and sneaky, I didn't notice it until it suddenly made a snort sound. That about made me jump outta my shoes, and even Bobby made a yelp.

I know that horse recognized me. Its black eyes glared at me and its ears, pointy like devil ears, reached out toward us like it was listening, and then the ears flattened back. The horse started making more snorts and waving its head up and down. I heard a hoof stomp too.

"Easy now, Dodger, we're your friends. Sparky, you don't happen to have any candy, cookies, any treats on you—something to give this horse."

"I'm slap outta the good stuff. Or any stuff. I'm starving, if you wanna know."

That horse made a lunge toward me, big teeth grinning and snapping. I fell back in the dirt, trying to get away. It kept reaching and snapping its teeth. If there was a horned beast, or eared beast, on Bunker Hill, it was this crazy horse.

Then we heard, "Hey, Bobby? Sparky? Is that you guys? Hey, Dodger! Settle down." A head peeked up over the back fence. "Don't worry. I'll get Dodger a carrot. He loves carrots. Be right back." Then the head disappeared. It popped back up again. "I'm not supposed to talk with you, Sparky. Double so now, especially since you're a multiple murderer and dance with horned beasts. My mom's a church goer, okay?" Head disappeared again.

Marigold.

His mom, who's married to Old Bob's nephew, fussed over him and treated him like a dainty flower. She didn't have any other children, so he was like her little baby prince. His clothes were always new and looked like they just got pulled off the laundry line and off the ironing board. Same with him, except for the ironing board bit. Always fresh washed. His mom gave him plenty of pocket change for as much candy as he could get his mitts on.

I'd heard Marigold was named after a movie horse Old Bob used to have. Maybe. But a more fitting name couldn't have been picked for him. You know the orange color marigold flowers have? That's him, from the top of his head all the way down to his toes. Every inch, that same orange color. Okay, maybe not as bright an orange as the flower, but you get the picture.

About now you're probably wondering how I know so much about every inch of Marigold, and maybe I gave a little bit too much detail just now, which Bookie said is never good because cops can always use it against you. I'm not sure cops would be interested in all this about Marigold, but Bobby would. It all started with me asking Marigold if he was orange like that all over. He said he was and I told him I didn't believe him. Of course, he said fair is fair, and if he showed, then, well.

This is something Bobby must never know.

I asked Marigold to promise—serious promise, like a secret to the grave—that he wouldn't ever, ever, ever, ever, never, never tell Bobby. He promised and so far hasn't said a peep. If you saw him and Bobby together, Marigold talked like nothing in the world was amiss. He was something of a gent, Marigold was.

I don't think Bobby would ever speak to me again if he found out. Or, maybe he would, but he'd have a broken heart about it. That I was sure of.

As mad as I got at Bobby about me being his girl and all that, I'd never break his heart. Not on purpose.

I felt bad about the whole Marigold thing. I didn't really plan it.

If I wanted to be honest—another thing Bookie said fell under the general heap of all the bad ideas in the whole world—it was kind of interesting finding out about how orange Marigold really was and all that.

But, like I said, Bobby must never, ever, ever, never know. Okay?

It wasn't too long before Bobby and me heard sounds coming from the horse shed. The demon Dodger turned its head sharp around to see who was coming in, but then turned its head back to fix me the evil eye one more time and snap its chompers.

"Good Dodger. See what I got ya. Yeah, you like that, don't you?" and so on from Marigold's voice in the shed. The horse turned its head back to the sound of Marigold's voice. There were horse sighing noises and other happy-horse sounds.

Then Marigold's head popped above the top half of the

horse door. He was smiling in his easy, happy way, like he always did. Ever since that thing happened which Bobby must never know about, I felt like Marigold looked me in the eye with an extra sly smile. Maybe it was my imagination. Or maybe not. In either case, I did my best to give him a bored stare, like I could care less how orange he was or anything. So far, Bobby hadn't noticed anything. I probably should stay away from Marigold altogether. But, he was fun sometimes. That's another honest statement.

Honesty. There it was again. No wonder Bookie didn't like me.

"I'm not supposed to talk with you." But he was still smiling. He said this a lot, smiling. His mom never approved of me. Well, I was a street kid who didn't take a bath if I could help it, so I could hardly blame her. She probably worried I'd smudge him.

The time I traded some of his fine candy stash for a rat skull I found under Mrs. Tomes' house was the end of the line for his mom. Marigold said she screamed and he admitted he did a lot of crying. It was so bad that for a while, Marigold really didn't talk to me. I believed him about the crying. Like I said, he can be a cry baby sometimes. When I'd spot him at the pharmacy after the rat skull business, his eyes looked puffy and he'd get away from me fast.

But that didn't last. He talked to me nowadays, but just had to be careful about it.

Bobby was all business: "Sparky, show him the photo."

I pulled the picture out of the front pocket of the overalls I was wearing and showed it to Marigold. The picture was getting a little banged up from its travels, but you could still see the people in it.

Marigold took it and his mouth dropped open. "Is that the dead girl?"

"It most certainly is," Bobby said. "But what we need you to do is look at the grownups in the photo, especially the man."

Marigold squinted at the picture. I could hear chomping and horse snorting in the shed. A swish of horse tail fell on Marigold's head. He brushed it away.

"Has he done work for your uncle?" Bobby asked

"Let me see. I think so. Yeah. My uncle found him on a movie set. He was doing extra work for a cowboy show where my uncle was training the horses. He wants to be an actor, like they all do. My uncle gave him a few odd jobs, but no more."

"Why?" I asked.

"Too lazy. Big head. Talks back. Came late to jobs or didn't show up at all. My uncle says it's a waste of time to help him anyway. He's pretty, but my uncle says he doesn't have the 'it' factor."

"The what?" Bobby asked.

"'It' factor. That's the most important thing to have if you want to be an actor in Hollywood. If you don't have 'it,' you just need to hang it up. But this guy, he thought he was a star or something and didn't have a clue he had no 'it.'"

"How do you know if you have the 'it' factor?" I wondered.

"You can't tell. There's no way to measure it or take a picture of it. 'It' just is there or not. My uncle can tell in one second if someone has the 'it' factor." Marigold got a dreamy faraway look like maybe he thought he had the "it" factor. But then he remembered the situation and asked, "Hey, did he kill that little girl?"

"We don't know," Bobby said. "We need clues and leads. Is this guy still trying to do acting? Is he working on movie sets now or something?"

Marigold scrunched up his face. "Nah, don't think so. My uncle said he was too lazy to work with horses or stunt work or anything else much."

"So your uncle washed his hands of him, huh?" I said.

"Kind of. He did get him a job driving for a lady. It's not a lot of work, only here and there. Enough to pay the rent, I guess. But my uncle says this pretty boy likes nice clothes and talked about buying a fancy sedan. He says this guy will never be happy no matter where he works, because he'll always be a bum without a nickel. And no one's going to pay a bum a wage that'll buy a fancy sedan. That's what my uncle says."

"Who is this lady he's driving for now? Does she work in City Hall?" Bobby asked.

"I don't know. My uncle calls her The Onion Girl. That's all I know."

"Onion Girl?" That sounded weird. Usually floozies had names like Peaches. A floozy calling herself Onion Girl wasn't going to win herself any sugar daddies. Or maybe she was no floozy. Maybe she was a for real girl gangster. Wow.

Marigold shrugged. "That's what my uncle says. Seems to mean something to him." He shrugged again in case we missed it the first time.

"The bleach job in the picture, is that The Onion Girl?" I asked.

Marigold frowned at the photo again. "Don't know. I don't remember ever seeing this one. But, she looks like a lot of girls that wanna be actresses. My uncle says starlets are a dime a dozen. This one has even less 'it' factor than the guy. I can tell," he said like he was an expert. "She won't end up being anything. Or, anything in the movies."

"She'll end up a floozy?"

"I think she already is one, from the looks of her." Marigold smiled at me. What was that smile about? Did he toss me in the floozy category too? Oh, boy. That thought made me mad. I'd have to sock him for sure if he thought I was a floozy. But I'd hate to sock him, with his pretty face—though that hadn't stopped me from cracking Bobby's nose. Socking Marigold might make him wanna tell Bobby what I didn't want him to tell too.

"Do you think maybe the grownups hoped the little girl would be a child actress?" Bobby asked.

Marigold didn't bother looking at the photo again. "Nah, she's got even less 'it' factor than the grownups. It's like she's hardly there at all. My uncle says kid actors have to have pizzazz." I'd bet Marigold thought he had five tons of pizzazz.

Bobby nodded, thinking about what Marigold said.

Marigold handed the photo back to him and turned to me. "So, Sparky, you're innocent then?" he asked, smiling again.

"Course I am!"

I said this a little too loud, because that horse whipped its head out the half open door so fast, it almost knocked Marigold over. "Hey boy," Marigold laughed. He pulled a carrot from somewhere, his pocket maybe, and stuffed it in the horse's mouth. It still stared daggers at me.

"That horse is dangerous. It bit me."

"Yeah, but you were throwing rocks at him. That's what my uncle says. He says even if you didn't kill that little girl, he wants to see you strung up." But Marigold was still smiling, so I could tell he didn't agree with his uncle on the stringing up bit.

But, okay. Got me. Maybe I threw a rock, or maybe a few rocks at that horse. I tried getting close to pet it, but it lifted its back hoof up like it was about to kick me. And then the parents doing the birthday party saw me and chased me away.

I just wanted to pet the horse, maybe sneak a ride with the rest of the birthday party kids.

So, I threw a rock. A few rocks. So what?

"You threw rocks at Dodger?" I thought Bobby heard about that. I guess not. Bobby gave me his not-happy face.

"I, well, I, you see, it, ah..." I was trying to come up with a story that wouldn't make Bobby even more mad.

Sometimes I was lucky. Or like Bookie said, sometimes the shiny coins of the good luck goddess sprinkle down. This time, it wasn't coins, but Marigold's mother. "Marigold! Marigold! What are you doing? Who are you talking to?"

Bobby and I ducked down fast. We heard Marigold, smooth as butter, say, "I'm talking to Dodger. I'm giving him carrots."

Then we heard his mom in the shed. "Come away now. That horse will get you all mussed. Be careful not to stray too close to the shed door with that dangerous girl running loose. I wish the police would hurry up and catch her." Then we heard her hustling Marigold away.

With Dodger's carrot supplier out of the picture, it turned its angry horse eyes back on me and started making unhappy horse snorting noises again.

"Let's scram!" I whispered to Bobby.

Keeping low so Marigold's mom wouldn't see us over the fence line, we took off. We slipped behind another fence into a backyard that was always empty because the lady who lived in the house was bonkers and did nothing but talk to her bathroom mirror all day. We could hear her soft voice but couldn't see her clearly through the white lace curtains that moved in and out her open bathroom window in the hot breeze: "Oh, yes, Charlie, I'd love to go there. You know how I enjoy dancing the cha-cha."

"Sparky, we need to go back to Creepy House," he said in his low voice.

"They'll get mad at me for running around. The goblin told me to stay put."

"I know. But they're really worried. Besides, we have to let them know what we found out. Maybe they'll have some ideas."

"Yeah, maybe. You know, I think Onion Girl might be a girl gangster. I don't know for sure. But, what else would she be?"

"Holy Moly. We have to tell them that."

"But we can't tell them everything. Tootsie doesn't want goblin to know about the City Hall car because then he'd know that she beat up the bad man to find out."

Bobby tapped the bug jar on his chin, thinking. "Maybe we can say that bookie told you."

"Nah, better leave him out. Tootsie doesn't like the sounds of him."

"No kidding."

"Hey, we'll say we found out about the car at the rooming house or something."

Bobby shrugged. "Okay. We must let Gilbert know somehow. We need his ideas and Tootsie's."

I wasn't sure if any ideas would come, but I did know I was starving. My stomach decided to growl, proving my point.

We worked out another game plan. Bobby would walk the streets, bold as a brass button. If any cops stopped him, he still had the bug in the jar, plus the extra ammunition of his for-real library card. When he got close to Creepy House, he'd duck into a back yard a couple houses away and sneak over, being careful not to muss his clothes. "I have to keep my parents in the dark. That's imperative."

Did I tell you Bobby likes to show off his big words?

And me? More crawling and scrambling. My overalls were still wet from the rain barrel I had to hide in, and they stank so bad, any extra dirt wouldn't make a difference.

Before we parted ways, Bobby leaned in close, like he was going to kiss me. I braced myself. But then he pulled back. "Sparky, you stink bad. Really bad."

Thank you, stinky slop-covered overalls.

He was about to leave again, but then he stopped and said, "What is it with you and Marigold?"

My heart turned to ice. Oh, no.

Chapter 11

What did Bobby suspect about Marigold?

My mind raced a hundred miles an hour. I came up with: "I don't know. I think he likes talking with me because his mom tells him not to and he likes that she doesn't know he's talking to me when he's not supposed to or something, and he knows but she doesn't know when she gives him candy money, but he knows."

Bobby peered at me but then, he bought it. "Okay. I just wondered." And then he was off.

Didn't I have enough problems already?

But first things first. I had to get back to Creepy House and face whatever trouble I'd get for running around like goblin told me not to, because my stomach was so empty and growling so loud, the crazy lady was liable to stop talking to her mirror and come out to investigate. So off I went in the opposite direction from Bobby.

There'd been plenty of times I was so hungry I felt like I would pass out. So hungry, I felt like my insides were going to eat my own stomach to make it stop growling. You'd think I'd be used to it, brush it off as no big deal. But let me tell you, that kind of hungry was something nobody got used to and you'd go a long way to not be in that kinda fix again.

The only reason I was in this hunger fix was because of the wanted murderer bit. Limited my usual ways of slipping around the Hill and looking for hand-outs. I had a real sweet hand-out deal at Creepy House, but even getting there had been tough lately.

My stomach was screaming so hard, it was all I could do not to go running out in the wide-open streets, taking the quickest way to Creepy House. I had to go slow, careful, to dodge all the cops that were prowling the Hill, looking under cars, peeping over fences. It was bad.

Had to bite my hand at one point to keep my stomach from making me bolt. I told my stomach, in a really quiet whisper, that if the cops caught me, and me included my stomach, the both of us'd be swinging in the wind. Didn't help. Made my stomach yell even louder.

About half-way to Creepy House, I was hiding under a pile of broken up orange crates at the side of an old hotel, when my loud stomach growling caught the notice of a local cat. This long-haired tom was a big guy, all black, but for a white face that swung around at the sound of my stomach. The thing with cats was you couldn't fool them. They could tell in a hot second what the situation was. This tom was no different. He knew there was something under those busted up crates, *his* busted-up crates by his hotel, a something that wasn't supposed to be there, and he was going to do something about it.

I could see him through gaps in the broken crates, and he could see me. He crouched low, and then sprang, hitting the crates and making the rotted wood snap. He yowled and started digging through the wood with his claws. I saw satisfaction written all over his big white face.

The tom kept yowling. I tried to make nice. "Good kitty-kitty. Good kitty." No dice. He got a good long swipe on my neck. It hurt! I almost started yowling.

"Hey, kitty, what'd'ya got there, huh?"

Oh, no. Could it get any worse? I knew that voice if I knew my Mug.

I saw the tom whip his face around. I couldn't see Mug from where I was hiding, but that cat sure could. It arched its back and started hissing.

"Hey, kitty, take it easy."

This cat didn't like Mug any better than it liked me.

The last I saw of that tom was him crouching, and then leaping at something. From the, "Hey! Crazy cat! Get off me!" my guess was the something was Mug.

I heard a yeow and a thunk, another "Crazy cat!" and the sound of big running feet. Mug-sized feet. Then I heard scurrying and, "Quit chasing me! You stupid, crazy cat!"

I waited until I heard Mug's feet run around the corner. Further away, I heard him yelling, maybe to other cops, "Get the cat off me!"

Ho, ho. That cat turned out to be helpful after all. While

Mug and the rest of the cops were busy with the cat problem, I shook off the broken crates and took off. Didn't want that cat running from the cops and straight back to its hotel and straight back to me with a hundred cops on its tail.

But I still had to travel slow, keep extra hidden. By the time I got to Creepy House's back yard, I was so hungry, the world was waving and swimming before my eyes.

I meant to slip down the cellar doors, try to clean myself up a little before reappearing, to make the goblin less suspicious. I should have known better.

Bobby came bursting out of the French doors in the sunroom.

"I thought the police had you! What happened to your neck?" Bobby grabbed me, all concerned but partly annoyed.

"Hey, I had to dodge cops, and this cat nearly blew my cover and attacked me and everything."

It wasn't too long after that Gilbert joined the action. "I told Mademoiselle you've come back to us at last. Mademoiselle was so worried!"

When I looked at his face, I was so surprised, I couldn't say anything. His face was red, the scar over his eye redder, and his eyes were puffy like he'd been crying, or snuffling at the very least. How about that? His face had gotten like that over Tootsie, when we disappeared to Court Hill Park to deal with bad man. Tootsie I could understand, but I didn't think anybody'd have that kind of reaction about me.

Nah, it probably wasn't about me. He was upset because Tootsie had gotten worried. Or, maybe they worried if the cops got me, I'd spill the beans on where I'd been hiding. Yeah, that's what the tears were about. I mean, no one really cares where I go or what I do. Well, except for Bobby, and that was more like being nosy and bossy and being a pill when I didn't obey orders.

Couldn't have been about me. Not really. Right? I wasn't sure what to say, what to think.

"Come, a nice hot bath is what you need."

Before I knew it, he'd scooped me up and was running with Bobby on his heels, straight to the bathroom. And Bobby was saying, "Yes, that's a good idea."

Not so! I found my voice. "No bath! No! I'm hungry! I want some a' those buns! I want those!"

"Sparky, you're in the worst mess I've ever seen you in. I told you how much you stink. You need to clean up. Now." Bobby again.

Goblin was made of softer stuff. Goblin, how could I have ever doubted you? "No, no, young man. If she is hungry, she will have something. Yes, my little Sparky, I have so many buns left from this morning. Mademoiselle said, 'Gilbert, cook away! I don't care if Doctor advises against it.' She hoped the smell of the cooking would bring you back here. We were so worried."

Bobby still had to have the last word. "I told her how worried everyone was. I told her she can't keep running around the Hill disappearing."

I would have said something real smart to Bobby, along the lines of, "Hey, I'm wanted and needed to clear my name and somebody had to do something, and it was your idea to take the side trip to Marigold, not me." But, I was so tired, and the promise of those buns made any kind of thinking fly straight out of my head.

Now I could smell them. Sure, I'd bet they were cold since this morning. But hot, cold, any which way, they had my name on them.

When we got to the kitchen, I wanted to leap out of Gilbert's arms, but he had to carefully set me down on a chair ("Ah, Sparky, so much wiggling."). I was wiggling, and practically bouncing in that chair.

It seemed like Gilbert was moving as slow as a sleepwalker, pulling the towel off the buns on the plate, bringing me a little plate, then a fork, then a knife, then a napkin, then a bowl of jam, then a little spoon for the bowl of jam, then he started fiddling with a second jar of jam. I couldn't take it any more. "Gimme those buns!"

Bobby gave me a look, but the goblin smiled at me and finally brought the plate of buns to the kitchen table. I'd grabbed three off the plate before it even hit the table.

Then the three were in my mouth, then the little spoon was full of jam and in my mouth too. It was getting crowded in there.

Bobby kept giving me looks and goblin kept chuckling. "You won't be able to swallow with no drink!" He brought a tall glass filled to the brim. I gulped it and it was the freshest, most ice-cold milk I'd ever drunk.

"Ahhhh." That was me. Happy and full of the best chow I'd ever shoved down my snout.

Didn't last.

Maybe because I wasn't used to drinking tall glasses of ice-cold milk and maybe because three big buns was two big buns too many for my stomach that'd been so empty and yelling, but I suddenly felt like my stomach was going to throw it right back out. Hey, stomach, I gave you what you wanted. What's all the fuss now?

I didn't have a choice but to sit frozen, with my mouth clamped tight, my eyes squeezed shut.

"Ah, Sparky, I think you ate too fast." Goblin was chuckling again, but I didn't think it was so funny. He wouldn't if I chucked it up all over his nice kitchen table with the nice forks and spoons and fancy jam. Or maybe he would think it was funny. I couldn't figure these people out.

Maybe because I wasn't talking, Bobby decided to fill the goblin in on what we learned from my boarding house adventure and Marigold.

"We found out some valuable clues today," he announced to Gilbert.

"Oh?"

"Yes. We may have located a suspect. We got information from a rooming house," and Bobby eyed me to let me know he was sticking with our story, "that this man might have driven a suspicious City Hall car on Court Hill the morning the dead girl was found. Sparky, show him the photo."

I was able to pull one hand away from my stomach to fish the photo out of my overalls pocket.

"This is the guy, and this is the dead girl," Bobby explained after he snatched the photo from my fingers. "Only, in this picture, she's not dead yet."

"Ah, this is very sad," Gilbert murmured. He paused and added, "There are things spilled on this photo."

"Sorry. But you can still see him. He may have fled town. We're not sure. He was trying to be a movie actor, but was a failure because he has no 'it factor.' So, he got a job driving cars for someone who might be an underworld figure. We're not sure. It's a woman gangster code-named The Onion Girl."

I had my eyes open by now, though my stomach was still mad at me. Gilbert looked like he was only half paying attention, but his eyes got sharper when Bobby mentioned Marigold's "it factor." When Bobby said, "The Onion Girl," he positively got bug-eyed and stuck his face close to Bobby.

"You said, 'Onion Girl'?"

"Yeah. Have you heard of her?"

Gilbert sat back, kept looking at Bobby, then threw his head back and made a huge sound.

I thought he was having an attack. Bobby and I looked at each other. I could tell by Bobby's wide eyes that he thought the goblin was having a stroke or caught rabies or something too.

He kept making the noise. Bobby and I kept looking at him, looking at each other.

As Bobby stood up to do something, Gilbert started coughing and leaned forward. He put his head and one arm on the table, and he slammed the table with his fist.

Rabies for sure.

"Are you okay?" That was Bobby. I could tell from his eyes darting around that he didn't have the foggiest idea what to do.

Gilbert made the sound again, but more quietly, more slowly.

He was laughing. That's what he was doing.

"Ha. Sorry, young man. Yes, 'Onion Girl.' I will tell Mademoiselle. She needs rest after," and he paused, "becoming very excited this morning."

Bobby gave me a look, a *I-want-you-to-feel-guilty* look. Hey, how was I supposed to know people would get "excited" about me disappearing in slop bins all night? No one's ever cared before. Except Bobby, but he knows I show up eventually.

"But," Gilbert grinned, "I must break her rest. She will want to hear this!"

Gilbert was up and going in a flash. We heard him trotting up the stairs, huffing because he was moving too fast. Then, "Mademoiselle! Mademoiselle! You must hear this! Come!" He sounded like I would if I'd found a huge candy stash for free.

Bobby sat back down and looked at me, eyebrows raised. "Onion Girl must be a really dangerous criminal. But why would he laugh? I don't understand."

My stomach still didn't feel normal, so I decided it was best to keep my mouth shut for the time being. All I did was nod. Bobby was right. It sure was a strange thing.

It didn't take long for sounds of movement to come from up above somewhere, muffled talking and two sets of feet coming down the stairs.

I heard Tootsie's voice. She sounded tired, confused. "What? I don't understand?"

"Hear the children say it! Wait!" Gilbert's voice. It sounded like he was holding back laughs.

When Tootsie came into the kitchen, she was pale; no makeup on today. She wore a long, loose gown that was mostly white, but with black sleeves. Dribbles of more black and also grey ran down the front of her gown, like someone had dribbled paint. But I could tell it was supposed to look like that. Sometimes fancy stuff made no sense to me.

Gilbert was right behind her, big smile on his face. "Go on, children, tell Mademoiselle what you told me."

Bobby looked at me. It didn't seem like he knew what to do. I wasn't sure either, so I shrugged.

Bobby shrugged back. He turned to Tootsie and Gilbert and told the story of the driver that Marigold said had no 'it factor.'

While he talked, Gilbert helped Tootsie into one of the kitchen chairs at the table. Gilbert started to laugh, but low and quiet, so he wouldn't drown out what Bobby was saying.

Tootsie's face seemed even more confused. She looked up at Gilbert, who was smiling. I could tell Bobby was even more confused too. As he talked and pointed to the blond man in the photo, he looked at Gilbert, looked at Tootsie, looked at me. But, hey, you got me. I was as deep in confused land as everyone else.

When Bobby got to the City Hall car part, her head whipped around to him, her eyes wide, and then I could tell he made an extra point of saying that we found out about it at some "rooming house." She stared at me and I winked, to let her know I hadn't ratted her out about our visit to Court Hill and bad man. She crinkled her eyes like she wasn't sure if she should be mad or not. She still seemed confused.

As soon as Bobby said, "Onion Girl," everything changed.

Tootsie shot up from her chair, slammed her palm down on the table almost exactly like Gilbert had done, and made a sound like a scream. Reminded me of her singing. Bobby jumped in his chair. I did too.

I realized she was laughing. I thought I'd heard the two of them laughing before, but I guess I hadn't heard nothing. Her and the goblin had strange ways of showing they were having a good time.

Now she was slapping Gilbert and they were both laughing. "Oh, my goodness! Isn't that the bees' knees, Gilbert?"

All Bobby and I could do is look at them, look at each other and trade some more shrugs.

Suddenly, Tootsie was full of energy. Her face had color, her eyes were bright. Whatever had been ailing her, Onion Girl cured her a lot faster than that vitamin doctor.

Tootsie even did a quick little tap dance while Gilbert clapped time.

After a bit more of their honky-tonk nonsense, Bobby cleared his throat and asked as seriously as he could, "So, you know this Onion Girl?"

This got them laughing all over again.

It took a while for them to calm down, so long as a matter of fact, that my stomach had finally settled. I made a big burp, and let me tell you, I felt so much better.

"Sparky, you're such a hoot," Tootsie smiled and pinched my cheek. Gilbert chuckled too. From the way Bobby's eyes darted back and forth among the three of us, I could tell he was having trouble deciding which one of us was trying him most.

"Could you tell us who The Onion Girl is? Please?" Bobby asked like he was about to run out of his last drop of patience.

Tootsie and Gilbert looked at each other, grinning.

"Onion Girl," Tootsie said to Gilbert, her voice light and happy. "Isn't it sad no one knows her name? She's only Onion Girl." Then they burst out laughing.

It took a while for Bobby to get a straight answer from those two, they were having such a good time laughing. In the meantime, I stuffed another bun in my mouth, almost got sick again, so had to sit with my hand over my mouth until my stomach stopped lurching.

Turns out this Onion Girl wasn't a gangster, wasn't a floozy, nothing like that. She was an actress from the old silent movies, just like Tootsie, except her real name was Sally Smiths, not Onion Girl. Her big scene was in a movie where she was chopping onions, began to cry from the onions and then began to wail about all the tragedy in her life, ran outside in the dark stormy night, fell to her knees begging to know "Why!"—she said this over and over on the cards with the words that the silent movies had—then she got sick and had a long drawn out and dramatic dying scene. She made a bunch of sobbing sad movies, so she was also called Sobbing Sally. But the onion chopping one was the most famous. So, The Onion Girl she was.

When they were telling us the story, they also called her "that cow." The girl had a lot of nicknames.

"We need to talk with her, question her. Does she live on Bunker Hill too? I want to knock on her door, be direct in confronting her." Bobby said, all serious-like.

Tootsie rolled her eyes. "That cow doesn't have the imagination to live here."

"She has no imagination at all," Gilbert added.

"It won't work if you try questioning her," Tootsie

explained. "She'll get all offended. You see, she imagines she's a movie star." Tootsie and Gilbert traded grins again. "No, I'll need to handle this. I'll tell her I want to visit, to catch up. Do you suppose she'll be curious, Gilbert, take the bait?"

"Onion Girl will be so happy anyone wants to talk with her. She has no fans."

"None whatsoever." Tootsie smiled big.

It was time for Bobby to head home with his bug in a jar and tell his parents about the library. He was in a pout about not being able to go to Onion Girl's place and question her.

Turned out, though, visiting Onion Girl wasn't something that was happening anytime soon. After Gilbert made calls over the next few days, he said Onion Girl was in Palm Springs, a patch of desert east of Los Angeles. She'd bought a house there. "I suppose she's tired of not being recognized in this town, so she had to go into hiding," Tootsie said full of satisfaction.

The long and the short of the situation was that Onion Girl wasn't going to be tearing back to Los Angeles just to talk with Tootsie. She'd be back when she'd be back. She still had her LA house. Her plan was to live there sometimes and here sometimes. Right now, she was in her "there sometimes" phase. In the meantime, we had to cool our heels.

This Palm Springs business might explain why the driver took one suitcase, but left the other behind, along with half his duds. He'd driven Onion Girl to Palm Springs, but he was planning on not being there forever.

I was not too thrilled about this Palm Springs business holding things up. But it sure was fine by Tootsie. "It'll give me time to prepare," she declared.

The next several weeks were like a military operation while Tootsie did her preparing.

Chapter 12

Tootsie's singing coach who didn't like me, Mr. Beele, now came every other day. She wanted him to come every day, but he decided her voice needed rest in between "our rigorous training sessions."

Every other day was still one day too many for me. I tried to keep hidden when he was around. I still overheard him asking her every time he came, "Is that Mysteeree boy-girl servant person thing still lurking about?" And every time Tootsie answered, "Yes, I'm having Mysteeree do all my washing now. By hand. It keeps Mysteeree very busy."

I'd like to wash the stuffings out of Mr. Beele.

Then there were the two tough looking broads who came to give Tootsie "health" massages and "face beautiful treatments from the South Seas." They wrapped her in hot towels head to toe and piled all kinds of stinky goop on her face and left her like that until the goop dried and the towels cooled down.

How did I know this? Tootsie talked me into trying one of the so-called "treatments." She explained me to the broads by saying, "This little girl is Sally Mae, my darling baby cousin visiting from Des Moines."

To be safe, I wore what Tootsie called a masquerade mask, which was a kind of satin sock that tied around my head with long black ribbons. It had two eye cutouts. Around the eyes were multicolored paste gems and chicken feathers colored green and purple. I liked it a lot, but I told Tootsie maybe it was too small to hide my face properly. "Oh, nonsense! The ladies will smear mud on your face soon enough." I supposed, but still, I worried. When the broads asked why I was wearing a mask, Tootsie told them, "Poor thing, she's so shy."

The goop treatment soaked the mask, made the feathers

fall off, and made me feel like a doomed chicken. Afterward, I was all red and my skin started peeling so I really did look like a doomed chicken, one that'd already been plucked.

"That's your youth glow coming through," Tootsie said, all delighted.

"But I'm just a kid! I don't need any more youth already."

"Trust me, Sparky, sooner than you think, you'll be wanting it bad."

She asked if I wanted to try more doomed chicken treatments. Those two broads had a bunch of different types besides the South Seas torture: French Royalty, Chinese Empress, New Mexican Heat, She-Pharaoh, Deep Jungle Mystery. The broads had a list like a crazy diner menu. No thanks.

"Fine but let me know when you change your mind."

Change my mind? Ha! Did I tell you those broads came every day? No rest from the face torture. Besides, what if they started thinking too much about who I really was? What if they noticed I was the wanted murderer? Nah. Too risky. It was better to spy at them from a hiding place.

Then there was a guy she called "Mr. Exercise." Gilbert called him "That Troy." Gilbert didn't seem to like him very much, but he still let the guy in the door.

Mr. Exercise wore an outfit like what acrobats wore at the circus. Not that I'd ever been to the circus, but I'd seen pictures. The tights fit him so tight, it was like he was naked and covered only with white paint. Oh, boy.

When Bobby got an eyeful of this character in his tights, Bobby decided he didn't like him any better than Gilbert did. "You need to be completely away, hide in her closets with your eyes closed when that man is around. I don't approve of him."

Bobby had been making regular appearances at Creepy House, I think to see if Tootsie and Gilbert would change their minds about letting him quiz Onion Girl. But as soon as he got a gander at Mr. Exercise, there he was, showing up every day at 10 am on the dot, when Mr. Exercise came. At least Bobby kept sharp about staying hidden, glaring at Mr. Exercise and spying at all the other goings-on from behind drapes and around corners, like me. No need to have Beele and the rest of the nosy parkers spotting him and asking questions.

I guess Bobby was telling his parents the library was in need of his extra urgent studying or something, because they eased up on their no-leaving-the-house rules. I didn't think the library was open every single day. I wondered how long it'd take his parents to figure that out, start asking questions, and clamp down on his comings and goings again. Or maybe they thought the library stayed open special for Bobby because he was such a champion book worm. Yeah, they might've thought that, being book worms themselves.

This was the thing about Mr. Exercise: to do the bending and stretching and jumping up and down and other crazy stunts, Tootsie had to squeeze herself into a pair of circus tights too. Except hers weren't white. They were leopard spotted, pink, shiny black with sparkles, purple and green, and, well, you get the picture.

Gilbert was not too happy about Tootsie wearing these tights in front of that guy either. But, Mr. Exercise said it was "a requirement to allow the body movement to properly circulate the youth mechanisms." And that was that.

I noticed Bobby had no problem staring at Tootsie in her tights. If truth be told, I wasn't sure if Bobby was coming by at 10 am on the dot every day to make sure I wasn't looking at Mr. Exercise or to make sure he could sneak a peek at Tootsie-with-Tights.

Mr. Exercise, Mr. Beele, the face torture broads weren't the end of the parade. There was the dance teacher (I could tell him and Mr. Exercise hated each other), the raw food diet lady who came with an overflowing plate of green things that Gilbert had to mash and strain into juice and he frowned the whole time, the hair lady who coated Tootsie's hair with avocadoes every day (I could tell her and the face broads hated one another), the hand lady who soaked Tootsie's paws in olive oil every day (I could tell she hated the hair lady and the face broads and vice versa), and then the "slimming man" who wrapped her in tight denim bands all over and insisted she get "more healthful rays of the sun like the eternally beautiful pharaoh queens of ancient times." I could tell everyone hated him. Except Tootsie.

This sun ray order created a problem. Vitamin doctor was visiting all the time now too and he banished any sun. Not a drop allowed. The face broads also forbade sun because they said it would turn her red (and their treatments didn't?) and brown and wrinkled like a cross between an old prune and an old floor scrubber. Just say the word "wrinkle" and you got Tootsie in a panic.

After much talking, shouting and tears, the experts agreed on a solution Tootsie was okay with. There were three spots on her lower back that were safe for sun. Any other place was a danger zone that could cause her to look like a wrinkled floor scrubber prune.

So, every three days—three being a number important to ancient pharaohs—Tootsie lay in the only spot of sun to be found in her jungle backyard, face down with denim bands wrapped around her and towels draped over every inch of her except those three spots. She got really hot in the sun under the denim and towels. This made the raw food lady happy because she said Tootsie was sweating out the fat.

When I told you everyone except Tootsie hated slimming man, that wasn't completely true. The raw food lady didn't hate him. In fact, they got along really well.

You see, I bumped into them in the cellar while hunting for strange and interesting things no one wanted and tossed down there. I also planned to retrieve Tootsie's shiny dress that I'd stuffed down into the barrel when I changed into the dog-goat outfit. I wanted to put the dress back in the closet before Gilbert noticed it was missing. But it wasn't in the barrel anymore. Later, I found it cleaned and back in her closet, along with all the wadded-up hankies and everything else I made a mess of. Cleaned, pressed, mended and back in place. Gilbert never said a word to me, but it must have been him. I think he had too much time on his hands.

So, with the dress not in the barrel anymore, I forgot that plan, and decided to do my poking around the cellar. I found a broken old tin box that might be good for something, a brass ball that might be from an old horse harness. It looked good, so I was about to pocket it. Then, whoops! I bumped into slimming man and raw food lady.

The two of them panicked and begged me to keep their "secret" and in exchange, they'd give me candy. "A lot of candy. Good candy. Not cheap stuff." That was from slimming man.

The next day, sure enough, on behalf of both of them, he slipped me a box of chocolates by the cellar door when no one was watching, except raw food lady, who was being a lookout. It was a fancy tin box with a ribbon and each little chocolate bon-bon inside was wrapped in paper cut like lace. Well, how about that? I zipped down into the cellar straight away and me and that box of candy lived a little spot of heaven.

Them seeing me made me nervous, let me tell you. But, the two of them were more worried about getting in trouble with Gilbert than thinking too deeply about who I was exactly. I must admit, that chocolate did ease my worries. It was so good. It made up, kind of, for my lost candy stash the cops might've had, or bad man might've eaten. Kind of.

I was dying to tell Bobby and share some of my good chocolate fortune, but that would have meant explaining where the fancy candy came from and getting those two characters in goblin trouble. For that kind of first-class chocolate pay-off, Sparky kept a secret. Even from Bobby.

Okay, I had that other secret. About Marigold. But we're not talking about that ever again, understand?

Let's talk more about why I was down in the basement looking for interesting old things no one wanted, when I bumped into raw food lady and slimming man. Gilbert said I could decorate my room with stuff I found around the house if I wanted. He said I could "personalize" my room.

My room.

That's right.

My own room. A first for Sparky.

That's the bed the goblin was telling me about before, the bed in the guest room he wanted me to sleep in instead of in her closets or wherever. Only now, Gilbert called it my room. My room.

I would have loved to tell Bookie about it. He would have laughed, but I think he would have been impressed. If I were still talking to him.

I could tell Bobby was impressed when he got a gander at my new room in Creepy House, but he didn't admit it. Instead, he said, "This is a good thing because it will teach you responsibility and the basics of keeping house. That will be very important for when we are married."

Not that again. Why did he have to ruin my moment?

This room of mine came to my notice the day when Tootsie and Gilbert told Bobby and me about Onion Girl. Later that day, Gilbert made me take a bath (again). To recover from the bath, I ate some more buns until I'd finally gotten rid of any worries about starving.

By this time, the afternoon was fading to evening and I was sleepy. So, of course, I went looking for Clara Bell and her flat leopard boyfriend with a plan to snuggle up with one or the other of the furry pair, though probably Clara Bell, because of the spat Tootsie was still having with that flat leopard.

But they weren't in the parlor where they usually were. I ran around looking for them until Gilbert appeared, smiling, and said, "Ah, she is looking for her pets, is she?"

"I think someone stole them," I told Gilbert. I was panting I was so out of breath from running around in a panic.

He laughed. "No, little Sparky. They are in your room. It's been prepared for you since yesterday. I thought you'd be back home by then."

All this talk was scrambling my brain. "Your room." What? The, "I thought you'd be back"—I could handle. A little dig at me for running off and disappearing when he told me not to. But, "home?" Sparky had no home. Room, home? What was this?

"Come follow me and you will find your friends," Gilbert smiled.

I was certainly curious, so follow him I did.

He led me through the sunroom, past the stairs with the squares, down a hallway I hadn't explored, to a room. It had colored glass windows like all the others and transoms that fortunately were open to make it less stuffy. Through the clear glass transoms, I could see green from her jungle garden, and a patch of sky here and there.

The room seemed huge to me. Or, maybe I should say, too huge just for me. I was used to sleeping in corners, slop bins, you name it. But here?

The walls were pale green and there was a carpet on the floor that was pale green with a pattern of blue squares that reminded me of the stair squares. The bed seemed too huge to sleep in. It had a white coverlet with a pattern on it that was hard for me to make out because it was also in white. On either side of the bed were two little tables and on each were two white lamps with ruffled shades. On the tables were books with pictures on the covers of little kids. Books! I knew I'd have to show Bobby those. He'd want to study them right off the bat.

Everything was so clean, so nice. There was a dresser that matched the two bedside tables. Above it hung a picture of a tree and sky with a puffy cloud. There, sure as Gilbert promised, was Clara Bell on one side of the bed, and the flat leopard was on the other, kind of shoved in the corner.

Gilbert was smiling. I think he purposely waited until I noticed the leopards weren't in the parlor to surprise me with the room. I sure was surprised.

"I get both leopards?" It was almost too good to be true.

Gilbert sighed. "Clara Bell could never be separated from him," and the goblin eyed the flat leopard. "It was always a mystery what she saw in him. Sometimes the female of the species is blind when it comes to the male," he said in a faraway voice.

Well, that sounded like a whole story for another day. None of my business, really. I had a room. A real room. And it was all mine, whether or not goblin approved of the boy leopard.

Mine, at least for now. Who knew how long this sweet setup would last for Sparky. For as long as it lasted, I'd enjoy it.

Apart from the leopards, the room did seem kind of empty, so Gilbert said if I found things in the house that I liked, I could bring them into "my" room. Of course, as soon as I showed Bobby my room, he gave me his housekeeping lecture.

I had a different idea about housekeeping than Bobby, which was why I was rooting around the basement for old junk to decorate my new room. But after the business with raw food lady and slimming man, plus the high-class chocolates, the old junk got swept out of my mind for the time being. Plus, I was getting nervous about too many people getting a gander at my wanted murderer face. Really, the two leopards were enough as far as decorating. I liked them lots. So furry.

The days of waiting for Onion Girl to return from Palm Springs dragged on. Not in a bad way. There was lots of food and I stopped waking up in a panic thinking I had nothing to eat. I liked the books in my room. I showed them to Bobby. He said they were "okay" but that he could read bigger books, so he wasn't interested in them. That annoyed me, but I still could spend hours flipping through them, looking at the pictures of the happy boy and girl and their happy family.

Gilbert was careful to hide the newspapers so I couldn't see any screaming headlines about my latest crimes. I think he told Bobby not to talk about my wanted murderer case too, because Bobby changed the subject whenever I brought up that we needed to keep investigating.

The worst part was goblin getting firm about me taking a bath every day. He even put new clothes in the room's dresser. They weren't costumes, but were clothes meant for kids. They were sailor suit style and I wasn't sure I liked them. Bobby said they were better than overalls, but he held my hand one day, looked me in the eye and said, "I wish you'd wear dresses more."

Maybe I was bored from hanging around the house all day, maybe I worried time was ticking by and I was still a wanted murderer, but I got annoyed and snapped, "I think you like tights. I see you watching Tootsie in her tights."

Bobby turned redder than I'd ever seen him, and his mouth hung open. Soon enough, he pulled himself together, held my hand more tightly and stared even deeper into my eyes.

"Sparky, when we're married, we can both wear tights for each other. I promise. But we have to wait until we're married. It's important that we wait. I insist on that."

"Yeah, but are you still gonna ogle Tootsie in her tights?"

Bobby took in a huge, deep breath, and said like it was the hardest thing he'd ever had to do, "Sparky, I solemnly promise that I will never again look at Tootsie when she's wearing tights."

Sure enough, after that Bobby stopped coming at exactly 10 am, and moved his time to 11 am, when all the tights business was over and done. He still gave Mr. Exercise dark looks as the man was leaving.

I was impressed that Bobby'd be such a gent, just because I asked him too. So, you understand why he couldn't ever know about Marigold, right?

A dress lady came by to "update" Tootsie's "look." As she said to Tootsie, "We're in a new decade, Mademoiselle. To keep wearing old things makes an old girl, yes?" That was another danger word for Tootsie: old. So, Tootsie loaded up on lots of new threads, making Gilbert work hard to find space in her closets. Maybe her old stuff was old, but she wasn't getting rid of any of it.

The new look meant slim satin and silk gowns in light colors. Lots of them. And "casual" looks, like "country girl" pants with legs so wide they looked like you'd trip on them in a minute, "athletic fresh" blouses with puffy sleeves, and sunglasses even indoors. "You are California, health, sunshine, outdoors and indoors. The pants are not just for the beach anymore. We are in modern times. All this Egyptian business, that is yesterday. That is out." Tootsie had to get new shoes with higher clunky heels. "Tall is more the modern look now. Tall and slim. No more of that short girl look."

Another hair lady came by to take a hard look at how out of fashion Tootsie's hair was. This lady did more of the "old fashioned equals old" talk, so Tootsie was putty in her hands. At first her and the avocado hair lady got into a screaming disagreement, which was really entertaining to watch from my hiding spot behind a huge Chinese vase painted with dragons, fire coming out of their mouths. Oh, that's another thing I learned: all of Tootsie's favorites, like leopards and dragons, were out of fashion. Couldn't have those on her clothes anymore.

The two hair ladies finally calmed down with an idea from the raw food lady. The solution was lemon juice, which frowning Gilbert had to make by squeezing out buckets of lemons, on top of the lemons and limes he was already squeezing per Dr. Vitamin's orders. The three ladies doused Tootsie's hair with the lemon juice. Then, while Tootsie was sunning the three ancient pharaoh spots on her back (wait a minute, wasn't all this Egyptian stuff out of fashion? —I guess not completely), she also sunned her lemon-soaked hair. The ladies had to carefully wrap towels around her face and ears to make sure she got no "sun injury."

After the sun treatment, the avocado lady did a double dose of squashed avocados in Tootsie's hair to "reverse the sun hair damage." Then, after rinsing out her hair with rose water, the new hair lady did a lot of puffing and fluffing of Tootsie's hair to give it the "California natural, just off the beach look." I guess. Her hair was lighter, not quite blonde or even dishwater blonde, but lighter than the black hair she used to have, pre-lemons.

The dress lady had a bunch of slouchy caps she called "new style berets."

Tootsie worried. "Make sure they don't cover my roots. I don't want anyone saying I'm going grey or coloring my hair."

So, the ladies arranged the beret by pinning it on the side of her head, almost covering one eye. "There," hair lady #2 said, "Everyone can see now your hair is loose, light and totally natural. Youth hair."

Well, natural except for tons of lemons.

Being cooped up in the house all the time, I noticed sometimes it wasn't too stuffy inside and was tolerable even. Other days, it was hotter and stuffier than ever, especially in the afternoons. One day, it got so stuffy, Tootsie started complaining. So, Gilbert went downstairs in the cellar to tinker with the "modern cooler," a big machine that lived down in the dark. He got it working. It did make the upstairs cooler in Tootsie's closets, until it decided to stop working again.

Gilbert called in a man who worked for the company that made the machine. The two of them got into an argument about the transom windows. "When you turn on the cooler," the man growled, "you have to shut all the windows. All of them. Otherwise, the cooler works too hard and conks out. It's not the machine's fault."

"Doctor says we must have fresh air!" Gilbert countered, getting upset. "To have the same air being pushed around in a circle, that is unhealthy."

"Yeah, well, that's nice, but your cooler will keep going kaput, mister."

And that's what it did. The cooler worked for a few days, the stuffiness got better, and then kaput. The repairman came back, him and Gilbert argued, and the more they argued, the redder Gilbert's eye scar got. The cooler worked again for a few more days. Then kaput again.

Like I said, all these people in and out, all the nonsense was funny, in a way. But I still had to keep hidden and spy on the comings and goings extra carefully, so no one would realize I was the wanted Prussian spy devil girl. Bobby did his best to keep out of sight too, so no one would connect any dots. Tootsie admitted she didn't completely trust all of her exercise, hair and clothes people either, so she stopped bugging me about getting face treatments or doing anything else that'd make me seen.

I was getting restless.

The final straw: the spiritual man. He came flowing into the house wearing all white robes, except for a gold medallion on his white turban. Gilbert ordered me and Bobby to be completely silent while he was upstairs with the spiritual man and Tootsie. "Doctor will watch both of you."

Oh, no.

So, there Bobby and me sat in the kitchen with the vitamin doctor, who was still dressed in a suit made of that expensive thin fabric, the kind big shots wore in the summer, but dark blue this time. He only wore dark colored suits: green, brown, blue or black. For some crazy reason I couldn't figure out, Tootsie trusted him completely. So he was allowed to see me and Bobby, but he'd already seen plenty of Bobby and a little of me the first night we met him, so in a way it was too late. Cats out of the bag.

I wasn't sure I trusted him.

While we were waiting for the spiritual man to get done doing spiritual things, the doctor gave us sly grins like he knew something we didn't know. Bobby glared at him. I did a lot of twitching in my chair. The guy hadn't said a word, but finally said to me, "You don't need to be so nervous."

Spiritual man was up there for what seemed like hours. I noticed the outside light fading through the transom window above the kitchen door. "Bobby, you need to go back home," I whispered to him.

"I won't leave you alone with that man," he whispered back.

I could tell the doctor heard every word, because he chuckled.

Bobby suddenly grabbed my hand, yanked me out of my chair, and started running. "Cellar!" he whispered loudly.

I got his drift, so started running with him. The doctor was hot on our heels. We flew through the cellar door, slammed it, and I slid the latch in place as the doctor thunked against it. He jangled the door knob and pushed. "Children," he said quietly from the other side, "don't be silly. I'm watching you for your own good. You mustn't get into any mischief. Listen to Gilbert if you don't want to listen to me."

Fat chance.

"Don't open the door, no matter what he says," Bobby told me.

"Hey, I'm not that dumb, Bobby."

Bobby nodded and then took off. I followed him to the cellar storm doors leading outside. After Bobby closed those doors, I slid a piece of wood through the handles on the inside, so even if the doctor went around to the outside, he still wouldn't be able to get me. I knew Bobby was now hurrying back to his house.

I fell asleep at my post by the barred cellar doors. Thunking from someone pulling them woke me up. I could see stronger light coming from the gaps between the double storm doors. It was morning. I sat up.

"Little Sparky, are you there?" That was Gilbert's voice.

I slid the wood away from the handles and pushed the doors while he pulled them. I looked right and left, but no sign of the doctor. I supposed he told Gilbert I was hiding down there.

"Come, hurry, Sparky. Onion Girl's housekeeper called. She is back, and she will meet Tootsie for tea. Today!"

Chapter 13

The show was on.

All of Tootsie's people, the vitamin doctor, Mr. Exercise, the dance teacher, the face broads, the raw food lady, avocado hair lady, hair lady #2, slimming man, dress lady, the hand lady, and even spiritual man were all upstairs fussing with Tootsie, getting her ready to meet Onion Girl.

After forcing another bath on me, Gilbert gave me a quick breakfast of the thick slices of toast and jam. I couldn't enjoy it because he kept saying, "We must hurry!"

I barely was able to swallow my orange juice when he pulled me to my room. There on the bed was the shiny blue prince outfit I'd admired the first time I went in Tootsie's closets, plus matching shoes, hat, and wig with brown curls.

"Change, quickly, Sparky. You will be a boy today, named René."

"From Des Moines?"

"What? No! You are French. You are Mademoiselle's French page. You assist her, wait on her. You will carry this fan to cool her. It is hot and it is summer, understand?"

He pointed to a long handle that had a bunch of ostrich feathers on top of it, kind of like a fan dancer fan. The thing was taller than me.

"But what if Onion Girl recognizes me?"

"She will not! She will be too much staring at Mademoiselle. Besides, Mademoiselle does not want to be alone with that cow. The woman makes her nervous. We must be careful of her nerves."

"But, won't you be there?"

"Of course, I will drive. But, I am the servant. I will stay in the kitchen. I will talk to the housekeeper, and if this driver man is there, I will see him too. I will discover what information they will reveal to me."

"But, I'm a servant too, if I'm fanning her, right?"

"Yes! But, listen. You must not leave her side, because you are fanning. You must understand your character. You must play your role to the tee. You are a little French boy who fans. I see you maybe as a baby of the circus. You have lived in many foreign lands, seen many exotic animals. You are used to difficult circus labor, which has made you stoic. You have no problem fanning for many hours, in the most intense heat. Feel your character!"

I must have been staring at Gilbert like I had no idea what he was talking about, because I had no idea what he was talking about.

Gilbert sighed and sat on the bed, but making sure not to crush the costume, which I was sure he spent a lot of time ironing. "Little Sparky, just be close to Mademoiselle. Move the fan. This will keep her nerves steady. She plays a part too. It is important that Onion Girl see her play it perfectly. And Onion Girl, of course, will be playing a part too."

It made no sense to me, but, okay, I'd go along with it. Hopefully, this time the blue satin boy disguise would work, and Onion Girl wouldn't go screaming to the police that she'd spotted a murderer.

Maybe Gilbert guessed what I was thinking, because he added, "Onion Girl is too vain to wear her spectacles. She will not know you." He winked and chuckled.

Then Gilbert was hurrying out of my room to help with all the Tootsie preparations. I heard his feet running up the stairs.

There was a mirror inside the room's closet door, so after I got into the disguise, I checked out how it looked. Strange, but not bad. The pants were too short, which I guessed was why the costume came with white stockings. The hat had one feather sticking out of it. But I did like the shiny blue. And the shoes had sparkles on them that matched all the sparkles sewn on the costume. I liked those sparkles, even if they were paste.

I heard more commotion from feet moving around upstairs. Then I heard lots of feet stomping down the stairs with the squares, and the kitchen door opening and closing a few times. Silence. Mr. Exercise and the rest of the people parade must have left.

After a few more minutes, Gilbert knocked at my door. He gave my getup a quick up and down. "Yes, nice. Now your face." He dipped a fat brush in a pot of face powder he held and swished the brush over my freckles. "Ah, it is far from perfect, but it will have to do." He quickly stashed the powder and brush on my dresser. "No time for perfect. We must go. Now!"

I followed him out my room, dragging the long-handled fan. "Come I will take it," Gilbert said.

Gilbert was wearing a beige outfit with high boots and a cap that reminded me of what jungle explorers wore in the movies. I wasn't sure if he meant to look like that, so I didn't mention it.

It wasn't even 10 am, so I knew Bobby wouldn't come by for another hour. "Hey, Gilbert, if Bobby comes and we're all gone, he'll panic."

"Don't worry. Doctor will be here. He can keep Bobby company until we come back."

"I don't think Bobby will like that much."

Gilbert sighed. "Doctor is a good man! He helps our Mademoiselle with vitamins. I do not understand your objection to him. But, never mind, we must see Mademoiselle make her entrance!"

Holding the feather fan in one hand, the goblin pulled me to the foot of the stairs with the squares.

Out of the shadows stepped Tootsie, her hand held up by the vitamin doctor, who stared at her with a much nicer smile than the one he used on me and Bobby.

Goblin dropped the fan and it clunked to the floor. He let go of my hand and began wildly clapping. "Bravo, Mademoiselle! Bravo!" He kicked me with his foot until I got the message. I started clapping, then added a loud whistle with both fingers in my mouth.

I guess Tootsie liked all the fuss. She beamed and nodded to me and Gilbert. With the doctor holding her hand up, she slowly walked down the stairs. She looked almost like a different person.

That beret was perched on the side of her head, nearly covering one of her eyes. Loose hair hanging out from under the beret covered the rest of that eye. The hair on the other half of her head was swept up and under the beret. Her hair was the same lighter color through and through. Not a trace of dark roots showing.

Her blouse had huge puffy white sleeves, but the sides of the blouse narrowed down sharp to her waist in a triangle of pale green and white stripes. I could tell she'd gotten thinner since all her exercise people started showing up, but this blouse made her look skinner than ever. The pants had a tight, high waist that added to the skinny look. Then the pant legs ballooned out super wide. Under them, I barely made out the white clunky shoes with super high heels. She did look taller.

Between the super wide, long pants and the clunky heels, I worried she'd trip and fall down the stairs. But she glided down each step like a pro. Maybe that was the dance teacher's work.

As she got closer, I could see her makeup was completely different. Instead of the white-white face with black Egyptian lines on her eyes, this face paint made it look like she'd gotten brown under the sun. How about that? After all the trouble of keeping sun off her face. The same brown paint was on her arms, neck and hands. Maybe that's why the doctor was holding just the tips of her fingers so carefully. It looked like she had no eye makeup on, no lipstick. But, maybe she did. Was there another something different about her face? Wait a minute. Yeah. Were those a few dots of painted-on freckles?

It was all so natural, it was hard to tell. I supposed that was the point.

When she reached the bottom, Gilbert was clapping even harder. "Oh, Mademoiselle, you are so beautiful, I am crying!" And he was. I saw the tears running down his face. His eye scar was that angry red color even though he was crying in a happy, not angry way.

She looked different, though I didn't think it was anything to cry about. But, I got the idea I was supposed to say something, so I blurted out, "Wow, Tootsie, you look like a kid on the beach." Which she sort of did, not that I'd ever been to the beach, but I'd seen pictures, and I don't mean just the one with the dead girl in it.

She threw back her head, a little—can't mess up the hair and beret—and laughed—a little—probably didn't want to mess up the face paint either. "Oh, Sparky, you're too much." But she seemed happy. So, that must have been the right thing to say.

With the doctor guiding Tootsie along, we all hustled out the sunroom doors and into the garage. I'd never seen Tootsie's car before, except as a big shape in the dark garage covered with lots of rugs. Now the rugs were off and even in the dim garage, the auto shone like the sun. It was a gold colored car with a front about a mile long. Maybe that's stretching things a bit, but it sure was bigger than any car I'd seen on the Hill. Even City Hall cars, even the huge sedan that Bookie said belonged to a boss from Chicago. This car was like nothing I'd ever laid eyes on before.

I must have been standing there staring like a monkey, because Gilbert tugged me and whispered, "Hurry. Sit next to me, up front."

He opened the driver's door and I crawled through to the passenger side. He was trying to figure out how to hand me the fan, but its long handle wasn't fitting. He was grunting and starting to sweat, his face was turning red, his scar redder.

"Is everything okay?" Tootsie asked. I heard tension in her voice.

Gilbert looked up. "Oh, we are just fine." He smiled, but still looked panicked.

The doctor was a smoother operator. He let go of Tootsie's hand to take the fan from Gilbert. "I see the handle comes apart quiet easily in several places." He pulled part of the handle off and another. Then he slid it across the seat to me. "The feathers fold together too. How ingenious. Fans do tend to do that, don't they?" He smiled at Tootsie, and I could see her shoulders and face relax. He slid the feathers across the seat to me. "You'll be able to put it back together, right?" the doctor asked me.

"Of course she will," Gilbert replied for me. "Everything is fine, Mademoiselle."

The doctor nodded and helped Tootsie into the car. Gilbert climbed into the front and roared that boat to life.

I'd ridden in cars plenty of times, like when Bookie was in a hurry to go somewhere and needed me to do something. But riding in Bookie's cars was nothing like this.

This sedan felt like butter. The seat was so soft, I could live on it and sleep plenty. The car was so big, it laughed over the bumps in the road like they were nothing. I was enjoying myself.

Tootsie wasn't. "Do you think my look is too different? I worry she'll think I'm chasing a trend. Being a clown."

"You don't look like any clown," I told her. "Clowns have red noses."

"Yes," Gilbert said, trying to make his voice happy, "that cow has always been like a pig. She has nothing on you."

"Yes, I suppose."

"You have class, Tootsie." I learned from Bookie that it's always a smart thing to tell a gal she's got class. With no class, a gal is just another broad.

Tootsie smiled a little smile.

But I could tell she was nervous.

Chapter 14

Onion Girl lived in the Hills above Hollywood. Gilbert had to slow the sedan down to go up the steep streets and around the looping bends. I'd never been up so high. Bunker Hill was high, but this was going more than a few rungs up the ladder. I got scared at first—I hate to admit—but then I decided I liked the thrill of it.

There were hardly any houses. It was mostly wild country. And down below, the city was laid out like a blanket. But up here, I caught sight of a rabbit on the side of the road, and then something else. "Hey! Is that a deer! I thought I saw it there!"

"Not a deer," Gilbert laughed. "That was a horse. There are people up here who live like cowboys and ride horses. But, yes, there are deer too."

"I used to ride here sometimes," Tootsie said dreamily. "Those were the days. It's gotten more crowded up here since then."

Didn't look crowded to me, but I decided not to point that out.

After curving around the side of a cliff, we came to a pair of tall, black gates. Gilbert stopped the car, got out and pulled a cord that rang a bell. He did this a few times. Then he leaned against his open car door and waited. I couldn't see anything beyond the gate, only an empty, scrubby hillside with a gravel drive heading up it.

I was glad he kept at least one door open so we got some air while we waited. When the goblin was driving, the car windows had to stay shut because he said wind might muss Tootsie's hair and outfit. The car was nice, but it sure got hot inside that metal boat.

After a while, a woman in a housekeeper's apron came

down the steep drive. She walked slowly, probably so she wouldn't slide down the gravel. When she reached the gate, the goblin tipped his hat and she nodded and smiled in a tired way. She pulled a key out of her apron pocket and opened the padlock on the chain holding the gates shut. "Mind if I ride up with you?" she asked as Gilbert helped her pull the double gates open.

"But of course!" Gilbert smiled.

He got back in the car, drove it forward past the gates. Then he got out and helped the housekeeper close them again. She didn't lock the padlock. "I'll only have to unlock it when you leave and walk back up the hill." She stared up the long, hot drive. "I'll lock it again in the evening when things cool down."

Gilbert opened the car door on my side and said, "Go on now, René, scoot over for the lady."

I didn't move at first because I forgot I was supposed to be a French boy called René. Then I remembered the René part. I don't know any French, but was I supposed to know French? Was I supposed to not know English? I wasn't sure, so instead of talking, I smiled, gave a thumbs-up, and scooted over.

"Ha, ha. He is still learning his English," Gilbert smiled.

The housekeeper slid in, Gilbert slammed the door, and we were on our way up the steep, steep drive.

"You're adorable," the housekeeper said to me while patting the blue satin cap on my head. Playing along with the don't-speak-no-English routine, I kept smiling and nodding.

In the back seat, Tootsie stared out the sedan window, saying nothing. She kept her arms and hands spread out, her finger tips barely touching the seat on either side of her. I think she was working hard not to smudge her brown paint. Maybe she was trying not to sweat in that hot car too.

It seemed like we went up forever, with nothing in sight except more rocks and scrubby plants. When we reached the top of the rise, all of a sudden there it was. Green lawn going on forever, a fountain pouring water, roses thick as you please, and a huge white house with arches and columns and a red tile roof. Wow.

"Still living in her ex-husband's place," Tootsie murmured from the back seat. "It was always too over the top for me. But she likes over the top, doesn't she?"

It didn't seem like she was really asking anyone in particular, so the housekeeper and Gilbert glanced at each other and didn't say anything.

Gilbert pulled under a large arch near a set of double

wooden doors with red steps. He helped Tootsie out of the car, all the while being careful of her paint. Then, he ushered me and the housekeeper out. It sure felt good to get out of the hot boat and feel some air on top of the hill.

Gilbert pulled out the pieces of fan. "You'll help René put this together?" he asked the housekeeper, worry back in his voice.

"Sure, sure," she said and started pushing the parts of the handle together. I folded the feathers out.

While we were fiddling around, Tootsie stood looking out at the views of hills and city and big sky with puffy clouds. I wondered what she was remembering.

After Gilbert made sure everything was under control, he drove the car further along the drive, toward what looked like garages. He seemed to know where he was going, like he'd been there plenty of times before.

The housekeeper motioned for Tootsie to come through the double wooden doors. Silently, Tootsie glided in. I followed, holding the fan up like a banner.

"Madame, Miss LaFemme," the housekeeper said as she showed us into a parlor. LaFemme? Must be Tootsie's last name. I supposed if I were really a fan, I'd know.

The parlor was completely different from how Tootsie's house looked. The walls were white, there was only one layer of carpet, and it was pale blue. The puffy sofas and chairs were blue and white. Lots more blue and white plates hung from the walls. I liked it. It was cheerful.

Except for the broad parked in the middle of the joint. She stood up and held out both her hands to Tootsie. "Ah, dear, you're looking so well. I'm so surprised and happy to see you." Nice words, but her smile had a sly edge, and her voice was deep like cigarettes and had a chuckle just out of reach. So, this must be Onion Girl.

"You are so kind," Tootsie said, reaching out her hands, but only touching Onion Girl's with her finger tips. Tootsie was a pro. She didn't forget about being covered with brown paint for a second.

"Please, dear, do have a seat." The two of them sat down. And stared at each other with sly smiles and said nothing.

One thing I noticed right off the bat about Onion Girl was that she had almost the same look as Tootsie. She didn't have a beret, but she had the same light-ish hair swept up and over to one side, the simple brown-from-the-beach face and hands, a puffy-sleeved and wide pant outfit with high clunky heels, except in a white and orange scheme, instead of white and pale green.

I wondered if she wore white and orange because she got tipped off Tootsie was wearing white and green. I wondered if she hadn't been in Palm Springs, at least for the last few weeks. Maybe after all the hair and face and exercise people were done working on Tootsie, they zipped over to the Hollywood Hills and worked Onion Girl over. Certainly seemed that way to me. I think they had to work harder on Onion Girl. She was thicker than Tootsie, and older. But all grownups look old to me.

The big difference between the two, besides the white and green versus white and orange, was the jewelry. Tootsie only wore a thick silver bracelet. I knew she had tons more of the real rocks, so I figured it was part of her going to the beach look. I'd never been to the beach, like I said, but something told me gals didn't usually hang out in the sand wearing their best gems and jewels.

Onion Girl, she was decked. Huge necklace of clear yellow and orange stones. Matching huge ear bobs and bracelets, three of them. Problem was, they were all paste. Every stone. Even from where I stood, it was plain to see. But from the proud way she moved her wrists around like she wanted the stones to catch the light, and the way she fussed with her ear bobs and necklace like she was practically pointing to them and hollering, "Look!" I don't think she had a clue they were fakes.

The two of them kept looking at each other with those smiles. I wasn't quite sure what to do. So I stood next to the puffy chair Tootsie was sitting on and fanned her with the feather fan—not too hard. I didn't want to mess up her hair and beret so carefully pinned in place.

Along the back wall, the parlor had windows and sets of double French doors. The glass was clear, not colored like in Creepy House, so I could see into the backyard, which looked lots bigger than Tootsie's. There were more rose bushes circling a huge stone tile patio filled with white painted metal tables and matching chairs with fat blue and white cushions. The middle set of doors was open and through them I could hear splashing sounds. Another fountain? Or did she have a pool? The thought made me excited. I'd never been in a swimming pool before. Bookie bragged to me that he'd been in lots, especially when he was in Chicago. I was getting the feeling that this Onion Girl had a lot more dough than Tootsie.

Was it the goblin who was splashing around in the pool? I tried leaning over to see the pool and who was in it, but I couldn't quite see and I nearly leaned the fan on top of Onion Girl's head.

So, I straightened up fast.

Onion Girl's eyes darted away from Tootsie and straight to me. She frowned and glared. "What is that thing?"

"Oh, René? He's so sweet, isn't he?" Tootsie said, like she didn't notice how annoyed Onion Girl was. "When I'm out driving, I have him hop out of the car and get things from the store, so no fans bother me. He takes so much pressure off me."

Onion Girl's eyes darted back to Tootsie. Her mouth dropped open in almost a sneer, but she quickly covered it with a sly smile. "Fans? Is that so?" The way she said it, it was like she was telling Tootsie she had no fans that'd bother her for nothing.

Tootsie stayed cool as cream. She cocked her head in an angel-like way and smiled sweetly.

The housekeeper reappeared with a tray full of a teapot, cups and a plate of cookies. I got excited, thinking of the cookies Mrs. Tomes' housekeeper makes, until I noticed there were only two tea cups. Oh, I forgot. I was the servant here, not the guest. No cookies and tea for me today.

The housekeeper silently poured out the tea, while Onion Girl and Tootsie went back to silently staring at each other. Onion girl took a sip of the tea, suddenly pulled back and spit it into her cup. Her eyes looked furious. She waved her hand to the housekeeper and then to a dish of crushed ice the woman had brought in with the other tea things. The housekeeper scrambled to dump several spoonfuls of the ice into Onion Girl's cup. Then Onion Girl waved her hand again at the housekeeper, like she wanted to brush her away. The housekeeper turned and ran out the room.

"Damn girl knows I don't like it that hot," Onion Girl muttered. She took a sip and didn't try to spit the tea this time. She squinted at me. "He's effeminate for a boy."

"You got a problem with that?"

Onion Girl laughed so hard, she came close to snorting up her tea. She had to put down her tea cup and saucer. "Why should I care? Half my husbands were effeminate."

With that settled, the two old stars went back to staring at each other in an unfriendly way. I kept up my fanning of Tootsie with the ostrich feathers. This was going to be a long afternoon.

I noticed Onion Girl was squirming in her puffy chair, like there was something she wanted to get out of her system, but didn't want to be the first to talk.

She couldn't hold it in. She leaned back with a new, I-have-something-to-brag-to-you-about smile.

"The Mayor and I are doing a fundraiser downtown by City Hall. He's so charming. We're close, you know," she practically purred. "Ah, and here's a photo of the two of us from another charity ball, 'Fashions for the Freezing.' Many poor with no overcoats benefited from this gala." She lifted a framed photo from a small round table next to her chair. She held it up so Tootsie had a good view. There Onion Girl was, with the guy who was in the papers lots, the Mayor, with his big pretty-boy grin and his slicked back hair. People said he looked like a movie star himself. He grinned big enough for one.

"Oh, and he gave me these baubles as a little thank you for making the event such a huge success. He's so sweet." Onion Girl waggled the paste bracelets and ran her fingers over the paste necklace. "Amber, topaz and yellow diamonds. A very modern look."

Tootsie looked at her with no expression.

If Onion Girl was ruffled, she didn't show it. She kept going. "It's such a plus to have a famous, serious actress at these fundraisers. I draw many more donors." From the way she made a point of saying "serious," I got the idea she was saying Tootsie was a joke. Tootsie's face didn't move a muscle. Onion Girl smiled and kept going. "We planned to have this new benefit for victims of the war: limbless veterans, orphans and the like. But no one cares about the war anymore. Old news. Rather like some careers," and she pointedly looked at Tootsie.

"Yes, rather like some careers," and Tootsie pointedly looked back.

"So, our gala will benefit the poor. The poor in general, you understand. We'll work out the details later. The main thing is the party. The theme will be a circus. Lots of color, animals, clowns. So fun. We're calling it, 'Circus for the Poor.' All the political people of any importance will be there, along with the Hollywood elite, which explains why I am spearheading this gala."

Tootsie snorted.

"Oh," Onion Girl said with a raised eyebrow like she suddenly thought of something, "I suppose you weren't invited, were you? Well, long out of the limelight. That does happen."

Tootsie's mouth got a hard look. "I think you're mixed up. I did get an invitation," and then Tootsie smiled, big.

I could tell by the surprised way Onion Girl's eyebrows shot up and her frown went down, that Tootsie was lying through her teeth. "Oh, really?"

"Of course, I'm so deeply involved in preparing for roles,

that I simply cannot risk being out in the cool night air. My voice, you understand. I must pamper it. The movies are all talkies nowadays. You did know that, right?"

Onion Girl puffed up like an angry cat. Her teeth were on the edge of her lip. But then she deflated and turned her barred teeth into a smile. Must be the actress in her. "I'm so glad you are keeping up with the latest trends in the world, Tootsie. Everyone thought you'd become a recluse." She added a little laugh, like a little knife, to make her point.

Tootsie gave her own laugh. "Idle gossip is the hobby of people whose lives have passed them by. Sad souls living in the past, growing older, growing fatter." Tootsie glanced at the Onion and gave a sad smile while sipping from her cup of tea. "Oh, and thanks so much for the cookies. I'm so sorry I can't touch them. I love my small figure and want to keep it that way." Tootsie practically smirked at Onion Girl.

Onion gal puffed up all over again, and I thought I caught what almost sounded like a growl coming from her coral painted lips.

I have to say, Onion Girl was not what I would call fat. Mug is fat. But he's proud of being fat because then he can throw his weight around. Onion girl? Okay, maybe she's not as tiny around the middle as Tootsie. But, fat? No. Maybe actresses have a different standard.

"Too bad no audience will ever see you after you trim down," Onion Girl smiled through her barred teeth. Oh, oh. Things were getting rough.

"Don't be so sure. I have so many auditions lined up. And I'm sorry, you must need glasses nowadays. If I trimmed down any more, I'd disappear."

"My eyesight is perfect. Now that you mention it, all the major studio heads will be at our Circus for the Poor event. I'll ask them about these auditions of yours. I hope they don't think you've disappeared already."

For a second there, I thought Tootsie was about to come out of her chair and clobber Onion Girl, from the way she balled up her fist. But she relaxed back into her chair again and laughed, "Oh, you were always such a comedienne."

Onion "serious actress" Girl didn't like the comedienne bit from the way her eyes got narrow and she peered at Tootsie.

Actresses.

I wasn't sure how much more I could take of their little war. My arms felt like they were about to fall off from fanning the ostrich feathers.

I heard a louder splash and then what sounded like something wet slapping on something hard, like the stone tile on Onion Girl's patio.

From the edge of the French doors, I saw the flap of a towel, an arm, a leg, and then the towel fell away. It wasn't Gilbert, that's for sure.

It was a young man wearing next to nothing, in what I guessed you called swim trunks. He shook his wet hair like a dog, and then moved his hands across his blond hair to smooth it down.

He smiled toward the French doors. Onion Girl, who'd heard the splashing and slapping feet on the tile, turned around in her puffy chair and waved.

"Oh, darling! Do come in!"

If I could've seen her face, I'm sure she was smiling too.

He walked through the open glass doors and parked himself behind her chair. The two of them clasped hands.

"Oh, sweetheart, you do love to swim, don't you?"

He grinned.

She turned back around, sure enough, with a huge smile, this time toward Tootsie.

"This is Dennis."

"I see," Tootsie said, cool as iced gin and not even a ghost of a smile.

Dennis leaned against the back of Onion Girl's chair and winked at Tootsie. Since Onion Girl's back was now turned away from him, she couldn't catch that wink. Onion Girl reached around and tugged Dennis' hand. "Sit down, sit down! Don't stand about, Denny." Her voice was sing-song, more like a little kid's. She sure did have a soft spot for this Dennis.

"Aw, I'll make your nice chairs all wet. Besides, I like where I'm standing." He looked Tootsie steady in the eye while he talked, but stroked the hair on the back of Onion Girl's head at the same time.

"Don't be silly!" But I could tell Onion Girl liked his hand in her hair, so she stopped protesting about him standing there. I wonder what she'd do if she saw him grinning at Tootsie behind her back. Probably breathe fire. Then send Dennis packing.

It was all I could do not to breathe fire.

Yeah maybe the clothes, or not-clothes, were different. Maybe the hair was slicked with water instead of pomade. But there was no mistaking the face from the photo.

It was him, the driver. The blond man in the photo on the beach with the bleach job and the dead girl.

I wondered if the bleach job knew about Onion Girl. Maybe. I'd bet anything Onion Girl didn't have a clue about the broad in the photo.

Maybe he was a dud as a movie star, but he sure was something else with the ladies. He looked like he thought he was a movie star, from the way he grinned and hung-over Onion Girl like he belonged. Which he did. Wonder what she paid him.

I inched back as much as I could and kept my head low, hoping to disappear and not have him see me. But he seemed to have only eyes for Tootsie and Onion Girl.

"Mayor know about your friend?" Tootsie asked.

My fanning stopped mid-swish.

Tootsie was playing it rough.

Onion Girl's mouth turned down, frowning. When she did that, she looked a lot older.

She recovered herself soon enough and put on a mean smile. "Oh, I'm sorry, Dennis. I didn't introduce you to Tootsie. She used to be in movies." I noticed she said "used to" extra loud. "That's been a while ago. I'm sure you don't remember her."

"Oh, I do," and Dennis the driver smiled at Tootsie while biting his lip, in a way that reminded me of how Marigold looked at me sometimes. His hand was still in Onion Girl's hair.

Onion's eyes creased, and she batted his hand away. He kept smiling and leaning against the back of her chair.

"Tootsie owes her career to me, Denny," she said, pulling herself together again. "A country girl from God knows where, and I gave her a chance. Felt sorry for her."

Tootsie didn't move, like she was wearing a mask.

"It was more my former husband who encouraged her. He was drawn to the naive girls that drift into town with only the clothes on their backs."

"Is that what he saw in you?" Tootsie asked, her voice like ice cold gin again.

For just a moment, Onion Girl bared her teeth and started to rise from her chair. Then she sat back down again and made a chuckle like nothing Tootsie'd say was worth the time of day to a door knob. The driver's eyes danced from one to the other. He was enjoying this show.

Onion Girl was opening her mouth to add her two cents, or twenty-two million cents, when Gilbert slipped through the doorway quiet as you please, and gave a little cough like a fancy butler in the movies. It was our signal that the goblin had gotten all the info he could get. "Mademoiselle? Our appointment. I'm afraid...?"

"Oh, yes, Gilbert, thank you so much. I'm sorry, darling, but I have this annoying appointment to pose for publicity stills. Such a bother. I'm sure you remember what that was like. Oh, well, we'll have to get together again soon. This was such fun!"

Whatever comeback Onion Girl had in mind died on her lips, as Tootsie was up in a flash and out the door with me at her heels.

Chapter 15

The doctor was waiting for us inside Tootsie's garage. The moment Gilbert stopped the car, the doctor opened the car door and helped Tootsie out. She fell into his arms and looked like she was about to pass out.

Maybe it was the heat. The goblin still wouldn't let me open the car window after we left Onion Girl's mansion. "Mademoiselle must not be in disarray. A fan walking on the street could see." Or maybe it was her nerves again.

All during the ride back to Creepy House, she kept her cool, straight face that'd she'd shown to Onion Girl. She didn't say a word.

Now, that face melted like ice cream that'd dropped to the street on the hottest day of the year. Her new face looked lost.

Gilbert was out of the sedan in a flash. He ran to her as fast as his stubby legs could go. With the doctor holding her up on one side and Gilbert on the other, the two of them walked her out of the garage and through the sunroom doors.

I could see Bobby inside. He ran up to them, and it looked like he was offering to help. Gilbert waved him away.

Me? They left me to my own devices back in the car. But, I'm used to that. I did have some trouble opening the car door all by myself. That thing was heavy! The sedan was high off the ground too, so it was another trick sliding off the seat and onto the ground, especially since I was wearing the blue prince outfit which I was sick of by now. Why'd I want to wear that thing? I should've realized the satin would be hot, especially on a long car drive in the middle of summer. Though I didn't know the windows would be rolled up tight the whole way.

I dragged the feather fan out of the car and toward the house. It thunked on her stone tiled garden path as I pulled it along.

"Here, let me help you with that." Bobby came out of the sunroom, pulled the fan from my hand, and dragged it inside. He left it propped up by where Clara Bell used to sit. Then we made a beeline for the kitchen. There was a plate of cookies that the goblin must have left for Bobby to keep him busy. It looked like half of the cookies were gone, since the other half of the plate had only crumbs.

Bobby shoved the plate towards me. I shoved one cookie in my mouth. Ginger. Nice.

"I wish you'd told me something was happening today," he said, pouting. "By the time I came, you were all gone. It was no fun sitting in the kitchen for hours with that doctor. I couldn't get anything out of him. He speaks cryptically."

"Speaks what?"

"In riddles or secret code."

"Oh, yeah?"

"Yeah. So, where were you?"

I felt like telling him more secret code, but since I didn't know any, I gave him the straight story. "We went to see Onion Girl. Don't get mad at me. I didn't get advance notice either. And look at this outfit they put me in. I'm supposed to be a French circus boy or something."

"That was dangerous bringing you there. Onion Girl could have recognized you."

"Nah. She only had eyes for Dennis."

"Who?"

"The driver. The one in the photo with the floozy and the dead girl. He was swimming in her pool, making himself at home, hanging all over her and making eyes at Tootsie at the same time."

"Scoundrel!"

"You said it. And Onion Girl is saying she's got something going on with the Mayor. She had a photo of the two of them. And she was draped in gems—totally paste—that the Mayor gave her. But from the way she was flashing them around, I don't think she had a clue they're fakes."

"Interesting. I'll bet the Mayor doesn't know about this Dennis."

"That's a safe bet. And say, she's going to some big charity shindig with the Mayor by City Hall. 'Circus for the Poor,' or some garbage like that."

"Sounds like something we should infiltrate."

"What?"

"Crash that party."

"Yeah, well, first I say we tail that Dennis and find out where he takes us."

"Exactly my thought!" It was Gilbert standing in the kitchen doorway. His face looked angry, his scar angrier.

This was music to my ears. I wasn't one to sit back and do nothing. I liked to take action.

Gilbert sat down at the kitchen table with me and Bobby. He told us what he learned at Onion Girl's place. "Miss Sally's housekeeper does not like this driver. She says he 'sponges' the lady's money. She says he is a 'bum.' There are some little treasures about the house, small antique boxes, candlesticks and the like, that have disappeared. But the lady does not want to believe this man steals. She even accuses the housekeeper! Every time the housekeeper asks him where he is from, he tells a different story."

"That's suspicious," Bobby agreed.

"He lives in Miss Sally's house now, so we will be able to find him," Gilbert added, "and follow him."

He laid the ground rules. We'd keep Tootsie totally in the dark. "This adventure today has taxed her nerves far, far too much. This must be our secret only."

Bobby demanded to come along this time. After thinking for a moment, Gilbert decided he could use an extra set of eyes and hands. "But we will go out at night. I think your parents will not believe you go to the library after dark."

Bobby got up from his chair and stood as tall as he could. "I shall sneak out of my window. And before doing so, I shall stuff clothes under my sheets in the shape of a sleeping boy. If they look in my room, they will not know the difference in the dark. They shall be none the wiser."

Atta boy. That's my Bobby.

The caper was set.

Gilbert picked a night when the doctor would be spending a lot of time giving treatments to Tootsie. Gilbert would keep the doctor in the dark too. "He has no secrets from her, so it's best this is a secret from him."

In Tootsie's closets, I found all-black pants and long-sleeved shirts for both me and Bobby. But when Bobby showed up as promised that night, he was wearing a white shirt and tie of all things. He didn't want to change into the black gear. "This is an important adventure, so I think it's best to be formal."

"Black is what all the burglars wear. It's easier to hide in the dark if we're dark too. Besides, that tie will get caught in something for sure, and your white shirt will stand out like a spotlight. The driver'll see that shirt and see us following him."

"I suppose. If black is the accepted costume, then we must go with that." He didn't seem too happy about it, but he changed into the black shirt.

I decided to drape myself with the flat leopard too. It was heavy, and the tail and back legs dragged after me. But it was an important disguise.

I'm glad Bobby thought so too. "If this Dennis wants to try something, seeing a big cat may make him think twice."

Gilbert wasn't so sure. "This is crazy, but we have no time to argue about this leopard. We must go and be back before Doctor realizes I am gone."

Bobby said, "It's a cheetah."

Gilbert threw up his hands, "Fine, keep the leopard, the cheetah, all the jungle animals." So, I got to take the leopard with me.

The goblin wasn't wearing his beige jungle explorer outfit he'd worn when we drove to Onion Girl's the first time. He was wearing all black too, with a black cap on his head, a lightweight black jacket, and black gloves. He shushed us and motioned for us to tiptoe after him out the sunroom doors and to the garage.

I wanted to sit up front with the goblin, but he whispered, "that thing," meaning the leopard, "must go to the back. What would police say if they see a dangerous animal sitting by the driver, yes?" So, Bobby rode up front. He shrugged to me like it wasn't his idea, but I could tell he was happy about it.

With Bobby steering the wheel, Gilbert pushed the sedan out of the garage with the engine and lights off. I could tell this made Bobby even more happy, but he tried keeping a casual face like this was no big deal for him and maybe he steered huge movie star sedans like this all the time.

Gilbert pushed the car down the alley until I think he got too tired. No kidding, Tootsie's car was huge. His face was red and dripping. After Bobby slid over to let the goblin back behind the wheel, the goblin said, "Okay. Now we put the show on the road."

As Gilbert drove down Bunker Hill and out of downtown, through the Hollywood flatlands toward the Hills, we put a rough plan together.

"We sit outside Miss Sally's house and wait," goblin said.

"Not right in front. She might see us and wonder what's going on," I pointed out.

"Yes, that's a danger. We should wait a house or two down," Bobby said.

"But there's no other houses around. Just lotsa brown dirt and dead weeds as far as you can see." And I was right about this. Around Onion Girl's house, it was empty.

Gilbert came up with an idea. "I will park where the road curves above the house. We can see who comes and goes and with hope, they will not see us."

We drove up into the Hollywood Hills. With the sun down, the car wasn't as hot as the last ride to Onion Girl's house. Goblin let us roll the windows down too. "Only, do not hang your arms out the windows like that, children. I fear you'll hit a post and it will take your arm flying off!" Okay, fine.

As we got close to Onion Girl's house, Gilbert cut the car's lights. Sure as he'd said, he drove just past the house and stopped where the road started to make a snake-like turn around and up into the brown hills. He backed up at an angle, pulled forward, backed up again, turned the wheels hard one way and then another, until he got the boat of a car turned around so it faced Onion Girl's house.

"Now we wait," he said.

And we waited. And waited. And waited.

We couldn't see the house, though a glow from its lights dimly cast down the hillside and the gravel drive. Someone was home. Then we saw a pair of headlights coming up the road. A small dusty sedan, worse for the wear with a missing front bumper along with a big dent where the bumper should have been, pulled up to the gates. A man climbed out and pulled the cord that rang the bell. His sedan's headlights lit him up.

"Mr. Beele!" Gilbert hissed.

Sure enough, it was Tootsie's voice coach going into enemy territory bold as a brass button. As I suspected, Tootsie's people were working for Onion Girl, too.

The housekeeper did her trotting down the steep drive to open the gate, and then rode back up with Mr. Beele. Not long after, we heard caterwauling echoing along the hillsides. Must be Onion Girl trying to sing. Let me say, she wasn't any better at the singing business than Tootsie. You know, I didn't think this Mr. Beele was such a good voice coach.

The goblin folded his arms and looked extra put out. "And how can I tell Mademoiselle about Mr. Beele's betrayal when I can't tell her what we are doing here?"

While Onion Girl was doing her caterwauling, I noticed

something. "Hey, that's a big car coming down the drive with the lights off. Engine's off too."

Sure enough, it was a huge boat almost exactly like Tootsie's, except beetle green instead of gold. It was coasting silently along the drive. There was enough light glowing down the hillside from the out-of-sight mansion to catch the sedan's shiny green color.

"That is Miss Sally's car," Gilbert whispered. But there was no Onion Girl at the wheel. She was busy caterwauling. Who was at the wheel was a young guy. Dennis, the driver. There was enough light to catch that blond head. What was he up to?

Dennis stopped at the gate and got out. The housekeeper must not have locked it again, because Dennis pushed it open nice and easy. He coasted past the gate and kept going, leaving the gate wide open. "Ah," goblin whispered, "this Dennis must know the housekeeper will not lock the gate until Mr. Beele leaves, and he must be planning to return and shut the gate before then."

"So no one notices he's been gone," Bobby added.

The goblin let the green car get a little way ahead. Then he released the brake and rolled forward silently, except for the stony dirt road crunching under the tires. Since the road was downhill from here, Gilbert kept coasting.

Let me tell you something about the Hollywood Hills. Away from any houses, the Hills were dark. Not a little dark, but dark, dark. Like locked in a closet at midnight dark. Okay, maybe not quite that dark, but you get my point.

Add to that a dirt road, narrow, with a cliff going up on one side, and a cliff dropping straight down, down, down on the other. One missed turn in the dark, and we'd roll down all the way to the Hollywood flatlands where we'd be flattened, too.

What about the deer or horses and cowboys we saw during the daylight? What if one of them didn't see us and ran out in front of the car?

I could tell Gilbert had all this on his mind from the way he leaned forward over the steering wheel trying to see better. He muttered in the foreign language he spoke sometimes. Bobby didn't say a word, but I'd bet he was scared. I know I was scared, so scared, I shoved a leopard paw in my mouth to make me feel better. And it did make me feel better.

Around one last bend, finally, we saw the lights from the Hollywood flatlands. Dennis turned on the green car's lights as he rolled into the streets below and must have started his engine too. Gilbert started his engine, but he kept the lights off.

As we followed Dennis, the goblin kept far enough back so we could see him but not lose him. Dennis drove to an area of newer apartments, duplexes, triplexes, fourplexes.

Dennis parked in front of a two-level duplex with a red-tiled roof. Gilbert rolled to a stop across the street and a couple of apartments down. Even though he was on the opposite side of the street, he parked so he was facing the same way as Onion Girl's car.

Dennis got out of the sedan, ran up the duplex steps to the top unit and pounded on the door, which was painted pale pink. When he got no answer, he started kicking the pink door and yelling, "Let me in!"

Finally, a woman with mousy brown hair cracked the door open. I could tell right off the bat, she wasn't the bleached blonde floozy in the photo with the dead girl.

"She's not here," the woman said. "Go away."

"I don't believe you! She's in there. Let me in!"

"You know she's hardly home. She's here, she's there, she's everywhere. You're not the only guy she hangs around with."

She tried closing the pink door, but he shoved his foot in. "She owes me money! I want my share. That's my money!"

"She owes me too, buster. Her half of the rent. If you see her, tell her I'll throw all her stuff out on the street if she doesn't pay up."

The woman slammed herself against the door to close it, foot or no. Dennis yelped and pulled his foot out. He limped down the steps.

Halfway down, he stopped and yelled back up at the apartment, "If I find out you're lying, I'm gonna to teach you a lesson. A hard lesson!"

Real nice guy, that one.

Gilbert motioned to Bobby to follow, and out the car they went. They ran across the street. I pushed the heavy car door open quiet as I could and wiggled out too. Didn't want to miss any action. With the leopard draped over my head and its tail and feet dragging after me, I followed Gilbert and Bobby, but not too close, in case they spotted me and ordered me back. I ducked behind another parked car to watch.

Gilbert may have been old and short, but he could move fast. He slammed into Dennis, knocking him to the ground. Dennis started kicking, but Bobby jumped on his legs. Dennis nearly flipped Bobby over with a big kick, but Bobby held on tight.

"We know you killed that little girl!" Gilbert growled to

Dennis. "You confess! I have police all around nearby!"

"Liar. I don't see no coppers anywhere, you old loser! Let me go!"

"Confess!"

"I was in Palm Springs. Sally can vouch for me. I don't know nothing!" Dennis yelled.

Gilbert said, "Then why you asking that girl for your share? We heard you demanding the money!"

Then the driver pulled away from Gilbert and swung his fist hard at his face, dropping the goblin to the pavement. Bobby tried hanging on to Dennis' legs, but he gave a big kick and knocked Bobby off. Dennis ran around to the front of the green sedan, slid in and started her up.

With Gilbert down for the count, and Bobby busy trying to revive him, there was only one thing left for me to do.

I ran back to Tootsie's gold car, used all my weight to pull open the heavy driver's door, scrambled in, and closed it again. I was in business.

I'd watched Bookie drive. He showed me how it worked: the clutch, the gears, where the gas pedal was, that sort of thing. Okay, so I was no expert and since I was short, being a kid, I had to do my driving a little differently.

I stood, and kind of hopped up and down on the clutch, the gas, and I bypassed the brakes. I was on a chase. Brakes weren't important.

I was moving! Fast, too. Oh, boy! I was thinking I loved this driving. Okay, so I wasn't going straight, more like weaving to the right, then to the left. But I was going. One of the back doors started banging, probably because I hadn't closed it when I slid out to follow Bobby and goblin. Whoops. Oh, well. Too late now.

It wasn't long before Dennis noticed he was being tailed. He panicked and swerved and sideswiped a bunch of parked cars. The noise of metal tearing against metal screamed. I saw sparks flying between the cars.

I admit I was thrown off balance by the sounds of the loud scraping and ended up sideswiping the same cars. More screaming metal on metal and flying sparks. I ruined Tootsie's car! But I didn't have time to think about the trouble I'd be in. I had to keep hard on the green car's tail.

Dennis tried turning left at the first cross street, maybe trying to lose me, but a little sedan was coming straight. He veered hard to miss the little sedan, but his back end hit that car and he swerved. Then I hit the side of the green car. It bumped up on a curb and rolled on its side with a loud clunk and sounds of breaking glass. Oh, boy. Tootsie's car bounced to a stop against the same curb. As it bounced, my feet slipped from the clutch and gas. The car jerked, and the engine cut dead.

Dennis climbed out the driver's side window. There was hate in his eyes. "I'll get you!" With his fists balled so tight the skin over his knuckles was white, he headed toward Tootsie's car, and me in it.

I took a chance. I shoved open the sedan door and rolled out with the leopard draped over me. I hopped up and down waving the leopard's arms and made my best, loudest roaring sounds.

"Jesus!" Dennis fell back, then scrambled up and took off running. I tried to follow, but that big guy had the speed. He disappeared into the night dark streets.

I heard loud huffing and puffing behind me and saw Gilbert limping as fast as he could while leaning on Bobby. When he got to the car crash scene and saw the scrapes along the side of Tootsie's car and the huge dent in the front bumper where I hit Onion Girl's car, he looked near tears and kept saying, "Oh, my, oh, my." I felt terrible and wondered how much a boat of a car like that cost, and if I could ever come up with that kind of dough to buy Tootsie a new one. Maybe, if I went back to second-story work.

By now, the lookie-loos were coming out of the apartments and little bungalow houses. There was a lot of, "What's going on? My rose bush got run over! My car got sideswiped!" The guy in the little sedan that slammed into the green car demanded, "Satisfaction!"

I wondered if the goblin expected something like this might happen, or maybe he always was extra prepared. He had a wad of bills at the ready that he pulled out of his black jacket. He peeled off bills and handed them to the complaining citizens. "Please, this is studio business. Confidential studio business. Please say nothing." While he handed out the cash, me and the leopard stayed in the shadows away from curious eyes.

When he ran out of cash, he said to me and Bobby, "Hurry, we must go now, before any police."

We had to get in the car through the front driver's side, leopard or no, because the passenger side was too dented from my sideswiping. Also, the back door I'd left open, even though it wasn't on the dented side, it still had gotten off kilter. Gilbert had a heck of a time closing it and didn't want to risk needing to pry it open when we got back to Creepy House. So, in the front we all piled. Luckily, the car still started, and Gilbert pulled away from the crowd of neighbors. Some yelled after us, "Hey! You didn't pay me!"

Gilbert had peeled off a bunch of bills for the man with the little sedan, but I guess it wasn't enough. He kept yelling, "I want satisfaction!" until he was too far away for us to hear anymore.

"What about the green car?" Bobby asked.

"If Miss Sally is such friends with this Mayor as she says, then he will take care of all this. Let us not worry. What is important is to keep Mademoiselle's name out of this." He glanced toward me, "And your face out of it."

Chapter 16

Sure enough, the next morning's papers were quiet as mice about two boat-like movie star cars crashing in the Hollywood flatlands. Not a peep. Guess Onion Girl really was chummy with the Mayor.

Gilbert didn't want to show me the papers at first, so I had to keep asking him, over and over, louder and louder, until he couldn't take it anymore. "Fine!"

There was still a story reminding "good citizens" to call the police if they spotted me. But it wasn't as big as the other stories, and only had one photo of a body covered with a blanket on some Los Angeles street. My latest victim. Three times as big was a photo of the grinning Mayor handing a doll to some TB kid in a hospital bed. She had a cute bow in her hair. Made me snort.

"The public always wants something new, something exciting. It is sad how they bore so easily, forget their idols for lesser talents," Gilbert sighed. "Soon enough, you will be yesterday's news. I have seen it so many times."

I hoped so. But would the cops get bored with chasing me too? I wasn't so sure about that.

Gilbert kept a bag of ice over his eye where Dennis slugged him, while he got on the phone to get a "metal man" over to the garage to fix the car. He told me, "If she asks, we will tell Mademoiselle that the dirt and stones from the Hills when we visited Miss Sally ruined the paint. The metal man is only re-painting. Yes? Remember that?"

Sure, I can keep a story straight.

The metal man came quick, and started banging on the gold car. The doctor prowled around, looking at me and then Gilbert suspiciously, but he didn't ask any questions.

Bobby was nowhere to be seen. Maybe he was lying low so

the parents wouldn't start realizing he wasn't in bed last night like a good little boy.

I was bugged that Dennis the driver got away from me. I was even more bugged thinking about the roommate in the duplex.

She knew something. I was going to find out what.

My idea came from a maid's outfit I'd seen in Tootsie's closets. It came complete with cap, apron, mop and bucket. It looked like it belonged to forty years back or so, but it clearly said, "cleaning girl." I added a black curly wig for good measure and patted on a nice thick layer of pink powder. Hopefully, that disguised me enough.

I'd ridden the streetcars plenty of times around downtown, but Hollywood was another story. It took me a while to figure out the lines to take, and I had to ask about ten people. I admit I borrowed a few coins to pay the fares from the dish of change Gilbert kept in a kitchen drawer. Hey, don't judge. It was for a good cause. Saving my skin.

Then it was more walking, walking. Did I tell you that half of Hollywood looks exactly the same? Same streets, same bungalows, same duplexes. Same, same, same. Finally, I was walking down the right street toward the right duplex.

I noticed Onion Girl's boat car was gone and the street swept of any broken glass. Even the sideswiped parked cars were gone. Was the Mayor getting them fixed too? Must be. Luckily, there were still squashed rose bushes. Otherwise I wouldn't have known I was heading in the right direction.

I spotted the pink door on the duplex's second story. This had to be it. I hauled the mop and bucket up the steps and tapped on the door. No answer. The pink door still had Dennis' shoe marks on it from when he tried kicking it open. I tapped some more and added, "Hello? Hello?" in my nice little girl voice.

The same mousy brown-haired woman cracked open the pink door. She stared down at me. "What the hell are you?"

"I'm the cleaning girl."

"I don't got no cleaning girl. Scram!"

I shoved the mop handle in the doorway as she was trying to slam it shut. "The other lady hired me to clean."

"What? She's got a cleaning girl now?" The roommate opened the door wide to let me in. "Fine, go ahead, clean away. Just don't expect a tip from me. Well, la-di-da and hot-tee-tot. A cleaning girl. Don't that beat all?" She swished the hem of her purple polka dot dress back and forth in a la-di-da kind of way in case I missed the point. "Wish she'd take a minute to pay me back rent while she's at it, the cheap bum."

I don't know much about cleaning anything. Plus, I was trying to pretend I'd been there before, doing cleaning for the bleach job. That meant I couldn't ask where the tub was so I could fill up my bucket and start mopping. So, I used the hem of my apron to dust tables, chair arms. The roommate peered at me.

Before she got too suspicious, I needed to get in my questions.

"Say, where's that little girl I saw here before? I like playing with her."

"That girl's not here anymore. Besides, you're supposed to be working, not playing. If you were working for me, I'd a' thrown you outta here and down those steps five minutes ago. You're a crappy cleaning girl."

"Did she move out with her ma?"

The roommate laughed. "That blonde's no ma to nobody. I don't know where she dug that kid up. Probably pulled her off the street, or found her where the orange pickers look for work. You know? Where the Okies dump their excess baggage." She mean-smiled at me like I must be dumped baggage too. Real nice gal, this one was.

With Dennis yelling for his share of the money last night, and him doing secret night-time driving for the big wheels, I decided to play a hunch about the little girl. "But she said her dad was rich, and she was gonna live the high life."

The roommate laughed extra mean this time. "Money didn't go to that kid, that's for sure."

"But isn't her dad going to keep her?"

The roommate laughed so hard, she snorted. "The Mayor ain't..." Then she suddenly stopped and looked at me with dark, suspicious eyes. "You ask too many questions. Get outta here, you nosy little snot nose!"

She pushed me out the door and threw the bucket after me. "Hey, I need to get paid!" That was worth a shot, but only got my mop tossed after me.

The bucket and mop rolled down the stairs and smack dab into the bleached blonde. The one from the photo with the dead girl.

She tripped over the rolling bucket and had to grab the stair railing to keep from falling over. When the mop clattered after the bucket, she grabbed it and threw it aside while swearing up a storm like a sailor.

The blonde wasn't dressed like a sailor, I'll tell you that. A fancy pastel dress like you see in the nice shop windows downtown, along with matching pumps with not a smudge on them, little beaded purse, little hat perched on her head. All so new, I saw the price tag hanging off the end of the purse. The price? The tag was too far away for me to see, but my best guess was not cheap. What I noticed most were the paste baubles: white and blue stones around her neck, her wrists, and matching white and blue stone ear bobs. Nice and sparkly. Nice and fake.

She looked up and spotted me, hate in her eyes. "You little..."

Suddenly, she shut up and her eyes got wide. She was staring hard at my face.

I reached up to my head and realized my maid's cap and black curly wig had slid over to the side, almost to my shoulder. Probably most of the pink powder was off my freckly face by now too.

The blonde recognized me. Oh, oh.

"You! You murderer kid!"

I heard the front door pop open. The roommate was listening.

"There's a huge reward on your head. You better watch yourself."

I heard the roommate's scrambling feet, then the click of a phone receiver. "That murderer kid is here! I get the reward, right? I called it in. She tried attacking me, and now she's attacking my roommate Sugar, Sugar Suvette." A pause, then, "That's an actress name, dummy. I'm an actress too. A lot better one. Delores DeLadomme. Remember me, brainless, when I'm famous!"

The blonde, Sugar, grinned at me. She must have heard the roommate ratting me out too. "Cops coming to get you. You'll swing in the wind, you stupid kid."

I took a chance and turned the tables: "You killed that kid, all by yourself! You waited until the driver was gone to Palm Springs, then you got the cash from the Mayor—blackmail cash— took a city car, then killed and dumped that kid."

Sugar's face got so red, I could see her burning up even under all her thick face paint. I nodded my chin to the paste jewels that she probably thought were real. "Guess it was worth it to ya, huh?"

"You're stupid, kid. Real stupid."

She pulled a little pocket pistol from her beaded clutch

with the price tag hanging out. She pointed the pistol smack dab at me. I saw her finger getting tight on the trigger.

I grabbed the wig and maid's cap from my shoulder and threw them at her face. I didn't wait another second before I turned and ran back up the stairs.

I heard the blonde shrieking behind me. Then I heard her brand-new pumps stomping up the stairs after me.

The roommate was peeking out the door with eyes getting bigger. Then she disappeared in a flash and tried slamming the door in my face. I took a "youch!" to the elbow to keep the door open. Had to. It was my only escape route, with the crazy blonde plus pistol hot on my behind.

Delores the roommate was fast. I had to scramble to keep up as she ran toward the back of the apartment. I followed the sounds of her tapping steps on kitchen linoleum and the slamming back door.

The roommate shut the back kitchen door so hard, I had to put some muscle into turning the door knob and pulling it open.

Just as I was running through the back door, I heard the blonde behind me screaming like an animal. The pistol went off. Can't mistake that popping sound for anything else.

I flew down the wooden back stairs in record time. I heard the pistol go off again. When I hit the patch of dirt at the bottom of the steps, I slid and fell on my side, which gave me a chance to look up at Sugar on the stair landing above. She drew a bead on me, but then stopped. She moved her eyes around and I could almost hear her thinking, *oh, oh, it's broad daylight, and look, there's a couple of snoopy neighbors out on the sidewalk staring, pointing.* She disappeared back into the kitchen.

I grabbed my chance and took off running. I saw the hem of Delores' purple polka dot dress disappear around the twin garages at the end of the yard. I ran after her around the corner of the garages and through the open side door. I saw her cowering inside the garage next to a stack of old, flat tires.

"Okay, you tell me what's going on!" I was out of breath, but still had to question this broad.

"I didn't know things would go like this. I didn't!" Dolores was panicking. I saw tears pop out of her eyes.

"Blondie got the money and killed the kid, didn't she?"

"No, I mean yes, she got the money. I think she planned it when her boyfriend was out of town, so she could take it all. He came around looking for his share last night."

"What about the kid?" I gave her a kick. She was ten times

bigger than me, but I knew that when the big characters panic in Bookie's office, they're putty in his hands. Delores was no different.

She yelped and kept talking. "The kid was alive when she got in that car with him. I swear it! I watched from the window."

"Him? The boyfriend, Dennis?"

"No! Listen, I don't know anything! I wasn't involved in any of this!" Then she suddenly stopped and said, "Hey, you're bleeding."

I looked down to where she was pointing at my arm. Sure enough, I was dripping blood. Didn't even feel it.

The second my eyes left her, Delores scrambled up, shoved me aside, and took off running out the side door.

I didn't chase her. Seeing the blood took all the fight out of me and it was like all at once my legs didn't have the pep to run. I sat down hard on the concrete garage floor, staring at my bleeding arm. How about that? Same arm I broke when bad man tricked me into climbing the rotted tree. Now it caught a bullet.

Maybe that's why the blonde didn't shoot again. She figured I was done for. I pulled off my maid's apron and wrapped it around my arm. I didn't know much about gunshot wounds. Bookie would, but he was far away on Bunker Hill, and besides, he wasn't my friend anymore. Even bleeding to death, he'd hand me over to Mug for that reward money.

I pulled myself up from the floor, and was stepping out of the garage, keeping an eye out for Sugar and her pistol, when I heard the screaming sirens of what sounded like a million cop cars.

Cop car after cop car pulled up on the street in front of the apartment, and in the alley behind the yard. I ducked inside the door so no one could see me, but I still had a view of what was happening through a garage window.

Mug pulled himself out of one of the cars in the alley, along with dozens of other cops. The nosy neighbors pointed and waved their arms around. I spotted Whisper-Whisper. Was he here because the roommate gave the blonde's name over the phone, and the cops knew she was one of the Mayor's girlies? And the cops knew to call Whisper-Whisper if a Mayor's girlie was in the picture? The girlie who knew the dead girl?

Sugar came charging out of the duplex, down the back stairs. She was yelling at Whisper-Whisper and Mug, telling them to, "Find that creepy little girl! What's the matter with you? You stupid or something? Can't find a snotty little kid?"

I guess she was so worked up, she forgot she still had that pistol in her hand. As she was waving her arms around, she was waving that pistol around too.

Maybe it was my imagination. Maybe it was because I was bleeding a little bit too much, but I could swear I saw Whisper-Whisper give a nod, not a big nod, just a little nod, to a young cop with a rifle. Then that kid cop raised the rifle and fired at Sugar. He must have been a crack shot, because a spot of red bloomed right over her heart. The red spot got bigger and bigger.

She looked down at it, shocked. She looked back up at Whisper-Whisper, opened her mouth like she was about to yell more insults, but then she fell forward, flat on her face.

Chapter 17

While all of them, nosy neighbors included, were busy staring at the dead bleach job, I took my chance to scram.

I kept telling myself that the bullet hole in my arm was only a scratch, that I wasn't really hurt so bad. But the back of my mind kept butting in and saying, hey, you're not feeling so hot, are you? And I wasn't. I wasn't sure how, but I made it back to the streetcars, back to Bunker Hill.

On the streetcars, I sat so my bloody arm faced away from the other riders. I kept my head down and looked at no one. I would have loved to take the Angel's Flight or Court Flight trams going up to Bunker Hill, but couldn't risk the cops. Let me tell you, that was the roughest climb up my Hill that I'd ever done. And the longest, since I had to keep ducking behind bushes and parked cars to hide when I spotted anyone nearby.

I made it as far as Bobby's house. I couldn't take another step.

He wasn't in the back yard. I hoped he was in his house, and not gone at the library. The room where Bobby liked to sit and read was on the ground floor of his house. I picked up a handful of dirt and threw it at the window. Whoops, the window was wide open, being summer and all. I heard the dirt fall to the floor inside.

Bobby's face came to the window. He looked annoyed, but then I think he saw my bloody arm. His eyes popped wide and he motioned his hands as if to tell me not to move. I couldn't move if I tried.

He disappeared away from the window. Maybe he was checking on what his parents were up to. Then he came back. He climbed out the window and hauled me up from where I'd plopped down on the grass.

"I'll get you to Gilbert and Tootsie. We have to be fast. You're bleeding."

No kidding.

Even though his house was close to Creepy House, it seemed like it took forever to get there. I kept falling, and he had to stop and heft me back up. Then we had to be careful no one spotted us, so had to stick to empty backyards and the alley.

For the last stretch, Bobby actually picked me up and carried me, though he wasn't that much bigger than me. He was huffing, puffing and staggering, but he made it to the sunroom doors. He pushed them open with his shoulder and dropped me on the layers of carpets. Youch!

The strange doctor was the first to spot us. What did I tell you? He was some cool customer, because his eyes didn't pop when he saw my bloody arm. He didn't react at all except to get down to business. "Get her into the kitchen," he told Bobby. "I'll fetch Mr. Grossman," which was what he called the goblin.

The doctor went out the sunroom doors toward the garage, where I could still hear the metal man pounding on Tootsie's car. The goblin must have been in the garage too. Hopefully, the metal man had fixed the car enough so the doctor wouldn't see how badly smashed up it had been and tell Tootsie.

After that, I think I was passing out and waking up. I remember Bobby dragging me to the kitchen by my good arm. I don't think he could carry me another step.

Then I remember lying on the kitchen table. Bobby was there, and Gilbert and the doctor. I heard the doctor say, "You're lucky. It must have been a small caliber. Otherwise, for a little person like you, maybe I'd have to amputate." He chuckled.

All of a sudden, I was in the downstairs bedroom, my room, with Clara Bell and the flat leopard. Outside the transom window, it was night dark. I closed my eyes, and then it seemed like a second later, the sky outside was noon-time bright. Then night again, then day. It was confusing, but I was too tired to think about it much.

I remembered the doctor had a needle, the kind doctors stick people with in the movies. It looked as big as a pistol, except with a point like a shiv at the end. Bobby was draped over me in the bed, sobbing. I never saw Bobby sobbing. Was it a dream? He was telling Gilbert, "We have to marry before she dies! She cannot die a spinster!"

Dying? Spinster? What? But I think I drifted off again before I could start panicking.

The next thing I knew, Tootsie was sitting on the bed and she was stroking my hair. She smiled at me. She looked like her old self again. She was back to wearing one of her strange outfits, a long, silky purple dress with lots of fringe. I liked it better than the beach girl outfit or whatever it was that she wore to Onion Girl's house.

"I'm so sleepy," I managed to mumble to her.

"Don't worry. It's only the vitamin shots. It's the latest discovery. They're helping you to heal."

"Oh, okay." And I was out again.

Slowly, my time being awake got longer than my time being passed out. The doctor came by too much for my liking. He didn't say much, but gave me his strange smiles. "Ah, and this will be your last shot." It was the shiv needle again. I wanted to dodge it, but the doctor was fast and I was stuck before I knew it. I was out like a light, but when I woke up, this time I stayed awake.

Gilbert made me a lot of hot soup that I had to drink up no matter how hot the day was, otherwise I couldn't get rid of him hovering around. Bobby came by too. He didn't say anything more about me having to marry him so I wouldn't die a spinster. Good thing; otherwise, he would've earned a solid punch to the kisser.

I told Bobby and Gilbert about what happened: Delores the roommate, Sugar the floozy in the photo nearly filling me with lead, then getting dropped herself, and the Mayor in the mix somehow. Gilbert shushed me and told me I must rest. I could tell Bobby was interested, but said, "Save your strength, Sparky. We'll go back to investigating when you're better."

I played with Clara Bell and the flat leopard. As I felt better, I wandered out to the garden and lay on one of the lounge chairs. I spent a lot of time staring at the jungle plants. My arm still felt tired, and I had a puckery kind of scar. But it was getting better.

One afternoon, Tootsie came out and talked me into letting her give me a "moon" nail polish job, where she only painted the middle, and left the pale part at the bottom of each nail and my chewed tips plain. She re-did it a few times in different colors.

In other words, I was bored out of my mind. As time passed, I worried about the trail going cold with the dead kid. Gilbert told me he called Onion Girl's housekeeper, and she told him Dennis the driver hadn't been seen since the night we chased him in the Hollywood flatlands. "Ah, Miss Sally is most upset. He left all his clothes behind. Custom tailored clothes she purchased for him at no small expense."

He probably was too afraid to go back to her house after he'd wrecked her car. And how could he get that far up into the Hills unless he hoofed it? That would be a tough climb. Probably the scene was getting too hot for him, and he ran and kept running out of town. Maybe he hitched a ride on a rail car.

I kept bugging Gilbert about letting me see the newspapers. I told him they would help me recover. Finally, he caved and let me see the morning papers, and again when the afternoon editions came.

There was less and less news about me and all my victims. One morning, there was nothing. Only a huge photo of the Mayor cuddling a puppy.

"You see," Gilbert said. "Always, they forget."

Maybe the papers forgot, but not the cops. I was still a wanted kid with a price on my head.

The day came when I couldn't take it anymore. I waited until Gilbert was busy in the kitchen, Tootsie was busy with two-faced Mr. Beele, and Bobby had left to go back to his mom and dad and cozy house.

I made my way upstairs. I was surprised at how tired my legs felt, when before I could run up those stairs with no problem. I dug around Tootsie's closets until I found a flowered dress that didn't stand out too much. I draped a scarf over my head. Not sure if that disguised me enough, but I hoped since I was out of the papers, no one would notice me. Hopefully, no cops would spot me.

I slipped out the garage, where Tootsie's car sat all nice and shiny like nothing had ever happened to it. Moving slow and easy, I made my way toward the park on Court Hill.

The first thing I noticed was the cops. There weren't any. Of course, Spooky was still leaning against his lamppost. Otherwise, nothing.

It could be a trick, so I wasn't letting my guard slip. Not for a minute. Not Sparky.

I heard voices when I got to Court Hill. I crouched to hide behind handy bushes and an old suitcase that looked like someone had thrown it there. It was popped open and empty except for one old sock. That made me remember Tootsie's trick. Getting shot must have made me lose some marbles. It wasn't smart to come here unarmed. I scooped up some stones from the ground and stuffed them into the sock.

I crawled closer, keeping low to the ground. I held the rock sock tight in my fist.

Up ahead I saw the boarding house where the bad man lived, and the bench where I found the dead kid. I meant to confront the bad man one more time. Maybe I was crazy, but what choice did I have?

Only, I didn't see just the bad man. There was another man, another voice.

Whisper-Whisper.

They were arguing. The bad man said, "You don't give me enough. How can I survive on the peanuts you toss me? Maybe I should talk, huh? Maybe so." I noticed bad man's face still had a pinkish mark where Tootsie whacked him with her silk stocking slugger.

It looked like Whisper-Whisper was trying to calm him down. He held up his hands toward bad man and said something, but I couldn't hear what.

Or maybe I stopped listening, because I noticed Whisper-Whisper's fingers, how long and thin they were. Long and thin, exactly like bad man's. And that wasn't all. They both had the same long, thin shape, same vulture-like neck. Only, Whisper-Whisper was younger, had bigger chompers, and more hair.

They were related. I didn't know how, but they must have been. Was bad man Whisper-Whisper's older brother? Cousin?

So, it was Whisper-Whisper who'd been paying bad man's rent. I saw Whisper-Whisper handing bad man a wad of cash. Bad man snatched it, but he frowned at it like it wasn't enough.

Well, well. It was getting clearer to me now. It was Whisper-Whisper who did the Mayor's dirty work, picked up the girl from the Hollywood duplex, gave the payout to Sugar, killed the kid and dumped her on Court Hill. Problem was, his brother or cousin, the bad man, was supposed to bury her or get rid of her somehow. But he was slow getting around to it because he wanted more cash. So slow, I found the kid first.

I guess I was too lost in my thinking and wasn't watching where my knees were scraping the ground. I scooted on top of a twig and it made a loud snap.

Whisper-Whisper's head whipped around and he started running, right toward me.

As I scrambled to stand, I made the mistake of putting my weight on my bad arm. Ouch! My arm gave way and I fell on my face. Whisper-Whisper was fast. He grabbed me and pinned me to the ground. My sock weapon dropped out of my hand. Whisper-Whisper tore the scarf off my head and laughed, low and quiet.

"Ah, it's you. I thought so. No one sighted you for so long, I thought you'd run away to another town. Or, more likely, were dead. That would have been so much easier for everyone." He yanked my arm up to look at the pucker scar the bullet made. "This is where she shot you, isn't it? Her roommate told me."

He twisted my bum arm tight. I felt like crying, but no way was I giving him that kind of thrill. I saw bad man jumping up and down, giggling, clapping his hands, enjoying the show. These loonies were two of a kind.

"Such a problem you are for a little girl. Such a trying, trying problem. Not the first time you've caused me time and trouble, is it, little girl? Wandering about, dressed as a goat, looking, searching for answers. What are you up to, you little bag of trouble?"

"You and that creep framed me! You know I didn't kill that girl! You did! I know what happened!"

Bad man booed, then got into another giggle fit. Whisper-Whisper chuckled. "Silly girl. You think too much. It's all a dog and pony show. Just play along. Nothing bad will happen to you. We'll keep you under wraps until this whole mess blows over. Then you'll be fine. It's politics. Nothing personal."

His voice was like honey, like how bad man talked when he was trying to trick you. I almost believed him. Almost. But it's tough to trick Sparky.

He was lying. I'd be fine? My foot! I was doomed. It was all over. I had to take a risk. And I did it. I twisted my head around as far as I could and bit the part that was sticking out the most. His bobbing Adam's apple.

His hands let me go in a hot second. He made a sound like he was trying to scream but couldn't quite get it out.

I ran like I'd never run. I looked behind me and saw Whisper-Whisper on the ground with his hands around his throat, and bad man was kneeling over him.

Rounding trees just outside the park, I nearly plowed into a big city sedan.

Chapter 18

A man got out from behind the driver's wheel of the city sedan. It was José. He must have driven Whisper-Whisper up to Court Hill. I know José saw me. But he leaned against the car and looked away.

I didn't stick around to ask questions.

Back to Creepy House I headed as fast as I could. When I got there, I snuck in through my usual back way, the sunroom. Funny how it became "usual" so fast. But I had to check myself—a street kid like me couldn't get too comfortable in any one place. I had to start telling myself that ten times a day. This nice setup I'd stumbled on? It couldn't last. So there was no point getting comfy.

I could hear Gilbert, Tootsie, and Bobby talking in the kitchen. Oh, oh. At least I didn't hear Mr. Beele, so he must've left already.

I felt wiped out from running, but I hurried to clean myself up in the big white bathroom, which I also was getting comfortable with. Tut-tut, Sparky. There you go getting comfortable again.

I threw on the sailor shirt and pants I was wearing this morning and tried to be cool as I strolled into the kitchen.

They hardly noticed me. They had bigger news.

"Circus for the Poor! She actually sent me an invitation! Can you believe it?" Tootsie was as excited as I'd ever seen her. She was laughing it up with Gilbert and Bobby. "Look how fancy the paper is!" She was holding a colored paper with sparkles on it.

"Ha! Of course, she sent an invitation. She is too curious to see if you will come, see what you will do," Gilbert said.

Bobby saw me. He jumped up and pulled me into the sunroom. "Sparky, remember how we talked about infiltrating this Circus for the Poor?" he whispered.

It was his idea, I remembered. And it was a good idea. "Yeah?"

"It's tomorrow night. I'll sneak away from home like I did when we tailed Dennis. We can spy and gather information."

"I don't know. Your parents are going to get suspicious."

"I think it'll be okay. They are starting to wonder, but I'll work it out. It's important that I go with you to help you, because I'm not sure you're completely recovered. But I know you want to start investigating again, and so do I. What do you say?"

How could I tell him about what I'd just found out? He didn't want me tangling with bad man, so he'd only get bent out of shape if I told him I'd gone to Court Hill again.

Then there was the danger. I know I saw Whisper-Whisper nod to the young cop as a signal to shoot the bleached blonde dead. Now I knew he probably killed the little girl. I hadn't figured out all the details, but the driver and the blonde must have been trying to blackmail the Mayor, telling him the drifter kid they found was his and threatening to make him mud to the voters by going to the papers. Whisper-Whisper, faithful creep he was, took care of that kid. Permanently.

Sugar did a double-cross, handing the kid over to Whisper-Whisper when Dennis was in Palm Springs so she wouldn't have to share the loot. The roommate probably thought she'd get a cut of the action too. Think again, Delores.

And the pay-out Whisper-Whisper gave the blonde? Some dough, sure. She had money to buy those new threads I saw her wearing. But mostly, I'll bet she was paid with worthless paste jewels.

I was already past my ears in trouble with Whisper-Whisper. But, Bobby was in the clear. Whisper-Whisper had no idea Bobby was alive and had a mom and dad and happy home. I wanted things to stay that way.

"Sure," I lied. "When you sneak away from your house tomorrow night, wait for me here. Then we'll have to talk about costumes. You know, disguises."

That made Bobby happier. Then he took off to get back to the parents and the house, to keep them from getting too suspicious.

I hated flat-out lying to Bobby. He'd come, wait and wait. By the time he realized I was gone, it'd be too late for him to do anything. I hoped.

All the usual characters: Mr. Exercise, the face ladies, the hand lady, the hair ladies, all of them, showed up in force before the day was over. They were back again the next day to see what magic they could work before the circus ball that night. A new one showed up I hadn't seen before, a guy with a beard who did things with her jewelry.

The dress lady stayed the night, doing her work on a few of Tootsie's gowns, tearing them apart and then putting them back together into, "something spectacular and not out of date." Or at least that's what Mr. Beele said when I eavesdropped on him talking with the spiritual man.

Gilbert was up bright and early the morning of the ball, getting himself all prettied up too. The face and hair gals had a go at him. The dress lady was still busy sewing away on the gown, sleep or no. So, her assistant made a few nips and tucks to Gilbert's beige jungle explorer outfit with the high boots. The getup looked the same to me, except not as tight. I think Gilbert used to be less round in the middle.

He was very excited, pacing back and forth. "There will be press. Lots of press, I think! This is an important night for Mademoiselle!" I heard him saying to the doctor.

With all the excitement bubbling away, I stayed low and out of sight as usual. Bobby came by in the afternoon, reminding me about our date for the Circus for the Poor, in case I forgot.

"We need to start talking about our disguises, Sparky. We need to start planning."

"Later. Come back after dark, when there's less people hanging around here."

He frowned. "But, that might be too late." He peered at me. I wonder if he was suspecting I was going to ditch him.

"I'm thinking about disguises right now. We'll be okie dokie, okay?"

"Okay." But he didn't sound too happy about it. Back to his house he went.

I didn't want to ditch Bobby and hated telling him stories. But it was true that I was thinking about my disguise. I was going to be a clown. Get it? Circus? Clown? Onion Girl said something about there being clowns too. So, I'd blend right in. I'd spotted a rack of clown outfits during one of my trips into Tootsie's closets.

I couldn't do much until the crowd thinned out. I got my signal when I heard a lot hands clapping by the stairs with the squares. Keeping low, I made my way there and slid to hide behind an ottoman.

There Tootsie was at the top of the stairs, taking in all the applause like she was drinking in life. And she looked alive, with color in her face that I don't think was only the face paint.

Her new-old gown was slim at top and then fanned out around her knees and draped down to her feet. The top part was gold, and the bottom was a pale green. She spun around, and you could see the gold part wrapped around the back kind of like a belt. The dress sleeves disappeared around the back too. What you could see was a whole lot of her bare back and the back of her necklace, or really, the front of it. She was wearing the necklace backwards, so a big hunk of all kinds of stones, mostly greenish, sparkled away and hung down her bare back. Even from my spot behind the ottoman, I could tell those jewels were the real deal.

The back of her short hair was pinned up with even more gems, green, gold with some pink ones and even black. She held up her arms, and there were more on her wrists and fingers. When she turned to the front again, the doctor was at the ready to lay her wrap over her shoulders. It was a whisper of fabric so thin, you could see through it. It had more gems sewn along the edges, mostly pink with a few green ones.

I didn't know the first thing about classy clothes, the real kind of high classy, but this outfit was something else. I noticed her face paint wasn't nearly as brown as when she was doing that beach look for Onion Girl, but still it was far from her usual white face and black Egyptian eyes. Her face had a shimmer to it, kind of like how her gold car looked, like she'd been buffed and polished.

She smiled a mile wide and did a few more turns as the whole crew oohed, ahhed, clapped, whistled, and hollered: Mr. Exercise, the dance teacher, the face broads, the raw food lady, avocado hair lady, hair lady #2, the hand lady, slimming man, dress lady and her assistant, spiritual man, and the bearded jeweler guy. No one clapped and hollered louder than the goblin. I saw tears in his eyes. Even the vitamin doctor was smiling bigger than I'd ever seen him. He was wearing a tuxedo, too. First time I'd seen him in anything but his thin suits.

With her arms still stretched out, Tootsie took the steps down slowly, her smile big. Now I could see Tootsie was a star. A for real star. If I didn't need to hide, I woulda stood up and clapped too.

Once Tootsie, the vitamin doctor, and the goblin made their way to the garage, and the gold car rolled out into the night, the crowded thinned.

Slimming man and the raw food lady lingered in the kitchen while she made him some kind of special juice. There was a lot of giggling coming from there. I didn't want to know.

I crept upstairs. That was another minefield, because the dress lady and her assistant stayed behind to clean up and put away their needles and threads and whatever. The jeweler stayed to mess around with the jewelry boxes and I guess to make sure no gems had gone astray. They were preoccupied with chattering about how swell their handiwork looked on Tootsie.

Good. That made it easier to make my way to the clown costumes. Most of the outfits were identical: pale green jumpsuit with puffy black buttons down the front, with matching pale green shoes and pointed hat with another black puff on top. I grabbed one that looked about my size. I found pots of clown face paint in a case nearby. There was a mirror inside the lid of the case, but not a lot of light. If I started clicking on more than the usual dim closet lights, the dress gals and the jeweler would know something was up. So, I made do.

I was no expert on clown paint, seeing as I'd never been able to scrape up enough nickels to go to the circus. I thought clowns had white faces, but this paint was the same pale green as the clown outfits. Must have been a reason for that, so I smeared it on thick. One thing I did know was clowns had dots on their faces. The case had a pot of black face paint too, so I was all set. To be on the safe side, I painted a whole bunch of black dots on my face, with a big dot at the end of my nose. I did remember the nose bit from seeing circus posters downtown, although I thought it was supposed to be a red nose.

I slipped down the steps, past the giggling in the kitchen and out the sunroom doors, into the alley and the night.

I hoped Bobby wouldn't be too mad when he figured out I ditched him.

Chapter 19

The cops were back to prowling around the dark streets of Bunker Hill. Whisper-Whisper must have told them I was on the loose again. There good 'ol Spooky was leaning against his favorite lamppost. He didn't move, but still, I was extra careful making my way down.

Even from the top of the Hill, it wasn't hard to spot the party. The whole area around City Hall was lit up. There were even search lights sweeping back and forth across the sky. It was something else.

When I got to the bottom, I could see all the speakeasys around City Hall were open for business and the well-dressed swells were going in and out. The streets were closed and were packed with the classy set, plus waiters carrying trays of eats that the high-end folks grabbed and stuffed in their snouts.

There were more clowns. None of them had green faces, but maybe there's different types of clowns. One clown was holding up a hoop and little dogs were jumping through it. I saw a lady in a sparkling dress standing with one foot each on the backs of one white and one black horse with feathers on their heads. Wait, over there was a high wire and people hopping around in tights like Mr. Exercise wore. I couldn't believe it. I hardly knew where to look. Over there was a real elephant. Men in tuxedoes and ladies in evening gowns that must have cost a mint were taking turns climbing on a ladder to the elephant's back for a short trot back and forth in front of City Hall.

I decided to make my way over there to see if I could sneak a ride. I confess, the whole reason I came down to this party slipped clean out of my mind. I guess circuses did that to people. Or me, anyway.

My mind got pulled back to reality when I spotted Tootsie.

Hard to miss her sparkles looking a million times brighter under all the lights. She was facing Onion Girl. Onion Girl was decked out in a shiny gold-colored gown. Her neck was weighed down with a bucket load of gems, all paste. Compared to Tootsie's sparklers, they looked doubly fake.

Tootsie and Onion Girl were both wearing their tight smiles and looked like they were trying to talk nice-like. I saw a few flashes from photographers taking their pictures. But it looked like most of the photo hounds were faced the other way, snapping pictures of the Mayor's grinning pretty face on a platform. He had his hand on a llama wearing a banner with his name and "Vote!" Oh, there must've been an election coming up. That's what this circus was really about, not a bunch of poor people.

Mug and some other cops were standing around the platform, guarding the Mayor, I supposed. But Mug looked like he wasn't watching the Mayor, but stared only at the girl in the sparkling dress standing on the two trotting horses.

Not too far from the platform, I spotted Whisper-Whisper. He was busy cooing to some high-rollers in tuxedoes. His big teeth were all a-smiling.

About now, I realized I didn't have a firm idea on what exactly I was planning to do at this circus party. But an idea came to me. I'd confront Whisper-Whisper in public. With all the swells surrounding him, watching him, what could he do to me? And everyone would know he was the real murderer. Sounded like a solid idea.

I marched up to him, pushed through the legs of the swells, and kicked Whisper-Whisper in the shins. The swells started laughing, sloshing the drinks in their hands. "Well, lookie that! Ha, ha. I think that clown likes you."

Whisper-Whisper was quick. Before I could get another kick in and start yelling that he's the murderer, he scooped me up by the arm, my bad arm, and hauled me away from the swells. "Excuse me, gentlemen." They laughed as he dragged me away.

I started yelling anyway, "This guy's the murderer! The murderer!" But I don't think anyone heard me. My arm hurt so bad, I felt tears in my eyes.

He pulled me into the shadows along the side of the Mayor's platform. He hauled me up to his face and shoved me against one of the platform's support posts.

"You don't learn, do you?"

"You killed that girl. She was just a little kid. You didn't have to do it. You could have dumped her in an orphan home or something." Up close, I could see the bruise from my bite on his Adam's apple. His voice sounded hoarse too.

"Bad things happen every day, Sparky. You can either waste your life fretting and worrying about the million sad little tragedies, or you can forget about them. Let them go. You can't do anything to change the world, Sparky. That's just the way things are. Besides, a kid like her, unwanted, abandoned, she'd have ended up dead one way or another anyhow. It hardly matters. Forget about it."

I squirmed and tried kicking him, but he was strong. I was about to holler, but he stuffed his hankie in my mouth. He caught Mug's eye and jerked his chin to signal Mug over.

"We'll put you away somewhere nice and quiet for a while until things blow over. After that, we'll probably keep you there. You cause too much trouble all the way around. Sneaking around dressed as—what are you? A clown with the plague? It's not good for kids to run unattended on the streets. They tend to end up dead." Whisper-Whisper grinned and chuckled. "By coming here, you saved the City from paying out the reward money. Focus on that. You're a good citizen."

This was looking worse and worse for 'ol Sparky. I knew when I was outside my weight class, and I was way outside. Pinned against a post, gag in my mouth, Mug on the way. My number was up.

I turned my eyes toward Tootsie. She was still in a tense smile trade off with Onion Girl. The photographers had lost all interest in them and were snapping pictures of the girl on the horses. I saw the vitamin doctor in the tuxedo standing behind her.

I don't know how, but she must have felt my eyes. She turned and squinted hard in my direction, then squinted harder. Oh, must've needed glasses like Onion Girl but wouldn't wear them either. If my arms weren't pinned, I would've started waving so she'd see me.

I saw her turn her head to say something to the vitamin doctor. He looked toward the side of the platform where Whisper-Whisper had me pinned, and now Mug was in on the act. "Okay, time to go, kid."

The doctor said one word to Tootsie. Was it "Sparky?"

With the photographers not interested anymore, Onion Girl lost interest in Tootsie and was turning away, her hand on the arm of an older man wearing a rug. Must be Dennis' replacement.

Then Tootsie said something to her. I wish I knew what it was, because it made Onion Girl whip around, fury on her face.

Then, I could hardly believe it, Tootsie hauled off and slapped Onion Girl so hard on the face, she stumbled back into the man behind her and his rug slid off.

Onion Girl got back to her feet in a second and jumped at Tootsie, her hands like claws. Tootsie's hands were all over Onion Girl, and they were in a flat-out fight.

The photographers whipped their cameras back to the actresses, and so many bulbs flashed all at once, smoke and noise filled the air.

Whisper-Whisper took this in, said, "Oh, my God!" dropped me like a sack of old potatoes, and took off running toward the fight, but not before grabbing Mug and pulling him along. Mug's face had exactly that lost look he had when the church lady was yelling at him about devils scampering around Bunker Hill. Battling movie stars wasn't something Mug knew what to do about either. But he trotted where Whisper-Whisper pulled him.

I fell hard from Whisper-Whisper's height, which was no joke. I was lucky I didn't break both legs on the street, but it sure felt like I had.

I pulled Whisper-Whisper's hankie out of my mouth and breathed in deep. That helped a little. It still took me too long to get to my feet. I didn't have my pep back from being shot. Whisper-Whisper squeezing my bad arm didn't help matters.

My plan was to slip around the back of the platform, out of sight, and then ditch this crazy scene and make my way back up Bunker Hill. I was way over my head. I was battling City Hall itself. I needed a better plan. I didn't know what, but I'd think about it after I was safe and sound in Creepy House.

I did feel safe there. Look at what Tootsie had done for me. She got into a full-out fight with Onion Girl to save my hide. Tootsie was more than okay. She was a first-class pal. Up there with Bobby. I could hardly believe it. Sparky was a lucky girl. Then again, maybe Tootsie just wanted the news hounds to take pictures. Yeah, that could be it. But maybe she wanted to save me too. Maybe.

My warm and cozy thinking about Tootsie and Bobby were wiped from my mind by movement. There, behind the platform, pretty boy Mayor had a floozy in his arms and was leading her away toward the shadowy alleys around City Hall. She was looking at some paste rocks around her wrist. "These are so beautiful!" Chump. The Mayor handed those fake beads out like cheap candy.

"So are you, doll," the Mayor cooed. "Let's go find someplace nice and quiet where we can have our own little party." She giggled.

This Mayor was some operator.

I decided to follow.

Here was my thinking. Okay, so Sugar the bleach job and Dennis the driver were blackmailing the Mayor, telling him this kid they found was really his from some affair Sugar had with him a few years back. Who knew if Sugar really had, but from how the Mayor seemed to operate with floozies right and left, he probably didn't remember. For all he knew, the kid was his.

This was the question. Did Whisper-Whisper say, hey, I'll take care of the kid for you, send her to some orphan home in trade for a bucketload of the fake jewels? Or did the Mayor suspect Whisper-Whisper was planning to get rid of the little girl in a more permanent kind of way to make sure she wouldn't pop up again, once Sugar tried pawning some of the bum rocks and found out they were fakes?

Or, did the Mayor tell Whisper-Whisper to kill the kid? Nah, I didn't think so. Whisper-Whisper was his handler, his manager. Anything dirty, Whisper-Whisper took care of, with help from his creepy older brother.

I didn't want this to be a wasted trip. I'd get some answers, maybe.

When the Mayor had the floozy in a nice and dark alley with Whisper-Whisper and Mug nowhere in sight, I took my chance.

"Hey!"

They were all wrapped around each other, giggling. The giggling stopped, and the girl turned to look at me. "What's that? Is it from a freak show?"

The Mayor stared at me, open mouthed, trying to figure out what I was and what I was doing there. I clued him in.

"Whaddya know about the dead kid? You know, that cute little girl cold as ice on the Court Hill bench? Huh?"

I guess I was thinking he'd babble, and if I was lucky, babble useful info, maybe finger Whisper-Whisper in a panic.

Didn't happen.

What did happen was something I'd never seen before, and I'd seen lots on the streets and in Bookie's place, let me tell you.

His face changed. Completely. Just like that. One second, the empty-looking pretty boy face, and then next, this twisted mask with black eyes like a cat gone crazy.

He shoved floozy to the ground. Her paste bracelet broke and the fake stones shattered. One smashed under her foot.

I turned to take off. I wished I could've moved like my old self, but still, I thought I was moving fast enough.

Mayor was faster. He grabbed me around my neck and head. What was he doing? He was trying to twist my head, break my neck!

The floozy jumped on his back and tried pulling him away. "Hey! Hey! It's just some little punk. Let the kid go!"

He growled. He really growled, and shoved her back down to the slime and trash and broken paste beads on the alley ground. She scrambled up and took off running.

This gave me just a moment to do something. My bum arm was free, so I reached up and shoved my fingers at one of his eyes.

He threw me off onto the hard ground, kicked me, then grabbed me again. I tried shoving against him with the bottoms of my feet, but he was way out of my weight class.

He dragged me to a manhole cover, then shoved it partly open with one hand. Strong guy. I didn't have a chance against this one. He stood, holding me by one ankle and kicked and kicked that manhole cover until it was all the way open.

I tried grabbing his leg, but he shook me off. I was more than hollering. I was screaming. At this point, I'd take Whisper-Whisper, I'd sure take Mug. I'd take Bookie, anybody, any rat. This guy was going to drop me down the hole.

He dangled me over the opening. I could smell the sewer down far, far below.

"Like it?" he said. "Want more?"

He let go of my ankle and I fell, but just as fast, he grabbed my other ankle. He laughed, low and quiet.

As I fell, I had just enough time to grab the edge of the manhole. I held on tight, my fingers like iron prongs.

"How long do you think you can hold on, Sparky? I'll drop your foot, and then I'll stomp on each of your fingers, one at a time, crushing them into bloody meat. Then you won't have anything to hold on with. You'll drop and drop, and on the way down, you'll think about me."

This guy was nuts. Even more nuts than bad man. I didn't know what to do except hang on tight, as long as my fingers held out, and keep screaming as long as my voice held out.

I saw movement in the shadows. Another green clown. Could it be Bobby?

Without thinking, I started hollering, "Bobby! Help!" As soon as it left my mouth, I knew it was a mistake. Bobby couldn't fight the Mayor any better than I could. We'd both end up dead, at the bottom of the sewer. We'd be washed away to the sea and no one would ever find us. Tough 'ol Sparky no more. I started to cry.

Bobby came running out of the darkness straight toward the Mayor. The Mayor let go of my ankle and I fell hard against the side of the manhole. I felt my fingers slipping, but they held. Good 'ol fingers!

Bobby hollered louder than I'd ever heard him, and his fists went flying at the Mayor. Bobby, sure, he's bigger than me and stronger, but no match for a strong grown-up like the Mayor. A crazy grown-up.

The Mayor grabbed Bobby around the head and neck like he'd done to me. I could see him stuffing a fine silk hankie into Bobby's mouth. Bobby was kicking like a first-class machine at the Mayor, but it wasn't doing any good. He was choking. Oh, no.

With my feet and my good arm, I was able to haul myself out of the manhole. If me and Bobby were both going to take the big hike in a permanent kind of way, we might as well do it together. And go down fighting.

I ran against the Mayor's legs, trying to throw him off balance, get him down. He did fall to one knee, almost into the manhole. This gave Bobby a chance to get his head out of the Mayor's hands. He pulled and coughed the hankie out of his throat, then scrambled around to the Mayor's back and starting pounding with all he had.

But I could tell the Mayor wouldn't stay down. He was already getting up, growling. He grabbed me by my bum arm, and then fell back onto Bobby, knocking the wind out of him. He grabbed Bobby's ankle and hauled him and me to the edge of the manhole. This was it. We were going down.

"There he is! Mayor's gone crazy!"

It was the floozy. How about that? And with her, was Mug.

When Mug wants to, he can move fast. He was all over the Mayor. Sure that was nice, but that made the Mayor drop me and Bobby. We both almost fell straight down into the manhole. We grabbed the edges and each other and were able to hang on. Good ol' floozy helped pull us out.

That was close, real close. But it wasn't over yet.

The Mayor was kicking Mug. "You're fired! I'll see you

clapped in irons! I'll see you floating down the river!"

"There, there, Mr. Mayor. There, there."

The Mayor might be a grown-up and a crazy wild one, but this time, he'd more than met his match. Mug pinned the Mayor's arms behind his back easy as you please, like he was a doll.

While Mug was dealing with the Mayor, the floozy was down on all fours, gathering up the beads from her broken bracelet. She picked up a half-smashed one. I heard her mutter, "Hey, what's this? Aw, nuts!" Then she threw the beads on the ground.

"You! Broad! Beat it!" That was Mug.

"Yeah, yeah. Thanks for nothing." She took off limping down the alley. I saw one of her heels was broken and her dress was torn. And not even some real rocks to show for it.

At least she'd come back with Mug to help a pitiful kid in trouble. Not many would have done the same. "Hey, thanks, lady!" I called after her. That was the least I could do. She waved her hand without looking back. Some people in this crazy world were okay.

Mug stared at me. My clown hat was gone and I'm sure half the green paint was off my face. I could tell he recognized me. "You. Get lost, you and your pal. Get lost and keep getting lost until you get lost some more." When we didn't move, he bent forward and yelled in our faces, "Scram!"

Bobby helped me up, gent that he was, and we took off running. "Wait," I whispered when we were around the corner. I peeked back into the alley and Bobby peeked too. There Mug was, frog marching the Mayor. "There, there. We'll get you a nice hot toddy. Hot toddy and your blankie and everything will be all right." The Mayor snarled and kept barking about firing Mug and "every useless bum that doesn't know I'm the Mayor! I'm the boss! You do what I say!"

"I know where Gilbert and the car are," Bobby said. "Let's go there and hide in the back seat." I could see he was limping, and I was too. But we made our way as fast as we could to the edge of the party, to where all the high-class automobiles were parked, drivers standing at the ready.

On the way, I filled Bobby in on what happened: Whisper-Whisper pinning me to the Mayor's platform, then Tootsie saving the day with her Onion Girl fight.

"I saw all the flashes from the cameras and heard shouting," Bobby said, "but I didn't know what was going on. Tootsie saved you."

"And you saved me, Bobby." I knew I'd get mad at myself later for telling Bobby this, by the soft way he looked at me. But it was the truth. He did save me.

When we reached the cars, we crawled low between the big wheels and bigger bumpers until we got to Gilbert. He was looking toward the lights, trying to see what the deal was with all the popping flashbulbs.

"Gilbert," Bobby whispered.

The goblin looked down and saw us. "What happened! You look terrible! Oh, my! In the front seat."

He hustled us in the auto. He pulled some hankies out of a drawer in the back seat, along with a bottle of what smelled like Tootsie's rose water. He doused the hankies and then wiped our faces and hands. Don't know if that helped much, but it sure smelled swell.

"We wait until Doctor comes, and then he will help you more. What happened? Did you have a fight with that Dennis?"

"No, it was the Mayor," I said. "He's the one who killed that girl. He's loony."

"A danger to society," Bobby agreed.

There wasn't time to give more details, because Tootsie showed up with the doctor behind her. Her hair was mussed, her wrap torn, and her gown as well.

But she had on a huge smile and beamed brighter than all the lights in that party.

"Oh, Gilbert, the press! Their cameras were going wild! Photos, photos, photos! Me and Sally got into a cat fight you can't believe!"

Now Gilbert lit up ten times more than the party. "A fight! Beautiful! You will be in the papers! I know it!"

"You are sure right, Gilbert!" she said as she slid into the back seat.

The doctor got in the back with her. "You'll be splashed in the newspapers most certainly," he told her, his strange little smile on his face.

She leaned back in the seat and closed her eyes, smiling. "Oh, isn't fame just too much sometimes? I miss it. I miss it so much. For so long, I wished it would go away. Then, it was gone, and there was nothing there. Nothing. A big lot of empty nothing. But, now I can taste it again. I can feel it."

Tootsie stopped yammering about fame suddenly, was quiet for a pause, and then said, "Sparky? Has anyone seen her?"

"Not to worry, Mademoiselle!" Gilbert said quick like. "She

is right here with me and her little boyfriend and both are fine. Perfectly fine." Boyfriend? What was goblin playing at?

Still, I sat up so Tootsie could see me over the seat back, then I turned around and waved to let her know I was okay. Bobby did too.

"Ah, see. Fine," the doctor said to Tootsie in his extra-soothing voice, the voice he never used on me.

Because it was night, Tootsie couldn't see the state Bobby and I were in until we got to the garage and Gilbert flicked on the garage lights.

"Oh, my. Clowns?" She paused and squinted to get a better look. "But what happened? You're hurt?" She turned and looked at the doctor. "I thought they were okay?"

Her happy face was melting. She looked angry and worried at the same time. I didn't want to see that happen, and I don't think Bobby did either. I saw Gilbert give us a nervous look. The doctor kept his face cool.

"We're completely fine. We were investigating, you know. Always investigating. And, yeah, I guess we wanted to see you and the press. Say, you gave me the break I needed when you hauled off and smacked Onion Girl. You saved me from a real pickle. And, wow! You got some good throws at that Onion Girl! The crowd went bananas."

"Absolutely bananas," Bobby agreed.

"Yes, they did, didn't they? So many people. So much press." She looked like she was trying to smile again, but, "Sparky, that man. He was trying to hurt you."

"Come, time to rest. You've had an eventful evening," the doctor said quietly. I saw him give a warning eye toward me and Bobby, like we'd better shut up.

The doctor hustled Tootsie back upstairs. Then he came down for a few minutes to help Gilbert patch and clean us up. They dealt with Bobby first, so he could sneak back home, and hopefully not make his parents call a five-engine alarm.

The doctor trotted back upstairs to Tootsie. Gilbert tucked me into bed and put Clara Bell on one side of the bed and the flat leopard on the other. I held Clara Bell's tail tight.

"I am so happy for Tootsie tonight," he said, "but I worry about this business with the Mayor. We will talk about it more later. Now you must rest."

My mind was whirling at a hundred miles an hour. What were we going to do now? The Mayor had power. Not Bookie power, not Mug power, or even movie star power. He had real power. No kidding, like Gilbert said, this was something to worry about.

Chapter 20

The last thing I thought before I finally drifted to dreamland was Bobby. Annoying as he was sometimes, that kid saved my life. Good 'ol Bobby. I'll never know why he thought so much of me. No one else did.

Wait a minute. Scratch that. Maybe nowadays, I had a couple more people who were okay with me. Hard to believe. Didn't know if they actually, really cared about me, but they seemed okay with me. At least for now. And that was something. A strange something. But there it was.

The next morning, sure enough, the newspapers were thick with screaming headlines—front page, don't ya' know—about "Movie Star Madness!"

Tootsie wasn't usually downstairs early for breakfast, since she didn't eat breakfast, but now she was in the kitchen. Her and Gilbert were turning the pages, looking at the dozens of photos and reading. The doctor came in with more papers with more photos and stories.

"Look, so much cleavage! You can see a ton of my cleavage, right?"

"Oh, most definitely," from Gilbert. "You are nearly spilling out. And here, more photos. You are so slim. So like a girl. Your gown—here is an entire article about how much it is of the latest fashion. And here, a department store promises to copy it. A cheap version, for fans to buy."

"Oh, fans. They can be too much. I hope I won't be overwhelmed."

But she smiled the whole time, and Gilbert and the doctor smiled, so I was sure she'd survive. Of course, they had to find fault with every one of Onion Girl's photos. "She looks like a has-been. Like yesterday's news. A complete cow!" Tootsie said. I don't know about that, but I wasn't going to say a peep to spoil

Tootsie's fun.

None of them mentioned the Mayor being the killer, but I didn't blame them. I suspected it'd been a long time, probably years, since Tootsie was in the papers.

Funny thing was, the big Mayor photo that was always on every front page, wasn't. No Mayor, not even a little tiny picture. Real funny.

Tootsie noticed I was rustling through the papers too. She sat back and gave me a steady stare.

"Hey, thanks again, Tootsie. You saved my hide," I said, hoping she wouldn't quiz me too much. Last thing I needed was her hunting down Whisper-Whisper with her stocking full of jewels. Maybe she could whap his brother, but Whisper-Whisper was a lot more dangerous. And powerful.

She grinned. "I should be thanking you," and she waved her hand at all the newspapers scattered around the table. "But, Sparky, are you sure you're okay?"

"Sure, fine."

She kept giving me her steady stare. Tootsie wasn't buying it.

"Oh! Onion Girl looks like your grandmother in this photo," the doctor said, smile sly. I knew he was only trying to distract Tootsie from my latest trouble, and it worked like a charm. Her head whipped around and, "Where! Lemme see!" Back into the papers she went.

Eleven o'clock came and went and no sign of Bobby. I wondered if his parents did finally get wise to his comings and goings. While the big people were busy gushing over the papers, I slipped away.

I did my usual sneaking through the back ways until I was in the bushes along the edge of his backyard. I waited for a while. My legs were plenty stiff from all the crazy goings-on yesterday, and they only got stiffer sitting in the twigs and leaves. I started thinking maybe this was a bad idea, when I heard the click of the back door and there Bobby was, book in hand. His face was bruised from tangling with the Mayor last night. Mine was too, but that's kind of normal for me.

He looked at the bushes. He heard me say, "Psst!" then sat next to where I was hiding.

He opened his book and spoke like he was reading from it. "I'm under house arrest. My parents discovered that I'd stuffed blankets and clothes on my bed to make it look like I was sleeping there. They were up waiting for me when I got back, late. They were not happy. I told them I was making a study of the night sky, but they didn't believe me. They think I'm joining street kid fights. They are very disappointed with me. I can go only as far as the backyard until further notice. No exceptions. I'm sorry."

"Hey, don't be sorry. I'd be a broken rag doll at the bottom of the sewers if it weren't for you. You saved my life."

He moved his eyes to look at me, then looked away, blushing.

Well, how about that?

Like I said, I'd probably be mad at myself later for blabbing all this sugar talk.

"Thanks," he said, a little crackle in his voice, though I could tell he was trying to pretend like saving my life was no big deal for the likes of Bobby. "I have to say I was feeling worried yesterday, like maybe you didn't want me to go with you. I came back to Creepy House early and kept watch. After most of those hair and whatever they are people left, I snuck back in and followed you up to Tootsie's closets. I saw where you went to get the clown costumes. After you left, I put on one too."

Bobby followed me through Creepy House and I didn't notice? Either I was getting really soft, or Bobby was getting to be a smooth operator, creeping around quiet as a cat. I was impressed.

"Sorry for ditching you, but I didn't want you to get in the trouble I'm in."

"Sparky, I told you I'll take the hangman's noose for you if it comes to that."

I didn't feel like going further along this line of talk, since it usually led to him jabbering about how we're going to get married and all that baloney. I decided to change the subject fast, to something we needed to talk about anyway.

"The Mayor's gotta be the one who killed the kid, don't you think?"

"I agree. He acted like a guilty murderer."

"I think after the Mayor killed the kid, Whisper-Whisper probably took her up to Court Hill for his brother to bury or toss in the incinerator."

"Brother?"

Whoops. I forgot I kept my trips to Court Hill secret from Bobby. He was going to get mad, but, too late, I'd spilled the beans on myself. Time to confess. But I didn't have to confess to everything. I admitted only that I saw Whisper-Whisper next to bad man and how much alike they looked, and how bad man was demanding more money from Whisper-Whisper.

"Sparky, I will tell you again. You must stay away from Court Hill. If you must go there again, I go with you. Understand?"

"Sure, yeah."

"See what happened when you went to the Circus for the Poor all by yourself? I need to be on hand to protect you, Sparky."

This was what I didn't like about Bobby: the lecturing, telling me what to do, thinking he's my boss. I wanted to tell him off. But we needed to figure out what to do with the Mayor first. Later, I'd give him a big ol' piece of my mind. Even if he had saved my life.

"Bad man wanted more money, so he didn't get rid of the kid right away. That's why I found her."

"I think that's exactly what happened. But we can't rule out Dennis the driver. He could have driven all night from Palm Springs, helped Whisper-Whisper with the girl, and then really floored it to get back to Palm Springs before Onion Girl noticed he was gone."

"Yeah. He had no problems borrowing her car the night we chased him. Who knows how much he was sneaking away from Palm Springs all the time? He might have been by that Hollywood duplex a bunch of times looking for his money before we tailed him. And hey, I'll bet Whisper-Whisper had Dennis drive the dead girl up from City Hall to Court Hill alone, so no one would know Whisper-Whisper was involved. Now that he doesn't need his help anymore, maybe Whisper-Whisper's been giving Dennis the bum's rush about paying, and that's why Dennis went to Sugar looking for the dough."

"That sounds right. Your Mug probably is involved with covering up the crime too. The way he marched the Mayor away, it made me think he's had to calm the Mayor down, keep his insane behavior under wraps, more than a few times."

"That's for sure. But how do we tell the cops the Mayor is the killer when the cops are involved too?"

"I've been thinking: we take this to the press. I will write a letter detailing the crime, naming the parties involved. I'll need you to mail the letters, since I'm under house arrest, as I said."

"I think the press will eat up the story. Yeah! I'll mail those letters."

"Just be careful. Mug will still be on the lookout for you. Maybe even more now because we saw what the Mayor is really like."

We made a plan to meet again at Bobby's backyard late in the afternoon. By then, Bobby would have his letters ready to all the newspapers he knew about, complete with stamped envelopes. One thing I could say, Bobby was good with particulars. He had some fine handwriting too, fine enough so the papers would think the letters came from a grown-up. It's a bad situation that newspapers and grown-ups in general don't believe what kids say.

Since neither of us knew what Whisper-Whisper's, bad man's, or Mug's real names were, he said he'd call them, "the Mayor's special handler," "the Court Hill man of known ill repute," and "the Mayor's special police officer protector." He said anyone familiar with City Hall and Bunker Hill should know who we're talking about. Sounded good to me.

Of course, he'd sign the letters "Anonymous." We agreed Mug probably didn't know which kid was the other green clown, so it was best to keep it that way. "Besides, if my parents find out I'm writing letters to newspapers about the Mayor being a killer, I think I'll be under house arrest for the rest of my life."

Back at Creepy House, the big people were still going through the newspapers and cooing. The jeweler was there. He'd taken the gems in Tootsie's hair and on her wrap from bigger pieces, like huge brooches and bracelets. Now he was busy putting all the sparklers back together again. There was a tense moment when he thought some gems were lost from when a bunch hit the street after Onion Girl grabbed Tootsie's hair. But the doctor had been sharp about scooping them up as soon as they fell. So, when the doctor emptied all his pockets on Tootsie's kitchen table, he found the little ones hiding in the corners.

Or maybe—ha, ha—he planned to keep the little gems hiding in his pocket corners if the jeweler hadn't noticed they were missing. But, I couldn't think too deep about that. I was on pins and needles waiting to get the letters from Bobby.

I couldn't take it anymore, so I cut out early and waited in the bushes for Bobby. By luck, he came out early too. He pulled out a stack of letters he had hidden in a huge old dictionary and slid them to me. "Be careful," he said. And then if he didn't slip a kiss! Lucky for me, it only reached me half way because of the iron fence posts and all the twigs between me and his puckering. Time for Sparky to take off.

I was extra careful. I was sure the Hill would be thick with a billion cops on the double-lookout for me. I saw a few, but that was it. Strange, but they could be hiding, trying to trick me. I kept my guard up when I slipped the letters into a mailbox on an empty side street.

That night, I could barely go to sleep. I knew the headlines would scream the next morning about the murdering Mayor, and I'd be cleared. If I was lucky, maybe some of the papers would even print apologies for their smear campaign against me. Starting the Great War? Killing millions of people? Come on. I wonder if Whisper-Whisper dreamed that up. Probably.

I felt bad about kicking Tootsie out of the front pages, but, hey, she had a good newspaper day. Now it was my turn.

The next morning told me: "Not so fast, Sparky."

I ran to the kitchen as soon as my eyes popped open. Whaddya know, but Tootsie was up early again. Her and Gilbert and the doctor were around the kitchen table again, leafing through the newspapers.

"Hey, let me see some papers too!"

Gilbert laughed and gave me some. "I tell you, Mademoiselle, she is such a little fan."

Tootsie smiled and tousled my hair. "Oh, Sparky. I'm hoping the studios will start calling again. I'm so bored not working. I want to be back in pictures so bad, it's like I've been starving for years." She moved her hand to touch a bruise on my face. She frowned. "You are a puzzle," she said to me. "You really are Mysteeree, aren't you?"

"The studios will call. You will see," Gilbert said, which drew Tootsie back to talk of studios and luckily rescued me from her quizzing.

While they were gabbing, I tore through the papers. Lots about what Tootsie wore, again, what Onion Girl wore, again, an interview with Onion Girl, gossip about her million and one husbands, a poem Tootsie once wrote about Paris, a picture of Clara Bell and the flat leopard when they were both still alive and living in Paris.

Yeah, nice, but the Mayor? The killer Mayor?

Nothing.

I traded that rag with the one the doctor was reading, then with the one Tootsie was reading.

Nothing. Nothing. Nothing.

Not even a big grinning Mayor photo, same as yesterday. Strange. But otherwise, nothing.

Maybe it was too soon. Yeah, that must be it. Come on, I only mailed the letters yesterday afternoon. I had too many ants in my pants. All I needed to do was wait for the afternoon papers.

That was some long wait. I stretched out on my bed and

flipped through one of the picture books Gilbert gave me, my favorite with the little girl and boy and their happy home. I usually got lost in it, but today, I had trouble paying attention. I twisted Clara Bell's tail so hard without even realizing it, for a minute there, I thought I'd made it snap in half. It was a bit bent, but mostly okay.

I thought about sneaking over to Bobby's place, but I worried he'd try kissing me again. Nah, I'd wait. That's all I needed to do.

A bunch of Tootsie's people came rushing back for some sort of emergency. The hair ladies were there, the face ladies, the dress lady and her assistant, the slimming man and the raw food lady, plus the spiritual man. Gilbert's face was bright red and pouring sweat while he ran around the downstairs, dusting, straightening.

All the running back and forth and shouting took my mind off the newspapers for a bit. What was up?

A truck pulled in front of the house. A pair of beefy guys carrying furniture came inside, along with a thin man who got into serious discussions with Gilbert about where this new furniture should go. I spied on the show from my hiding spot behind one of the huge Chinese vases.

"Everything is wrong! Everything is last decade! It is too overdone, too ornate. The modern look is sleek, like a greyhound, like the most exquisite ocean liner. All this must go!"

"That is too much change for Mademoiselle. She rather likes all her things. I am not so sure," Gilbert said, frowning.

"Think of what the reporter will see! Think of what the reporter will write in the papers! Do you want him to say that she is a doomed recluse living in a sad museum from the silent pictures?"

"Please, not so loud. Yes, you have many points. We will think up something. Let me think..."

It took a lot of thinking and more shouting, and then the doctor came down and put in his two cents. Finally, they figured out what to do.

The sunroom was the only place with "actual light" because the widows weren't all colored glass. "Light is modern!" from the thin man.

The beefy guys cleared everything out of the sunroom and hauled it down to the cellar. That caused me a fright when the guys got to the vase I was crouching behind, but I was able to scramble away in time and hide behind the velvet drapes hanging around one of Tootsie's portraits in the hallway. Then I had to scramble away from the velvet because the thin man decided the hallway had to be emptied out too.

It was getting too dicey inside the house, so I darted outside, and watched the happenings from behind jungle leaves in Tootsie's garden.

"There must be a clear path of modern design from the front door all the way to this sunroom. Everything else must be cleared and what we cannot clear, we will block with screens and light colored, modern fabric hangings."

More beefy guys showed up and another thin man who was the first thin man's assistant. There was more shouting, "Hurry! Hurry! This reporter will be here any minute!" from both thin men.

All the vases, the chairs, the tables, the statues, the peacock feathers, the bookshelves went down into the cellar. The beefy guys got on ladders and tacked yards and yards of billowing white cloth where the ceiling met the wall, and let it fall loose all the way to the floor. Then they tacked more on the ceiling because that was painted in colorful patterns too. "Loosely! No! Loose! Like a tennis tent!" I didn't know what a tennis tent was and from the looks the guys gave the thin men, they didn't know either. But after a lot of trial and error and shouting, they got it right.

Then the guys dragged in a huge white carpet and rolled it to cover the layers of Tootsie's multicolored rugs. With the thin men pointing directions, they set down a white sofa, a pair of white chairs, and what looked like a clear glass table smack dab in the middle of the white rug.

The room looked so different, I could hardly believe it.

"Tootsie must understand, this is only temporary. As soon as the reporter goes, all of this goes," Gilbert said to the doctor.

"Yes, I'll talk to her," and the doctor disappeared, probably to find Tootsie.

Then Gilbert was hustling the thin men and the beefy guys out of the house. "The reporter must not see you! He will be here right now!"

Almost as soon as the thin men and crew were gone, Gilbert went rushing toward the front, and came back to the sunroom, not with a man, but with a woman in a blue suit and little blue cap-like hat perched on her head. She had a notebook. The reporter.

"Please, Madam," and he showed her to one of the chairs. "Miss LaFemme will be down soon. Shall I find you something to drink?"

"Nah, that's fine. Thanks. I'll just keep myself company here." She yawned and leaned back.

It was no "soon." It was a good half hour, at least, before Gilbert came back with Tootsie.

She was wearing the same beach outfit she wore when we went to Onion Girl's house. Same hair, same face paint too. She was all smiles. She took both the reporter's hands in hers like they were old pals, and then made herself at home on the white sofa. From how she sat, I could tell she was being careful to keep her brown-painted hands from smearing the white sofa.

If she was shocked at how her sunroom changed, I couldn't see it. Cool as cucumbers. Now that's some acting.

"It's so wonderful that you could stop by and visit me."

"Yeah, part of my job, ya' know. Nice place you got here."

"Why thank you. You're so sweet." Tootsie's eyes looked around the room, but quick. "My inspiration for the look is the ocean. Sun on the sand. I wanted it to be simple, clean."

"That's the style nowadays, or so I hear. You look different from your movies. That on purpose?"

"My look is a reflection of how I've been feeling. I've been spending a lot of time outdoors lately, at the beach, catching the sun. It's a healthy life."

"You look like you've gotten some sun. Say, what'd'ya think of the things Onion Girl said about you? That ya' wouldn't'a had a career if not for her discovering you and all that?"

Tootsie laughed.

This was going to go on all day. I could tell. Or at least longer than I wanted to wait. I needed to see the afternoon papers.

I slipped through Tootsie's jungle and made my way back to Bobby's yard. The second I saw his face, I knew it was bad news.

Chapter 21

Bobby moved so he sat close to where I was hiding in the bushes on the other side of his backyard fence. This time, he wasn't puckering up for kissing. He was frowning.

"It's here," he whispered, holding up the afternoon edition. But the front page had the same baloney about Tootsie and Onion Girl's fight. And no photo of the Mayor kissing a puppy or a baby, or cooling his heels behind bars. Nothing.

Bobby flipped and flipped the pages until he was almost to the last page.

"Wait a minute. Murdering Mayor gets buried in the back?" I said.

"Shh!" Bobby's eyes darted to his house. His parents must be prowling near the windows. "It says that the unidentified girl found dead of tuberculosis weeks ago on Court Hill was a runaway from a children's home."

"TB? Wait a minute. That's not what they said before."

"Keep it down. It says, 'Let this serve as a lesson for all disobedient children who are considering running away.'"

"That doesn't make any sense."

"Hold on. There's more." Bobby ran his finger down lower on the page. "It says the Mayor contracted tuberculosis and will be going on an extended rest cure. It's not known when he'll come back."

"Is there anything about me?"

"Not a peep." Bobby turned the paper around so I could see how small the blurbs were about the Mayor and the little girl. And no photos.

"That isn't right. The Mayor is just wiggling out of this."

"I know, Sparky. I know."

Then there were sounds like someone moving around in

the house. "Bobby? Who are you talking to?"

Bobby shoved the newspaper against the fence and then trotted back into the house. "Coming, Mama."

I waited until I heard the back screen door close with the soft click. Then I waited a bit more before I reached my hand through the bushes and iron fence posts to grab the newspaper. I took off.

I hid in another yard behind a bin for garbage scraps. I looked over the newspaper top to bottom, right to left, and stared at both those blurbs until I felt like my eyes were burning through the paper. I wasn't much of a reader, I'd admit that to you. But I understood enough. A minute ago, I was a crazed murderer that needed to be rounded up. Now? There was no murder, and everybody suddenly got the TB.

If there was no murder, then I couldn't be wanted, right? I decided to test this out. I wandered openly down the sidewalks. I passed Spook leaning against the lamppost, which didn't have my wanted poster anymore. Spook didn't move, but that's normal for him.

Then I spotted Mug. I tiptoed up behind him nice and easy, then hauled off and whapped his back end with the rolled-up newspaper as hard as I could.

Mug may be big, but he's a fast one. He spun around like a crazy top, club in one hand, and the other was like a claw ready to grab. When he saw me, he looked so mad, I could almost see the steam come pouring outta his ears. But he didn't do a thing, like he'd lost his bad dog license all of a sudden.

"You! Beat it!"

"Not 'till you tell me what's going on with this TB baloney. If that girl died of TB, how come I was a wanted murderer? How come the Mayor has TB now too?"

"Scram or I'll haul you in for..." he gave me a quick look up and down, "walking around barefoot in public!"

His claw hand made a grab toward me. I hopped back, just out of reach. "Where's my candy box? Did you give it to the bad man? Did you? He said he had it!"

His eyes were burning, but looked a little confused. And then in a second, his eyes popped, and I could tell he realized what I was talking about. Mug made a growling sound, but like he was buying time. Hmm.

"You ate my candy!"

Make no mistake, the look swimming past his face looked like pure guilt to me.

"You owe me candy!"

He roared, "That does it! You're coming in!" He lunged at me.

I got the message and took off running.

I ran to the alley behind Marigold's house. That horse was hanging its head out of its horse house. It flattened its ears and snapped its teeth at me. I kept my distance and peeked over Marigold's fence.

There he was playing with big wooden blocks painted all different colors. They looked new. Let me tell you, Marigold had all the best toys, lots better than those fat dictionaries Bobby's parents dumped on him.

"Psst!"

Marigold looked up and instead of being happy to see me, his eyes popped like he got a seat in the electric chair. "Go away! I'm not supposed to talk to you!"

"It's okay. I'm not a murderer anymore. The newspaper says the girl died of TB." I waved the newspaper.

"I know that. I still can't talk to you. You're a bad girl and you're a bad affluent, or something like that."

"I'm not leaving until you tell me what's going on."

His eyes popped wider. "I told you everything I know about the driver. Go away! My mom got all suspicious last time you were here."

"What happened to him, the driver? Did he come around here?"

"No! Uncle Bob got mad because he heard that guy ditched the job he got him with Onion Girl after he tried stealing her car. Uncle Bob said he probably hopped a train out of town or something. He said with his pretty face, he'll find himself another sugar mama, or sugar daddy soon enough. That's all I know!"

Then Marigold started crying. That's the thing about Marigold. He's kind of a baby.

That devil horse started stamping its feet and snorting. It glared at me.

Sounds from the house, and a mom-type voice, "Marigold?"

Then another voice, "Who the hell's there! What the hell's going on!" Old Bob.

Time to scram.

I passed a group of kids I used to play with. I saw the twerp who yelled for the cops when this whole mess started. He spotted me and started singing, "Murderer! There goes murdering

Sparky skipping down the road!" The rest of them laughed.

I owed the bunch of them a punch to the guts and a knock to the snout. But I had other plans. So I only lunged at them with a big, "Boo!" That shut them up, for now.

Then I took off running to my Bookie. He was the real test. If he didn't care about turning me in for reward money anymore, then I knew for sure I was in the clear.

Bold as a brass button, I strolled in through the five and dime to the back room that my Bookie used as his office. Oh, sure, all the eyes in the store stared at me, but no one said a thing, did a thing. When I stepped on Bookie's rug, the squeaker under it made its loud mouse toy sound so he knew someone was coming.

"Look who's here. Our little Spark." Bookie grinned at me when I stepped into his office like nothing was amiss. I could tell by the hunched way he was sitting behind his desk that he'd pulled his piece out and was hiding it in his lap in case the visitor stepping on his squeaky rug wasn't a kid like me. He relaxed, sat back and laid his shooter on his desk. It was a new one I hadn't seen before, bigger.

"You ratted me out." I gave him my hard look.

"Aw, come on. I gave you the tip that got you in the clear. You should say thanks."

"I almost got caught. You said you didn't care if my little feet were twitching at the end of a rope!" I started feeling the tears in my eyes, in my voice. I had to stay steady. Tough girls don't start sobbing.

He laughed. He actually laughed. "Don't cry, Sparky."

"I'm not!"

"Fine. Listen, I knew you'd wiggle out of that one. And you did. So, no harm done, huh?"

He reached across his desk and tweaked my nose, and smiled at me and crinkled his black eyes, only just a little, but still. He'd never done that to me before.

He had a point. He did get me the clue that led me to Onion Girl, the bleached blonde, the Mayor, that got me in the clear. And I did get away from Mug, but that was thanks to the dog-goat outfit, not Bookie.

"Yeah, but if I didn't get away, you made sure you'd get my reward money."

He shrugged. "So?"

Nothing I could say to that.

He leaned back in his chair again. "Another thing. If you sneak up on me like you did before," and he moved a thumb behind him to the barred window above his chair, a window I noticed was covered with sheet metal now, "I'll plug you full of holes, and then I'll add a few more holes in case you didn't get the message the first time. Got it, girlie?"

His smile was gone. No more crinkle in the black eyes. That's my Bookie.

"Got it."

"Good."

I turned to go. "Well, I'll see you around then. Just stopped by to let you know you're a rat." But I said this in my friendly voice, to let him know I was kind of being okay with him now. Kind of.

"Oh, ho, ho, Sparky. Aren't you forgetting something?"

Forgetting what? Oh, right. That.

"I own you. I own you until all your costs and expenses and trouble and whatever else I can think of is reimbursed to me in full. And don't forget the interest." He must have seen my face sinking because he chuckled. "Remember that lunch I bought you in Chinatown? That was some expensive chop suey. It's on your tab now."

"Hey! That was a cheap joint. There were flies all over the place."

He gave me his extra hard look. "I don't like that you called me a rat too. That adds to your tab." He picked up a thick envelope from his desk and threw it at me. I caught it, like old days. "Run this over to Chum-Chum's place. Be quick about it."

I stood there not moving.

"Well? Whatcha waiting for, huh? I have lots more for you to do. Lots and lots. I own you. Don't forget it, Spark." He glared at me some more and then barked, "Scram!"

Don't need to tell me twice. Off I ran.

Chum-Chum operated out of one of the speakeasies by City Hall. So, I could take care of this package, and do some more snooping around while I was in the neighborhood.

As I strolled nice and easy down my Hill to City Hall, I made a mistake of passing by the church that had me pegged as the horned devil. "There she is! The demon girl! Help! Help! She's attacking!"

Okay, maybe I did throw a rock, but that's only after the screaming started.

I ran past Mug. "Hey, you!" But, too late, the angry church folk were coming fast toward him. Last I looked back, he'd taken off in the opposite direction, trying to escape them. Ho, ho. I kept running.

Down at City Hall, the usual cops were hanging around. They ignored me.

Chum-Chum was in the back of his speakeasy doing his usual talking to his goldfish in his baby voice. "How's my girl? How's my baby doll today?"

He noticed me when I dropped Bookie's package on his desk. Chum-Chum's desk was always so full of papers and stacks of money and half eaten sandwiches, I knew Bobby would want to start cleaning it up like it was an emergency. Not that I'd want Bobby to know I was in places like Chum-Chum's.

"Well, look who's back in business? Yeah, I heard there was an interesting boat going floating down the river." And he started making his weird laugh, like a cross between a horse and a baby. "Hear that doll, an interesting boat!" He was talking to his goldfish again, so I took off.

I walked into the City Hall car park like I owned the place. José popped out from behind his stand. "Get out of here! It's dangerous!"

"I'm in the clear. The girl died of TB. Don't you read the papers?"

"Get out! Now!"

Too late. José looked up and shut his mouth. I turned and saw what he was staring at. Whisper-Whisper. That guy walked in like he owned the place. In his case, he really did.

"It's okay. I'll have her leave. She won't come around here no more."

"Beat it." Whisper-Whisper said this so low and soft to José, I barely heard it. Next thing I knew, Whisper-Whisper grabbed me by my bum arm. I yelped.

"Come on now, I'll make sure she goes." José was pleading.

Whisper-Whisper leaned in close to José's face. Next to José, you could see how much taller Whisper-Whisper was. He loomed over José. He still had a red mark on his Adam's apple where I bit him. He was probably still mad at me about that.

"Beat it." He whispered, but José jerked back like he'd been whipped with a pipe. José took off running.

About now, I was realizing it was a big mistake to come here, strolling straight into the lion's mouth. The mouth was about to come snapping down on me.

But I couldn't stop. "So, what's this baloney about TB? Why isn't the Mayor behind bars?"

"You're not too bright, are you?" He was still whispering. He hauled me up by my bum arm until his nose was in my face. Boy, did my arm hurt. But I wasn't stopping.

"You're covering everything up, because you had Dennis drive the kid up to Court Hill for your brother to bury. But your brother wasn't fast enough, so I found her instead. You could swing for that. Being an accomplice. That's what you are."

"You don't know when to shut up, do you?"

Bookie's told me the same, so I supposed it was probably true.

"It's gotten to a point," he whispered, "where what you know outweighs anything else. Not that you really know anything. But, there's too many foolish hearts in this world. Too many soft souls. There should have been two floating down the river this morning."

"That what happened to Dennis the driver? He's floating down the river? I wonder what will happen when Onion Girl finds out and complains to the Mayor. Huh? Then what?"

"You are the stupidest little girl I know." He started twisting my arm. "Still hurts, doesn't it? Such a shame you hadn't bled to death." He twisted more. "The Mayor. Do you have any idea how hard it is to find a pretty, trainable monkey to smile for the cameras? It's grueling, thankless." He gave another twist.

I didn't want to, but I started squealing. Like a little pig. Guys lots bigger than me did that when Bookie started in on them. Though I heard Chum-Chum gave it worse.

I felt like a little baby, but I couldn't help it.

I heard footsteps pounding into the car park. Whisper-Whisper turned to look, and I looked too.

It was José, with Mug in tow. I guess Mug must have escaped the church folk and made it back to City Hall.

Mug didn't say a word, but gave Whisper-Whisper a look. A Mug all-business look. A Mug about-to-crack-your-head look.

Whisper-Whisper chuckled. Then he dropped me down to the concrete floor. Oh, that hurt.

I felt like I could barely move, but I took off running in a hopping kind of way because I hurt all over. I wasn't sure what just happened, but I wasn't sticking around to find out.

Was Mug the soft soul Whisper-Whisper was talking about? It made no sense. Mug would just as soon whap me with his club than look at me. But, then again, Mug always waved his club at me, but he never actually whapped me. Could he really have had a soft spot for Sparky, the trouble of his life? It was too crazy to believe. And what was this business about training monkeys?

Sitting on a curb past City Hall, where the street started to rise up the Hill, I spotted the hobo. I scrambled over to him.

"Mind if I sit by you for a minute?" I was scared out of my mind, I hate to say. He was somebody to hide behind, somebody who'd never given me trouble.

His eyes smiled when he saw me. "Aw, sure, kid. Take a load off for a while."

I huddled up next to him. Like I said, I was scared. I was out of breath and my arm hurt like fire.

"You okay?"

I nodded but couldn't speak.

"I wish you wouldn't hang around this place. Too many bad elements in and around City Hall. I'd offer you something, but I've only got one kind of sauce today, and it's not for kids."

I looked at what he was drinking. It wasn't homemade hooch from a jar, or even a bottle from Canada hidden in a paper bag. This was a fancy bottle of the French stuff. I knew what it was. Champagne. Chum-Chum made a pretty penny selling it to the big wheels who went in and out of City Hall.

The hobo saw me staring at it. "Ah, yes. I got a taste for this fine brew while I was away in France during the War. After what happened—my girls—I suppose I indulged too much. Until I had no more funds to buy this kind of drink."

I kept staring at him.

He laughed low and quiet. "I did a favor. This is my reward. I didn't do it for the drink, you understand. That girl. You know that girl?"

Was he talking about the dead kid on Court Hill? That was the only one I was thinking about.

"I thought you said you didn't see nothing," I pointed out.

He kept talking like I hadn't said a thing. "She was alive when he drove her up the Hill. I saw her, moving. Then he drove down, alone."

Alone? "You mean some young guy? Or you talking about Whisper-Whisper?" Maybe this meant Whisper-Whisper killed the girl up on the hill. Maybe that's why the Mayor wasn't in jail.

"I think a lot about my girls. If I hadn't been in France, maybe I could have done something to save them. My sergeant told me that was crazy talk, that I couldn't have done a thing. But I'll never know."

The hobo looked at me. "Same for this girl. It was strange

he was driving such a little thing up the Hill so early in the morning. It didn't seem right. I should have jumped in front of the car, anything to stop it, give the kid a chance to get away. But I didn't. And then what happened?"

He took a swig. Some of the bubbly stuff dribbled down his chin. "I made it right, or as right as I could. The champagne only dulls the pain. That's all."

I was more confused than ever. "I just saw Whisper-Whisper, so I don't think you took care of nothing."

"He did get me the champagne. For the favor."

"For the interesting boat going down the river?"

"Interesting boat? Interesting way of putting it. But, yeah."

"Who did you see in the car with the girl?"

He looked down at me. "That pretty face. That's who I saw."

"You mean Dennis?" Ah, the driver did speed from Palm Springs to kill the girl all by himself.

He shrugged his eyebrows. "I don't know any Dennis. I do know the Mayor. That pretty face is hard to mistake." He took another swig. "You should go back up the Hill. Safer there. I'll watch you, make sure you get up there okay. I used to be a soldier, you know. I could have kept one little girl safe. I could have."

I took off running again, or as best as I could for being banged around so much lately. I made my way back to Creepy House. I still snuck through the yards and alleys. With all this crazy City Hall business, I still didn't think it was a good idea for the brass to know where I was hiding out.

Bookie was probably waiting for me, thinking I was coming straight back after my run to Chum-Chum. I'm sure steam was coming out of his ears. I shoulda gone to him, played nice. But I couldn't do anything right now.

Maybe the hobo imagined he'd seen the little girl. He was a drunk. No doubt about that. Still, would Chum-Chum let a bum like him swill his fine French champagne out in the wide open, bold as a brass button, if the bum'd stolen it? I don't think so. And it was Chum-Chum who'd laughed about the interesting boat. That settled it for me.

I sat in Tootsie's jungle yard for a long while. Through the French doors, I could see her sunroom was back to normal. No more white carpet, no more white cloth draped over the ceiling and walls. I liked it better the way it was, crowded full of old mismatched stuff.

I guess I was only half right about what happened to the

little girl. The Mayor offed her all on his own. The money bad man wanted was to keep quiet. Now I was sure he saw everything. Whisper-Whisper was only there to mop it up. The plan was to pin it on me and then maybe stash me in an orphan home where no one would see me ever again. When I found out too much, Whisper-Whisper wanted me to go the way of Sugar the bleached blonde. And he probably wanted me dead for making him find another mayor, another pretty, trainable monkey. But Mug had a soft spot. How about that? I guess Whisper-Whisper's power only went so far with the cops.

Whisper-Whisper didn't do such a good job training his monkey. One thing's for sure. That monkey wouldn't ever be coming back from his TB rest cure. The hobo took care of that.

This was crazy. I'd have to run all this by Bobby. Not today. I was too beat. Tomorrow.

I finally went inside. I heard much excited chatter from the kitchen. It was the goblin, Tootsie, the doctor and Mr. Exercise. A studio called that afternoon. An audition. They were making a plan of action to get her ready.

"This is like a miracle!" I heard Tootsie say. "This is so wonderful! I am so happy!"

"When you are happy, I am happy!" That was Gilbert. I could hear a break in his voice, like he was trying to keep from crying.

I made my way to "my" room. Wasn't my room, never was. Tootsie was back in the movie business again, life was moving on. I wasn't wanted anymore. As long as I steered clear of City Hall, I didn't have much to worry about apart from keeping Bookie happy. It was back to my old life: sleeping in cellars, running for Bookie. This had been nice. But nice never lasted for kids like Sparky.

I said good-bye to the leopards. I hadn't come with anything, so there wasn't anything to take with me. The leopards were too big to drag with me, much as I wanted to keep them. I decided to take my favorite picture book the goblin gave me. It would make me remember this place for the lonely times. Otherwise, I'd only take the sailor suit on my back.

Later, when everyone was asleep, I'd sneak to the kitchen for some food for the road. Then I'd be off. They probably wouldn't notice I was gone for a long time. They'd be busy getting Tootsie ready for the movies.

I fell asleep, and when I woke, the moon was shining through the clear glass transoms. Time to go. In the kitchen, I grabbed some bread left over from the morning. Didn't want the weird little onions and other strange things Tootsie ate. Then I made my way out the sunroom's French doors.

I was usually quiet as a mouse, but maybe getting shot and almost offed by the Mayor and Whisper-Whisper made me unsteady on my feet. I tripped in the doorway and dropped the picture book. It bounced on one of her jungle plants and then thunked onto her stone patio.

When I was scooping it back up, I heard a sound from up above. I turned and saw one of the colored glass windows upstairs opening. First time I'd seen that happen.

Tootsie stuck her head out. Her face was covered in goo, and more goo oozed out from under a turban wrapped around her hair. The goo looked like something the face broads and the hair ladies cooked up. She squinted into the dark.

"Sparky? Is that you? Are you leaving? But you don't have to go out and investigate anymore. Aren't you in the clear now? Doctor told me."

I thought about not saying anything, pretending like the noise was a stray cat, but I did owe her plenty. She'd been awfully good to me, being a street kid and all, wanted for murder and the whole bit.

"Ah, yeah, all clear. So, I don't need to hide in your place anymore. Good news, huh? Just getting out of your way. Moseying down the road. Thanks and all. You and Gilbert"—I almost said "goblin"— "have been really swell."

I started making my way into the bushes.

"Wait! Sparky!" She disappeared from the window. I heard sounds from inside the house. Faster than I could have ever thought, she was flying through the sunroom doors. She slid to a stop on her knees and grabbed me tight. She was crying, which made the goo run faster. It dripped on my face.

"Sparky! Don't leave! Please don't leave. I couldn't cope if you were gone. You've helped me so much. Oh, please!"

I helped her? How?

Before I knew it, Gilbert was there, all fussing and worried. In the bathtub I went. When I came out, the doctor was there giving me the unhappy eye. The goo was off Tootsie's face, the makeup was on, a different turban sat on her head, and a different fire breathing dragon dressing gown draped around her. But even with face paint, I could tell her eyes were puffy from crying.

They all hustled me back to the room with the leopards waiting for me. Gilbert whispered close to my ear, so Tootsie couldn't hear, "Please, little girl, please stay. Please."

Gilbert tucked me under the covers along with the book I dropped. The covers were too warm for the summer, but so soft, so nice, so I didn't mind. Tootsie clung to me for a long time, until the doctor persuaded her to let go.

Then they were gone.

The moon watched me through the clear glass transom windows. All was quiet. The bed was soft. The leopards were by my side. I gotta say, it sure did beat sleeping in a basement with rat skulls and dead people's suitcases.

But why would anyone want something like me in their house? It made no sense. Well, it was a puzzle I couldn't solve tonight. The last thing that went through my mind before I fell asleep under the moonlight was I'd run it by Bobby in the morning. See what he thought.

I dreamed about the little girl. I dreamed she had toys even nicer than Marigold's and people to look after her, wherever she was. I hoped that was a true dream. You never knew, but I hoped it was.

Epilogue

I spent some time visiting my old hangouts and hideouts on the Hill. So much'd happened lately, it felt like I'd been gone years and was traveling down memory lane. I checked out my crawl space where my dog-goat outfit got caught in the cop's barbed wire booby trap. The barbed wire loops were gone.

But something else in the crawl space shadows caught my eye. Could it be? My candy stash box! My name was still on it, not scratched off like bad man said. So, he was lying. I shoulda figured.

I opened it. My candy was gone, but it in its place was different candy. Not my usual candy choices, but still, it was all right. Something was sticking out of the candy. I pulled it. It was a torn bit of a cop evidence tag. Merchandise with those tags showed up in Bookie's office once, so I knew what they were. I dug around in the candy, but didn't find anything else.

Well, how about that?

ABOUT THE AUTHOR

Over thirty of Rosalind Barden's short stories have appeared in print anthologies and webzines, including the U.K.'s acclaimed *Whispers of Wickedness*. Mystery and Horror, LLC has included her stories in their anthologies *History and Mystery, Oh My!* (FAPA President's Book Award Silver Medalist), *Mardi Gras Murder*, and four of the *Strangely Funny* series. Ellen Datlow selected her short story "Lion Friend" as a Best Horror of the Year Honorable Mention after it appeared in *Cern Zoo*, a British Fantasy Society nominee for best anthology, part of DF Lewis' award winning *Nemonymous* anthology series. *TV Monster* is her print children's book that she wrote and illustrated. Her satirical literary novel *American Witch* is available as an e-book. In addition, her scripts, novel manuscripts and short fiction have placed in numerous competitions, including the Writers' Digest Screenplay Competition and the Shriekfest Film Festival. She lives in Los Angeles, California. Discover more at RosalindBarden.com

9 781949 281033